NED BEAUMAN
GLOW

SCEPTRE

Ned Beauman was born in 1985 in London. His debut novel, *Boxer, Beetle*, was shortlisted for the *Guardian* First Book Award and the Desmond Elliot Prize and won the Writers' Guild Award for Best Fiction Book and the Goldberg Prize for Outstanding Debut Fiction. His second novel, *The Teleportation Accident*, was longlisted for the Man Booker Prize and won the Encore Award and a Somerset Maugham Award. He has been chosen by the *Culture Show* as one of the twelve best new British novelists and by *Granta* as one of the 20 best British novelists under 40. His work has been translated into more than ten languages.
www.nedbeauman.co.uk

First published in Great Britain in 2014 by Sceptre
An imprint of Hodder & Stoughton
An Hachette UK company

First published in paperback in 2015

1

A CIP catalogue record for this title is available from the British Library

Paperback ISBN 978 1 444 76553 3
eBook ISBN 978 1 444 76554 0

Printed and bound by Clays Ltd, St Ives plc

Hodder & Stoughton policy is to use papers that are natural, renewable and recyclable products and made from wood grown in sustainable forests. The logging and manufacturing processes are expected to conform to the environmental regulations of the country of origin.

Hodder & Stoughton Ltd
338 Euston Road
London NW1 3BH

www.sceptrebooks.co.uk

As to what hour it might have been I had no idea, except that it must have been some hour of the night. But it might have been three or four in the morning just as it might have been ten or eleven in the evening, depending no doubt on whether one wondered at the scarcity of passers-by or at the extraordinary radiance shed by the street-lamps and traffic-lights. For at one or other of these no one could fail to wonder, unless he was out of his mind.

'The Calmative' by Samuel Beckett

Only let the material interests once get a firm footing, and they are bound to impose the conditions on which alone they can continue to exist. That's how your money-making is justified here in the face of lawlessness and disorder. It is justified because the security which it demands must be shared with an oppressed people. A better justice will come afterwards.

Nostromo by Joseph Conrad

LONDON, ENGLAND,
MAY 2010

DAY 1

12.49 a.m.

When he first sees her, Raf is sitting on a washing machine about to swallow an eighth of a gram of what is apparently a mixture of speed, monosodium glutamate, and an experimental social anxiety disorder medication for dogs. That, anyway, is what it sounded like Isaac told him, but the music in the laundrette is pretty loud and he wonders if he might have misheard. The powder has been divided between two cigarette papers and then the cigarette papers have been folded up and twisted to make those tight sealed parcels that always remind him of pork wontons, and Isaac has already gulped down his wonton, but Raf still has his in his hand, because he can't stop staring at the girl by the door. She's half white and half something else, maybe half Thai; and she has one of those faces where the entire bone structure seems to ramify from the cheekbones in such a way that the result looks like a 3D computer graphic from the eighties because it's composed of such an economical number of sharp, flat planes, except that the angles are confused here by strands of long black hair escaping from where she's pinned the rest of it up at the back of her head; and she has a small mouth folded towards a natural semi-pout that must be a good shape for when she's pretending to disapprove of something while trying not to laugh; and she's wearing a black hoodie unzipped over a slouchy grey vest. There are about sixty people dancing in the corridor of space between Raf and this girl, like a rush-hour Tube carriage that's learned to vibrate to a determinate rhythm, and he considers pushing through them all to talk to her – 'Will you immediately become my wife?' – but then Isaac knocks him on the arm with a

plastic water bottle to hurry him up. Without breaking surveillance, he takes the bottle, puts the wonton in his mouth, washes it
down with a gulp of water, and leans over to shout in Isaac's ear,
'What did you say was in this?'

'What?'

'What did you say was in this?'

'Speed, monosodium glutamate, and an experimental social anxiety disorder medication for dogs.'

'What's social anxiety disorder?'

'What?'

The sound system isn't even that loud but the room's so small that
the treble pushes at the sides like a fat toddler stuffed into a car seat.

'What's social anxiety disorder?'

'I can't hear you. Come outside.'

Raf reluctantly follows Isaac out into the little paved yard behind
the laundrette where a few people are chatting and smoking. Upside
down in the corner is one of those white polypropylene slatted-back
chairs that colonise faster than rats, lying there in the incredulous
posture of an object that is almost impossible to knock over but has
nonetheless found itself knocked over.

'What's social anxiety disorder?' Raf says again. From here he
can't see the girl.

'Shyness, basically.' In recent years, Isaac explains, a lot of
American vets have started to diagnose the condition in pet dogs,
and as a result a range of competing psychiatric prescriptions have
now been brought to market. As for the rest of the mixture, he has
no explanation for the monosodium glutamate, unless that's just to
bulk it out, although in that case it's difficult to say why, out of all
the available inert white powders, the manufacturers have chosen to
use monosodium glutamate in particular. (Raf almost wonders if it
could be a joke about the wontons.) And it has some speed in it
because everything has some speed in it.

'What's it going to do?' Raf says.

'It's like really bad ecstasy.'

4

For a long time Raf had thought of ecstasy as a substance so synthetic it was almost a pure abstraction, so it surprised him to learn from Isaac last month that the reason there's no good ecstasy in London at the moment is that two hundred and fifty drums of sassafras oil, which in the old days was thought to cure syphilis, were confiscated at a port in Thailand. To find out that ecstasy – like cocaine, like opium, like marijuana – comes from a plant that grew in the ground is to find out that angels have belly buttons. (Speed, by contrast, is made out of ephedrine, which can be extracted from certain shrubs but nowadays is almost always made out of laboratory chemicals instead, so like some theorem in vector algebra the drug owes nothing to the outside world, unless you followed the chain all the way back to the hydrocarbons they take out of crude oil.) Strange, too, to think of the million flirtations that won't be consummated, the million dawns that won't be watched, the million comedowns that won't be endured just because a guy in Laem Chabang neglected to pay a bribe or another guy refused to take one. No politician at a WTO conference ever had so much power. The drug trade, Isaac told him, is the first globalisation of the emotional life.

'When is there going to be good ecstasy again?' Raf says.

'Maybe never,' says Isaac. 'We need to get hold of some glow.'

'What's that?'

'You know, that new stuff. Barky said it was the best thing he'd ever taken. Ever in his whole life.'

'Does he still have any?'

'I think so.'

'Is he coming here?'

Isaac shrugs. 'His phone's off.'

The reason the owners of this laundrette are allowing a small rave to take place here tonight is so they can sell drugs to the crowd, but all they have is cocaine, ketamine, and a new ecstasy understudy called ethylbuphedrone that you can buy legally over the internet from laboratories in China, none of which are of any interest to Raf.

Looking around, he feels, not for the first time, a mild bitterness that he wasn't born twenty years earlier, when a night out would have been all about snowy Dutch MDMA in a giant import warehouse near the M11, a drug culture so good that people wrote memoirs about it, instead of these self-administered double-blind trials in a twenty-square-metre urban utility. How was London reduced to this?

Quite soon, Isaac follows him back inside, and Raf sees that a boy and a girl have stripped down to their underwear and climbed inside one of the big spin-dryers to kiss, their skinny limbs struggling for purchase on the inside of the drum like test subjects in some astro-nautical study of the sexual possibilities of small cylindrical spaces. They, at least, have taken something good, or maybe not something good but at least something they've never taken before. The DJ is playing a track that Raf has heard on Myth FM a lot. He climbs up on top of the dryer, above the perspiration troposphere, to look around for the girl from before, but he can't see her anywhere so he just stays up there to dance.

2.12 a.m.

When Barky does arrive he still wears flecks of shaving foam on both ear lobes like little pearl studs, so maybe, like Raf, he got out of bed only a short while ago. In his wallet there are three more wontons wrapped up in a shred of orange supermarket bag, one dose of glow for each of them. About half an hour after Raf took that previous compound, he started to feel a change, but so weakly that he wasn't even sure, like when you go into a room and you think you can feel a cold draught but no windows are open and it might just be your imagination. Then it was gone again. So he's excited about trying Barky's novelty, and he's about to swallow some and get back up on the dryer when he feels a touch on his arm. He turns.

It's that same girl.

She leans to talk into his ear and he watches a soft shine skate across the film of sweat on her clavicle.

'What is that?' she says, which is a lot better than the expected 'Why were you staring at me like a psycho before?' She must have seen him take the wonton from Barky.

'Glow,' he says.

'Is your friend selling it?' She has an American accent.

'No.' But there's no way Raf is going to leave it at that. He's had girls flirt with him just for drugs before, of course, and maybe that's what she's doing, but in that case she doesn't know the rules, because there's no empty smile, no hand alighting provisionally on the small of his back. Plus, what if she is? He once slept with an Icelandic girl he met like that at a party. So he hopes he's not being a total dupe when he says, 'Do you want some?'

Now she does smile. 'No, that's OK.'

But he takes her hand and presses the wonton into it. 'I've heard this stuff is amazing.'

'What?'

Should he suggest they go outside so they can hear each other? No, not yet. 'What's your name?'

'Cherish,' she says, or that's what it sounds like. Is that a name? 'What's yours?'

'Raf.'

'Do you have any water?'

'Just a second.' He turns to Isaac, but he doesn't have the bottle any more, and Barky doesn't have one either. Raf thought he saw a half-empty lemonade up on one of the washing machines, but he can't see it now. And when he turns back, the girl has vanished again, like the ambiguous chill of the pedigree psychotropic. He asks Isaac and Barky where she went, but neither of them were watching. And Barky doesn't have any more glow to spare.

5.37 a.m.

Raf stumbles out of the laundrette to find himself engulfed in flow-ers. It's as if some phenomenological anode inside him has been swapped with its cathode, so that every sensation is replaced by another of exactly inverse quality and equal intensity: petals for skin, perfume for sweat, cold for heat, silence for noise, anthocy-anins for disco lights. Only after a moment does he realise that on Saturdays there's a flower market on this road, so they're unloading the tulips and daffodils – and sure enough, just at that moment the silence is broken by the trundling of a steel trolley as it comes down a ramp behind him. He breathes in deeply and then walks on down the road to the bus stop where he can catch his night bus.

Isaac and Barky have already left the rave. For a while, they said they weren't feeling anything from the glow, and Barky also had a gram of ethylbuphedrone, so they all resorted to dabbing some on their gums, which always reminds Raf of rubbing salt and pepper into a flank steak. But then straight after that, too soon for it to be the ethylbuphedrone, the other two had run out into the yard and started vomiting ballistically over the concrete. Between spasms, Barky said the glow they'd taken must have been fake. It occurred to Raf that if he hadn't even heard of glow until tonight, and yet some opportunist was already selling a fake version, he must be badly behind the times. And then he realised with horror that somewhere the American girl was probably throwing up too because of drugs he'd pushed on her, and she only had about half Barky's body mass, so a poison could kick her twice as far. Even if he ever found Cherish again, she'd never want to speak to him.

Now, coming down from the ethylbuphedrone, Raf just feels bleached and fidgety, and he decides he probably didn't have a chance with her anyway. When the bus finally arrives, its windows are bright like a goods vehicle hauling not flowers to market but bulk photons. He gets on, nods to the driver, beeps his Oyster card, and climbs the spiral staircase up to the top deck. What he sees there

8

startles him so much that he forgets to hold on to the vertical hand-rail, so when the bus halts at a junction he nearly topples forward.

A fox sits there, about six rows back. Every hair in its orange coat burns with a separate flame, and the reflection of a street light outside the window is curled up inside each of its round black eyes like a pale girl in a spin-dryer. Raf has never noticed before that the white fur of a fox's snout and belly is sprinkled over its eyes, too, to make two oversized brows, and as it considers him this one wears an expression of detached scientific interest. The animal couldn't have got past the driver, he thinks, so it must have jumped on at the exit doors when someone got off. As the bus accelerates again, he sits down, and the fox turns from him to look out of the window. A scent reaches Raf's nose, muddy and petroleous, a savage hydrocarbon with no derivatives. No other passengers get on, and when the automatic loudspeaker announces in her broken diction that they've arrived at Camberwell Green, the fox jumps to the floor and trots downstairs to disembark.

6.20 a.m.

For the first six months that he lived in his current flat, Raf honestly believed that the corner shop at the end of his street was run by one Iranian guy who worked twenty-two or twenty-three hours a day. He's been in there at every time there is, and it's always the same face at the till just like it's always football playing on the TV fixed to the wall over the wine gums. Raf did introduce himself once, but the next time he went in the guy didn't even acknowledge their new familiarity. Then about a week later he glanced inside on his way past and he saw both owners arguing about something. Like a twist from a bad murder mystery, they were twin brothers. Today, Raf buys three bananas and a carton of orange juice, enjoying the care-ful, almost clerical way the guy at the counter wets the tip of his middle finger on a soggy foam pad like a prosthetic gland to help peel open the plastic bag; and then Raf walks down to his block of flats, where an old stained mattress leans against the wall by the entrance, ready for rubbish collection the following week. The number of mattresses people leave out here every month seems wildly out of proportion to the human capacity of the building, like the waste product of some secret industrial process.

Even if it weren't for the drugs, he knows he wouldn't be able to sleep for another nine or ten hours, but he's so worn out that he gets into bed for a while anyway. The heavy black curtains are still closed from when he got up around eleven, so the room is in total darkness except for the red LED on his stereo, and around him are all the paraphernalia of his malady: eyemask, acoustic earmuffs, white noise machine, and about two dozen soiled earplugs scattered under the bed like the droppings of a hamster that eats only packaging foam.

The name of Raf's condition is non-24-hour sleep/wake syndrome. He was sixteen when he started to notice that his sleep patterns were even more fucked up than the average teenager's, but it took four different doctors before he got his diagnosis. In a healthy brain, your eyes tell your hypothalamus when it gets dark and when it gets light, your hypothalamus tells your pineal gland when to secrete melatonin, and the melatonin makes you fall asleep at about the same time every day. The normal human circadian rhythm is set at twenty-four hours to match one full rotation of the earth. But Raf's is set at about twenty-five hours. It's like his brain is wearing a novelty watch.

Most people who have non-24-hour sleep/wake syndrome have it because they're blind, so their hypothalamus never finds out where the sun is. But with Raf it must be something else, and no blood test or EEG has ever been able to determine exactly what. Serotonin is the precursor, the sassafras oil, of melatonin, so it could be that he has a mutation in the genes that make the enzymes convert one to the other, although that would imply that he has a lot of excess serotonin sloshing around in his brain, which is the same thing that happens when you take MDMA, and it's not as if he feels euphoric all the time. It could also be that something's awry in his suprachiasmatic nucleus, an office of his hypothalamus the size of a grain of rice.

Whatever the cause, the effect is that each morning he slips one more hour out of sync with the rest of the world, as if he's taking a short westbound flight every day of his life without ever leaving London. At the beginning of his cycle, waking up at eight in the morning is easy; after four days, it's like waking up at 4 a.m.; after eight days, 8 a.m. is about when he needs to go to bed for the 'night'; after fifteen days, it's towards the end of his 'afternoon'; after twenty days, it's towards the end of his 'morning'; and after twenty-five days, he gets another normal day. His cycle isn't precisely twenty-five hours, he's not made of clockwork, but it happens to work out too close to make any difference. He would be more at home on Mars, where the length of a solar day is twenty-four hours and thirty-nine minutes, near enough to his own cycle that he could probably make up for the discrepancy with a lot of naps at the week-end under the dim glitter of Phobos. Last year, a woman at a letting agency, not quite following an explanation that he already regretted attempting, said to him, 'Wow, twenty-five hours – you must get so much done!'

And non-24-hour sleep/wake syndrome has no known cure. He's tried light boxes, hypnotherapy, and vitamin B12 injections, but nothing works. For a few months he took melatonin tablets, and that did help a little bit, but a doctor told him that the longer you kept taking melatonin, the more you'd have to take to get the same effect, just like MDMA, and that after a while the melatonin would start to shrink your pineal gland in the same way that testosterone supplements could shrink your balls. The pineal gland, he's read, was once a blush of photosensitive cells on the forehead of an eyeless fish, but since then evolution has yanked it inside the skull. He doesn't want to lose his antique monocle, his shuttered window.

Raf had once hoped to become the first person in his family to go to university, but in the end he left school before his A levels because for about two weeks out of every four he couldn't stay awake in lessons. He's never had a real job. And he doesn't think he'll ever get married. Isaac says he should just trawl the sleep disorder support messageboards for a girlfriend who has the same syndrome. But the problem is that nobody else is likely to have his exact cycle. And, perversely, the closer his cycle was to that of a hypothetical lover, the more it would drive them apart. If hers was twenty-six hours against his twenty-five hours, they would synchronise every six hundred and fifty hours (by which time he would have lived through twenty-six subjective days and she would have lived through twenty-five). But if she had a cycle of about twenty-five hours and fifteen minutes against his cycle of about twenty-five hours, they would synchronise only every 2,525 hours (by which time he would have lived through a hundred and one subjective days and she would have lived through a hundred) which made his basic estrangement from the normal circadian rhythm look trifling in comparison.

In other words, their cycles would be mutually inverse for weeks at a time before they lumbered back together, as if each were going away on long business trips into the other's night. And their mutual synchrony would itself only synchronise with Greenwich Mean Time – making them indistinguishable from a normal couple for long enough to eat breakfast, lunch, and dinner together at the correct times – every 60,600 hours, or about every seven years, or about every two and a half blue moons. What if one of them had flu that week? Plus all this is to disregard the gravitational pull that each would exert on the other's cycle. Raf can make these calculations easily because back when he was trying to teach himself programming he adapted an open-source biorhythm generator into a new application to graph where he'll be in his cycle at any given time and date in the future. He'd planned to use it to schedule important appointments. But the life of a guy with non-24-hour sleep/wake syndrome is not exactly bursting with those.

That's not to say he's been single and friendless all this time. He's twenty-two, which is an age when a lot of people still play polyrhythms with their bodies for days at a time; drugs help with that. His last girlfriend was a DJ, like Isaac, so she might play from midnight until four and go to bed at five, or she might go to bed at eight in the evening and go back out to play an afterparty at four in the morning, or she might stay up all weekend and then sleep all through Monday. To make two tempos match up a DJ normally just needs to twiddle a pitch control, but in real life they didn't synchronise very often; for her, though, that was true with everybody she met, so Raf was at no disadvantage. Sometimes they'd improvise a sort of laggard domesticity: when she got a minicab back to her flat at dawn he'd already be cooking a curry, and they'd eat it on her balcony as the sun came up, go for a walk through the dewy park nearby, come back to fuck and smoke weed and watch DVDs until lunchtime, fall asleep until it was dark again, and then meet some friends in the pub. She was gorgeous, with big green eyes like smashed jade, but what he loved most was her detachment from the world: she was vague, almost vaporous, bemused by everything but surprised by nothing. He'd never been so happy for so long.

Then, in March, she told him she'd decided to move to Berlin. Raf waited for her to reassure him that the flights were cheap enough that he could visit her every couple of weeks, which was about as often as they got to see each other properly anyway. But then he realised that no invitation was implied. That conversation was the most practical he'd ever seen her. Afterwards, he found out from Isaac that she was already seeing someone new, a Brazilian techno producer who was known for playing fourteen-hour DJ sets. Isaac hadn't intended to tell Raf about it, but he'd taken two good pills that night, and he can't keep secrets when he's high, which is why most of the time he does his conscientious best to avoid hearing secrets in the first place, like a spy revoking his own security clearance.

These six weeks since she left have been like the lowest point of the worst comedown from the filthiest Chinese amphetamines anyone has ever had, although at least for once in Raf's life it's as if social expectations have shifted to synchronise with his own cycle: he's been dumped, so it's natural that he sometimes sleeps all day and drinks all night. Mostly, the change seems external, not internal. The shift is in the world around him. When you take good ecstasy, it feels as if the drug can pump from solid objects a joy that has always been hidden there inside them but will otherwise seep to their surface only very gradually. Now he feels the opposite: those same objects are desiccated, as if you could stand there with your tongue out for days and not a drop would fall. And it isn't getting any better.

Once, Isaac admitted he was scared that one night he might take so much MDMA that all the serotonin receptors in his head would burst like the turbines of a dam and after that last flood he'd never be able to take pleasure from anything again. That's how Raf is now. And while Isaac keeps saying he'll get over it, this despondency feels both permanent and territorial, as if joy might still exist some-where but will never come back to these specific streets, this specific desert, even though she doesn't even live here any more.

Five days ago, climbing the staircase to his flat, a staircase he now loathes because of all the times he kissed her there, he wondered what it might be like to leave London himself, and just thinking about it gave him such a mighty feeling of relief he decided then and there that in a month he would leave London. He's given notice on his flat. This morning, Saturday, he has twenty-five days left, one cycle, before he says goodbye to the city where he's lived all his life. He hasn't told Isaac yet or even chosen where to go. Berlin sounds fun, and cheap, and it's the only place he's ever heard of where apparently it's considered normal to go dancing right after you get out of bed, but of course it's also the only place that's forbidden. There's a part of him that hopes something will happen to change his mind this month, but donating an emetic to a beautiful girl isn't it. Or maybe a fox on a bus is a start, but it's not nearly enough.

2.35 p.m.

Every day Raf has to carry a Staffordshire bull terrier down a ladder. At first she used to wriggle but now she sits so happily on his shoulders that sometimes it feels as if she's reluctant to get down off her bony palanquin. Rose is four years old, black all over except for a white cravat, and for the last thirteen months she's lived on the roof of an eighteen-storey council block, guarding a radio transmitter bolted to a wall. In a chemistry lesson at school Raf was once shown how to do chromatography, where you watch the different pigments in a smear of anthocyanin extract bleed different distances up a grid of filter paper, the same way they test for MDMA in the blood, and he sometimes thinks of a building like this as a giant chromatograph for the streets below, with nothing soluble enough to reach the very top but police sirens and motorcycle engines and on hot days a faint prickle of smog. The skyscrapers across the river are cramped together into one narrow band of the horizon's curve, a string of paper dolls, as marginal and unconvincing as one of those tourist board graphics where they cut and paste a dozen famous silhouettes into a greatest hits compilation.

Like all pirate stations, Myth FM have installed their aerial on a separate building from their studio, parasitic off the lift's AC supply like a tick deep in a scalp, because otherwise if an Ofcom van triangulated the signal they could wreck the whole operation with a single raid. The studio needs only an uninterrupted line of sight in order for the link box they've pried out of a satellite TV dish to beam the audio by infra-red up to the main rig. But this also means there's no one around to guard the transmitter, which is worth nearly a grand, and there are a lot of other pirate stations in south London who'd rather steal a working box than build their own. Theo, the genial forty-one-year-old proprietor of Myth FM, has paid off the caretaker to let him keep two heavy D-locks on the door out to the middle part of the roof, and in the past he's even experimented with razor wire and electrified scaffolding poles around the rig, but the problem is that the sort of cunts who would know what to do with a stolen radio transmitter are, by definition, self-taught engineers with a lot of persistence, and they can get around anything you invent. So Theo adopted Rose. Maybe you could cut her down with knives if you were lucky, but only an idiot would start a fight with a full-grown Staffie on a roof with no parapet.

Theo's original plan was to leave the beast up on the roof, feed her twice a week, keep her hungry and resentful; but he loves dogs, and he just couldn't restrain himself, especially after Isaac told him he had a friend needing cash work. Rose now lives in a sort of shanty cabin nailed together out of tarpaulin, cardboard, insulating foam, and whatever else Raf could haul up the ladder to the roof, with a tub of rainwater next to a pile of old blankets that Rose can nudge together into a bed, and the lift machinery as her noisy neighbour. During the winter, Theo even put in a small electric heater on a timer switch, plugged into the same mains cable as the transmitter nearby, although he made Raf swear never to tell anyone. He sometimes jokes that he should move some students in there and charge two hundred quid a week.

Every day, Raf takes Rose downstairs in the densely annotated lift and gives her a long walk. He knows she must be lonely and bored up there, and he doesn't like it any more than Theo does, but she was hardly living in luxury with her previous owner: the scars on her snout and her milky left eye confirm what Theo has only hinted at in that respect. Also, as earnestly as Raf has tried to understand this animal, he's still never got the sense that she cares about being walked or fed on any sort of regular schedule, which is good for him, although he tries to make sure that most of the time he takes her to the park when there are at least a few other dogs around. Whatever the opposite of social anxiety disorder is, she has that.

Theo's always pleased to see Rose, so today Raf decides to take her over to the Myth studio itself, which is on the fifth floor of a shorter council block down the road with pairs of white concrete balconies running up the right-hand side like tick boxes on a questionnaire and iron railings around the sides that mark off a buffer of grass between the building and the street. (Raf has never understood the point of those token lawns – no one ever sunbathes or plays frisbee on them, but the council still has to mow them all summer. They might as well just put down AstroTurf.) From out in the corridor, under the jittery halogen, Flat 23 looks normal, but in fact its front door is reinforced and soundproofed, and there's no point knocking: you have to dial a phone number. Today the door is unbolted by Dickson, a stocky guy with a shaved head and a wardrobe full of *Scarface* T-shirts who works for Theo. He looks down at the dog and shakes his head. 'You can't bring that in here.'

Dickson's never liked Rose, and as a result Raf's never liked Dickson, but this is unprecedented. 'What? She always comes in here.'

'No animals. New rule.'

'What does Theo say about that?'

'Theo's not here.'

'Where is he?'

'Away.'

'Away where?'

Dickson is shifty and hostile at the best of times, so it's hard to be sure when he's lying, especially when they both know that they shouldn't be chatting like this with the door open, but he does not convince Raf when he says, 'Kingston. Family wedding.' Raf doesn't remember Theo ever mentioning cousins back in Jamaica. Perhaps he's lying low for some reason.

'You have to pay me, at least. It's been a week.'

Dickson seems to be willing to break his 'new rule' if it will get rid of Raf faster. Inside the flat the stench of skunk is so solid you could boil it for stock. At the end of the hall is the door to what would once have been the lounge, with a marker-pen sign taped up that says 'Pay before you Play!!' DJs on Myth are charged twenty quid an hour for their slots, money they'll make back later in club bookings once their names get known. Isaac used to say the internet would make the pirates obsolete, but Raf never believed that, and there are still at least seventy stations active in London, an invisible and inter-penetrative confederacy. Until everyone has a broadband connec-tion in their car, and next to their kitchen sink, and in the cheap hi-fi they just bought from the pawnbroker – which, admittedly, might be just a matter of time – the internet isn't going to kill pirate radio. The same goes for the digital switchover. What's more likely is that only the legal stations will make the transition, abandoning the dusty lecture halls and ballrooms of the FM dial to a squat party that can go on for ever.

Raf is friendly with almost all the DJs at Myth, so he doesn't bother to ask permission before he tugs Rose down the corridor and pushes through the door into the cramped studio. The curtains are drawn, but you can see the bump in the fabric where the link box leans up against the window like a cat pressing its nose to the glass. On the wall is a whiteboard with the week's schedule; in the corner, for reasons Raf has never discovered, is a pub fruit machine; and at the far end of the room, where the turntables and tape decks and microphones and mixer and computer knot their roots under the desk, Raf expects to see Barky or Jonk or one of the other DJs who sometimes play Saturday afternoons – but instead, glaring back at him, there are two men he's never seen before. He's not quite sure what ethnicity they are, but they remind him of the girl from the laundrette: maybe they're Thai, if she was half Thai. In the studio there's always a radio tuned at low volume to Myth FM so the DJs can hear straight away if there's a problem with the signal, and what this pair is playing is some sort of synthesiser torch song with a shrill woman singing in a language Raf doesn't recognise. He doesn't know much about foreign pop music, so all he can say to himself is that it reminds him of something you might hear while eating noodles in a restaurant. This is not what Myth FM usually broad-casts. The song comes to a tearful end, and one of the men turns back to the microphone to talk in what sounds like the same language as the vocals. Raf steps back out of the studio and shuts the door.

'Who are those guys?' he says to Dickson.

'They're doing an afternoon community programme.'

'Really? Which "community" is that?'

But Dickson hands him his wage for the week without a reply. Raf gets paid more than he probably deserves for walking Rose, but it's still not enough to live on, so he also does some freelance graphics programming. He's good with computers and he always had a knack for maths, so he was able to train himself out of textbooks, but he's not by any means a born coder and with nothing much on his CV he can still only get boring, repetitive work. At the moment, he's helping out a Polish company with lighting models for a program that an Australian property developer has commissioned to give online tours of unbuilt houses.

In the nineties, you didn't have to worry so much about virtual light – it was always just flat and even, like in southern California – but now that it's technologically possible to render it with a degree of realism, lighting is more important than almost anything else. Raf finds it amusing that a lot of the last generation of video-game programmers must have gone into the industry expecting that maybe they'd specialise in rifle ballistics or motorcycle handling and instead found themselves becoming as intimate with chiaroscuro as the most studious Florentine portraitist's apprentice. And sometimes, up on the roof after a day at his computer, looking down at the Myth transmitter, he thinks how strange it is that light and radio are both electromagnetic waves, differing only in relative size – light is a chihuahua, maybe, and radio is a Great Dane (and infra-red is a Staffie like Rose) but somehow they're all still the same species.

3.21 p.m.

In Isaac's spare bedroom live three Japanese fashion students who answered an ad he put on a listings website. There's only a double bed in there, and it doesn't look as if there would be space for three girls, even these slender ones, but that's not a problem because like the Iranian corner shop on Raf's road they are a twenty-four-hour operation. Every single time Raf visits Isaac's flat, day or night, without fail, one is asleep, one is awake, and one is absent; when he passes their bedroom he half expects to see a whiteboard on the wall like at Myth, dividing their shifts. He's never quite memorised their names, and he suspects Isaac hasn't either. Today, the girl painting her nails at the table by the front door is wearing combat boots and a dress that looks like an umbrella blown inside out, and the girl dozing on the futon is wearing gold plimsolls and a man's tuxedo jacket about five sizes too big for her. As always, they are magnificent. Stooping to unclip Rose's leash from her collar, Raf sees a huge bouquet of tulips resting in the kitchen sink.

'Who's that from?'

'By the time we left the laundrette the second time, the flower market had started,' says Isaac. 'Those kids from the dryer insisted on buying me those. They said I was beautiful. Hello, dog! Hello! Hello! Hello! Hello! Hello! Hello! Hello! Hello!'

'But you and Barky went home before I did.'

'We went back later on. We felt better.'

'Why didn't you call me?'

'Your phone was off.'

Last night, before they ate that first portion of wontons, Isaac told Raf that he had something exciting to show him in Walworth, but he wouldn't expand on the oxymoron. After the dog and her friend have sated each other's tactility, Raf puts the lead back on Rose and they take her downstairs to Isaac's car so they can drop her off at home on their way. As usual she resists the back seat as if it were a vertical plummet. Someone's windscreen must have got knocked through outside Isaac's block of flats, because in the gutter there are diamonds of safety glass with which this morning's rain has mingled an alluvium of damp white blossom and a few fronds of synthetic wig hair caught on a chicken bone, like the shattered remains of a tribal fetish.

'I was at Myth earlier,' says Raf as Isaac starts the car. 'There's something weird going on.'

'Yeah. I got a call from Jonk about it.'

'What did he say?'

'You can't believe anything that fucker tells you. Do you remember when he said he met that guy who could shoot electricity out of his fingers?'

'Yeah, but what did he say?'

Late on Wednesday night, Isaac explains, Jonk apparently left Myth FM after his two-hour slot, wandered across the road to the playground, and sat down to smoke a spliff on one of those plastic sheep they have on wobbly springs for the kids. Through the trees, he could see Theo walking down the street, and he was about to shout a greeting when a van pulled up right beside Theo. It was just a grimy white builder's van, 'NO TOOLS LEFT IN THIS VEHICLE OVERNIGHT', but the two men who jumped out of the back wore some kind of hi-tech goggles and were dressed all in black. Theo, taken aback, said something Jonk couldn't hear, and then they pulled him inside the van and slammed the rear doors. The van drove off, and the strangest thing, Jonk claimed, was that somehow the engine didn't make any noise at all: apart from the soft crepitation of tyres on the asphalt, it moved in total silence, headlights sweeping across the playground like the blank eyes of a wraith.

3.51 p.m.

They park outside a salvage yard with a sign that says 'WHOLESALE IRONMONGERS', radiators and baths and sinks piled in their rusty dozens behind the fence like an old house multiplied in a broken mirror. The next building down on the left is a medium-sized warehouse built from grey steel panels with a pitched roof and sliding garage doors at the front, generally looking as if the most exciting thing it could possibly hold is cardboard boxes full of spare parts for machines that make more cardboard boxes. Isaac leads him round to the back of the warehouse, where two green wheelie bins lean their open lids against a brick wall, empty but for a can of Coke and some wisps of cling film. A padlock that must have been snapped with bolt cutters lies on the ground beside the back door.

Inside the warehouse it's dark so Isaac takes out a torch and shines it around. In the corner there's a row of four portable toilets, and at the far end there's a metal shelving unit, but apart from that the building is vacant. Raf sees tyre marks on the ground. 'What are we doing here?' he says.

'I'm going to put on a rave.'

'We're right off Albany Road.'

'So?'

'Someone drives past, hears the music, calls the police, they're here in ten minutes.'

Isaac smiles and shakes his head. 'Go back outside and close the door.'

'Why?'

'I'm going to bang on the door as hard as I can with the torch, all right?'

Raf does as he's told. After a minute or so, he hasn't heard anything, so he presses his ear to the door, and that way he can just make out a faint percussive sound as if Isaac is tapping at the door with one gentle knuckle. He opens the door again and finds Isaac with the torch in his hand and his arm drawn back in a walloping posture. Raf can't believe it at first, so they repeat the experiment, this time with Isaac on the outside, banging on the door again with the heel of the broken padlock. Then they each move ten paces sideways along the wall, then ten more, and it's the same. Vibrations can't penetrate. The warehouse is soundproofed, like Myth FM, but much better.

'Why would anyone soundproof a warehouse?' says Raf, looking around at this simulation of his own skull when he's falling asleep sealed in his eyemask and earmuffs.

'I don't know. It's perfect, though. Hire a generator, lights, sound system, more Portaloos. Make sure everyone queues round the back. The police could walk right past and they wouldn't know there was anything going on. You could fit four hundred people in here.'

Four hundred dreams pushing into the skull. 'No more parties in laundrettes.'

'Yeah.'

The thought does give Raf great pleasure. 'How'd you find it?'

'You know Finn is always cycling around looking for new places to squat? He says he's found five of these already. Warehouses that get put up overnight but by the time he spots them they're always abandoned already. I checked the satellite view on Google Maps and he's right. The photo's only a month old but this was a petrol station then.' And indeed this sterile prefabricated structure feels no more attached to the ground than a plastic tub you flip over to trap a rat running across a kitchen floor.

Raf takes the torch and walks farther into the gloom. Towards the middle of the warehouse something black is coiled on the ground. He picks it up.

'That's a speaker cable,' says Isaac. 'Someone must have left it behind.'

'Does that mean there's already been a rave here?'

Isaac looks disappointed for a moment. 'But we would definitely have heard about it.'

Where the speaker cable was lying there's a stain that Raf might have taken for another tyre mark, but now he sees it's more of a rufous colour. He kneels down. 'Hey, look at this.'

'What?' says Isaac.

Raf scratches at the stain with his fingernail. 'I think it's blood.'

DAY 2

11.40 a.m.

The sooty scabs of chewing gum and the sycamore seeds trapped in pigeon shit make every paving stone in south London look like an unlabelled map of some distant volcanic archipelago, and when Rose browses along with her nose on the ground Raf sometimes imagines that she's not tracing a scent but rather searching for the one unique slab that can correctly locate a priceless bone one of her ancestors buried. Today he's taken the dog farther north than usual, almost into Bermondsey, where the streets are empty on a Sunday and the many new offices and flats wear visors of wood or aluminium as if to shut out Myth FM and all its influence. He's waiting with her at a pedestrian crossing when he sees a photocopied notice taped up at the bus stop nearby.

'Did you see me get knocked off my bike at this junction?' A date and time. 'Badly injured. Not at fault. Need to take driver to court to pay for dental work and new bike. Didn't get number plate but driver was in white van with engine that didn't make any noise (!). Looking for witnesses. Please call Morris.' And a phone number.

4.59 p.m.

There's a sort of famished muscularity to bicycle couriers that you also see in gay men who've kept on clubbing for a few years too long, and the dozen standing in this pub look as if they all have resting heart rates so slow that by any strict definition they're medically dead. On the phone, Raf admitted that he hadn't seen the accident, he just wanted to know more about it, so Morris said that Raf was welcome to come down later and buy him a pint. He has short dreadlocks under an orange baseball cap, and if he wasn't easy enough to pick out from the stitches in his forehead and the plaster on his broken nose, then he would be when his smile reveals a black doorway where his front teeth once were.

'The prick went right through a red light,' he explains after Raf has introduced himself and brought back two lagers from the bar. 'I was making a turn and suddenly he just gunned it. My bike's fucked up even worse than my face. Using my girlfriend's at the moment. Lucky she's tall.'

Raf has always envied couriers for the MRI scan they take of their city, front tyres like toroid dog noses, a dead leaf's difference in the height of a familiar kerb felt somewhere in their sinews when Raf himself probably wouldn't even notice an extra few inches; and because, like pirate radio, they were supposed to get squashed under the internet, but didn't; and also because he once saw a game of bike polo and it looked like a lot of fun. 'So the engine didn't make any noise?' Raf says. Until he saw that photocopy at the bus stop he hadn't believed Jonk's story any more than Isaac had.

'Yeah. Not just quiet like a Rolls. Silent.'

Raf's pint tastes a bit cloacal. It's that time of the early evening when the slant of the sunlight makes every pane of window glass look as deep and scummy as an old fishtank. Raf has to stop himself from yawning: he woke up at 1 a.m., so he'd like to be in bed by now. 'Has anyone else called you?' he says.

'No. Except there was one other bloke, same as you, said he didn't see it happen but wanted to hear about the van.'

'Why?'

'Didn't say.'

'Who was he?'

'Didn't say. And he didn't want to come here to talk to me. I started to wonder if maybe he was the driver wanting to find out how much I knew.'

Now Raf feels as if he should certify his own motivations. 'I've got a friend who might have had some trouble with the same van.'

Morris shrugs. 'You can have that other bloke's number if you like.'

DAY 3

The guy on the phone had an accent so posh that Raf was surprised when he suggested meeting in the McDonald's on Walworth Road. And when Raf said that if he wanted fast food there was a Happy Fried Chicken opposite that also served burgers – the 'chicken' in the logo on the signage there looks more like a nervous baby dinosaur wearing a glam rock wig – the guy still insisted on McDonald's. Raf comes in out of the drizzle and walks over to the only person in the room wearing a suit, who sits alone at the table farthest from the window with just a bag of chips on his tray. Pop music drools from the ceiling and the lights are bright enough to scorch the melatonin out of your brain.

'You're Raf?' He's in his mid-thirties, with a keen aquiline nose, and the manner of someone explaining that he would sack you if he possibly could but he just doesn't have time this week to look for your replacement. During their conversation, however, Raf will begin to wonder if hidden behind this impatience there isn't also something shaped like fear, which is not to say that the impatience is fake, because it's real, but only that it's been deliberately propped up right at the front. And every so often he glares around as if he's disgusted to find himself here breathing in beef grease, even though it was his own stipulation. Just now he mispronounced Raf's name, with a long vowel instead of a short one (people often guess it's either Mediterranean or Sloaney, when in fact there's nothing but south London in his family for a long time back, and that includes the grandfather on his mother's side who took up this variant on Ralph for reasons the younger Raf can never remember). However, instead of making a correction, Raf just nods and sits down; and instead of offering a name in return, the guy just says: 'You have some information you want to share about the white vans?'

It hadn't occurred to Raf that there was more than one. 'A friend of mine's gone missing. Someone supposedly saw him getting pulled into a white van that didn't make any noise.'

The guy waves him on. 'Right. And?'

'That's all I know.'

'That's all you know? You didn't even see it yourself?'

'No.'

The guy leans back in his seat. 'Well, this was a waste of time. On the phone you made it sound like you could actually give me something.' Only now does Raf notice what looks like a dried ketchup stain on the lapel of his jacket. The guy sees him staring and looks down, then brushes at it pointlessly with two fingers. 'From lunch. Bloody annoying. I only picked this up from the cleaners on Friday.'

'What are the white vans?' says Raf.

'Stay away from them.'

'Why? They're just vans.'

The guy looks around and then leans forward again to answer almost in a whisper, even though a nearby table of teenagers are cackling loudly enough over a mobile phone video to cover anything he might say. 'They're not just vans, actually. They're camouflaged military vehicles. They have hybrid engines so when they're running off batteries they don't make a sound.'

'What? Military?'

'Yes. Not British Army, though.'

'Who, then?'

'I can't tell you that. But they're kidnapping people. Mostly Burmese men, but some others. Such is the general reputation of white-van drivers, of course, that to most Londoners it couldn't be less surprising to learn that they might have someone tied up in the back, although we'd be more likely to expect a weeping schoolgirl.'

Raf is baffled. 'Burmese men? Why?' He thinks of the newcomers at Myth.

'I can't say any more.'

'How do you know all this?'

'I work for the British government.'

'What, like, MI6 or something?'

The guy shakes his head. 'Not MI6,' he says, his tone suggesting that somehow his job is even more secret than that. 'The important thing is, if you hear any more about any of this, then call me straight away. And if you want to give your friend the best possible chance of coming back alive, don't talk to anyone else about any of it.' He grabs a last couple of chips as he gets up, his unbuttoned jacket revealing a stowaway paunch, and when Raf follows him back outside he sees that the clouds have cleared. 'My God, that place is awful,' the guy says. He's about to cross the street when he halts abruptly and Raf turns to see why.

A white van is coming towards them, sun reflecting in the windscreen so Raf can't make out the driver's face.

The guy hurls himself back into the restaurant, almost knocking over a boy in a tracksuit, but Raf doesn't react as fast, so he's still standing there when the van brakes right beside him. The rear doors don't open, though, and when the lights at the crossing change and the van drives on, Raf can hear the tired growl of an ageing diesel engine just like any other. On the back, in the grime, with index fingers, someone has written 'I WISH MY WIFE WAS AS DIRTY AS THIS' and someone else 'SHE IS WITH ME' and someone else '<u>WERE</u> AS DIRTY'.

DAY 4

2.27 p.m.

Raf is at Isaac's flat playing an Xbox game in which the virtual New York has its own diurnal cycle that lasts only forty-eight minutes, with light-modelling a hundred times more sophisticated than anything he's ever worked on. He tells Isaac what he heard the day before, but he has to admit for all he knows the guy in McDonald's also responds to every lost dog notice he sees with a story about ethnically specific kidnappings. After Isaac insists on switching the television over to the cricket, Raf starts leafing through a stack of the Japanese girls' quasi-pornographic fashion magazines.

Raf and Isaac have been best friends since they were at comprehensive school together when they were fourteen. Isaac's biological parents were alcoholics and he'd been taken into foster care when he was younger, but his new family were a gas giant of warmth and tolerance, and he always stayed out of trouble – except in the sense that he used to deal a lot of weed and pills, but nothing nasty ever came of that, and Isaac would probably disagree with the Southwark Council Family Support and Child Protection Office on whether it constituted 'trouble'. He started DJing on Myth when he was nineteen in slots that weren't so much graveyard as necropolis, but he didn't really get to know Theo, or introduce Theo to Raf, until last year.

Raf thinks back to a night in January when he and Theo stopped at Isaac's flat to pick up a spare CD deck on the way to a house party. A few weeks earlier, Isaac had been looking around on the internet for a site that would sell him dried psilocybin mushrooms by post when he'd come across one that instead sold fresh

Gyromitra esculenta, a type of false morel used in Finnish cookery. Isaac is fascinated by these false morels, firstly because they are pinkish, bilobed and furrowy like a human brain, and secondly because they contain a precursor chemical called gyromitrin, which breaks down in the liver to a toxin called monomethylhydrazine, which was a component of the hypergolic propellant used in the Apollo Lunar Modules. Monomethylhydrazine is a toxin because it blocks the production of γ-aminobutyric acid, or GABA, an important neurotransmitter that you can buy in tablets as a treatment both for social anxiety disorders and for sleep disorders. But Isaac has spent his entire life swallowing pills without asking what's in them – all kids do that, and a certain set of adults – so naturally he is cocky around fungus.

When Raf and Theo arrived in Isaac's kitchen, he took three cans of beer out of the fridge and explained that he was cooking a traditional Finnish false morel omelette, but he wasn't going to offer any to his guests because with gyromitrin there was some risk of headache, vomiting, diarrhoea, jaundice, delirium, coma and/or death, although many tough old Scandinavians did eat the mushrooms raw without reporting any sickness whatsoever and in this case he'd parboiled them for so long that he was pretty sure he'd ingest only the very minimum amount of gyromitrin necessary to meet the goal of the experiment, which for the historical record was to show that he had metabolised rocket fuel in his own body. He sang part of the 'GABBA GABBA hey! GABBA GABBA hey!' verse from 'Pinhead' by the Ramones. But then Theo snatched up the frying pan and said he wasn't going to let any idiot eat poisonous mushrooms in his presence, and somehow the scuffle ended with him scraping the entire omelette into his mouth, choking down about half, and then vomiting into the sink. When it was over, Raf asked Theo why he didn't just tip the omelette on to the floor. Theo shrugged and said he'd panicked. (A few weeks after that, Isaac learned from a message-board that, like a confused ecstasy dealer, the site from which he'd ordered the false morels wasn't selling real false morels but instead real morels falsely advertised as false morels. Real morels, which are harmless ascocarps used in Provençal cuisine, do contain hydrazine, which was a rocket fuel in the Nazis' experimental Messerschmitt 163, but the problem is that they contain it from the very beginning, without the intervention of human biochemistry, which doesn't excite Isaac.)

Even if the expedient was impulsive, the impulse itself was characteristic for Theo, who is a born rescuer. There was the time Barky got in trouble with an ecstasy wholesaler who supposedly had ties to the Serbian mafia, and Theo not only let him hide in his flat for a couple of weeks but also redeemed half of his debt by bartering away a block of daytime radio ads for the dealer's brother-in-law's motorcycle workshop. There was the time Theo needed a sentry for Myth FM's single most valuable asset, and instead of just training up one of the Staffie puppies that are always oversupplied around here, he bought Rose, in effect a slightly faulty adoption dog. And there was the time he rescued Raf, too. Raf had begun to give up hope of ever finding any ongoing employment that didn't involve just sitting alone in his flat doing piecework and wondering why he was alive. He didn't want to be one of those sleep disorder patients who become nothing but vassals of their illness, but he could see himself going that way, and he had no idea what to do about it. Until this recent break-up it was the lowest point of his adult life. But then Theo heard about this from Isaac, and gave Raf a job that not only let him roam the streets but even exploited his peculiarity as a minor asset: if Rose was walked according to any regular timetable, then it would be easy to work out when the Myth FM transmitter was next going to be vulnerable for half an hour, but no one without a copy of Raf's own home-made calendar application could predict his pseudo-random arrivals.

Raf can't help dividing the world into the people and institutions that are friendly to his disorder and the ones that are hostile to it – like a fox nesting behind a bus depot, he's a creature making the best of an environment to which he is in some respects maladapted. So he feels an extra gratitude to his omelette-gobbling boss, maybe a unique one, on top of the friendship that's developed between them over the past year. Should he believe the worst about what's happened to Theo? He doesn't know. But he won't if he can possibly help it.

DAY 5

1.51 p.m.

The next-of-kin information you see on signs under railway bridges – 'IN CASE OF EMERGENCY: IF YOU WITNESS A VEHICLE STRIKING THIS RAILWAY BRIDGE PLEASE CONTACT RAILTRACK' – has for a long time made Raf hope very dearly that before he dies he will witness a vehicle striking a railway bridge just so he can finally call one of those engraved telephone numbers. On this rainy afternoon, walking Rose not far from his flat, the dirty ground under one of those bridges is a tintype of the dark belly above: from the square of dry asphalt you can make out its girth and from the inner grid of pigeon shit you can make out its iron ribs. Past the bridge is a basketball court, and from the way Rose strains forward Raf knows straight away that she's scented something. Then he sees the fox sitting on the waist-high wall at the edge of the court, and just like when he got on that bus on Saturday, he's so startled that he forgets his grip and the leash slips out of his hand as Rose shoots forward, snarling. She jumps against the wall, claws rasping at the brick, and what's strange is that the fox is only a few inches out of her reach and yet it doesn't even flinch as it looks down at her. It's as if the fox has calculated that it's safe and therefore has no reason to be alarmed, even though Raf knows that's not how animals operate. The fox lets the wave crash against the wharf for a bit longer and then turns round, jumps down, and canters off across the court into some bushes. Rose keeps on barking loud enough to snap a glottis until Raf picks up the lead again and hauls her away. 'Good job, girl,' he says. 'You definitely scared it off.' He turns right at the end of the road, intending to go back to his flat to pick up an umbrella before he carries on the walk,

34

and what he sees then is a lot more surprising than any sanguine fox.

A white van. Two men dressed all in black. And that same girl from the laundrette who said her name was Cherish. The rear doors of the van are open and they are pulling her inside.

Without even thinking, Raf runs forward. Rose is still riled so of course she keeps pace. When they're just a leash's distance from the men, she goes for them like she went for the fox. And the guy on the left pulls from a thigh holster what Raf recognises from many hours on Isaac's Xbox as a semi-automatic pistol with a silencer, maybe an M9. He takes aim at Rose. 'No!' shouts Raf. Then the guy on the right puts a hand on the other guy's arm, shakes his head, and says something Raf can't hear.

As Raf tries to reel Rose back, both men get into the van and slam the rear doors behind them. The van accelerates away, silent if it weren't for the squeak of its tyres on the wet road, and Raf watches as it turns left by the primary school on the corner and is lost from sight.

He looks back at the girl. Like the butt of a torch on a warehouse door, his heart is banging in his chest so hard that he can hardly believe it's not audible. 'Cherish, right?' he says.

She's wearing the same black hoodie but the hood isn't up so her hair is straggly from the rain. 'Yeah.' Rose jigs around Cherish's legs, all her violent energy transduced, until this new friend bends down and starts scratching her under the chin.

'Do you have any idea who those guys were?'

'No.' She takes a long breath and puts a palm to her own chest. 'That was . . . Fuck! I feel like I just ran a race or something.'

So the guy in McDonald's was telling the truth after all, Raf thinks. He wonders again where Theo is now. 'Do you want a cup of tea?' he says.

'Yeah, but I think I might cry in a second.'

Raf shrugs. 'OK.'

2.16 p.m.

Raf doesn't clean his kitchen very often, so the floor is sown with sesame seeds and there's a grouting of cumin power in almost every cranny. All the cupboard doors are made of that cheap painted chipboard that's so lightweight they never quite feel as if they're wholeheartedly shut. He turns up Myth FM on the radio and brings the two mugs of milky tea over to the table. 'I just remembered . . .'

'What?'

'The fake glow I gave you. Did you throw up? I'm really sorry.'

'I never took it,' says Cherish. Her hoodie is drying on the radiator. 'I had to leave right after I met you. Lucky escape, I guess.'

Raf blows on his tea. 'Have you ever had real glow?'

'A few times.'

'What's it like?'

'A lot like MDMA. But it lasts longer and it's a lot more . . . Don't ask me what the word is. And it does things to the light. That's where the name comes from.'

'Like magic mushrooms?'

'No, not really. Any electric light you look at, you see this . . . I don't know. But you can't look away. Once I saw a guy in the street outside a party just standing there watching the traffic lights change like it was the most spectacular thing he'd ever seen.'

'Only electric lights?'

'Yeah.'

The contrarian hypothalamus won't necessarily accept that you're seeing what the visual cortex has decided you're seeing, but instead insists on making its own private analysis of the heliometric data it gets from the optic nerve: that's one possible explanation for Raf's syndrome, but it might also mean that sometimes the hypothalamus knows the truth about light when all the rest of the brain is fooled by a hallucinogen. Out in the corridor Rose is dozing with the side of her face squashed against the skirting board. Raf knows that every minute he lets the dog idle in his flat is another minute that Myth's transmitter is unguarded, and he already feels guilty. But for all anyone knows he could still be out walking her.

'It's weird that I saw you again,' he says.

'Yeah.'

On Myth they're playing an ad for some club in Brixton: 'Remember, dress to impress: no hats, jeans or trainers.'

He hesitates. 'I was really, really, really hoping I would,' he says.

'Yeah?'

Raf feels as if their adrenaline is still here with them in the room but it's started to expand, thin out, condense on the window like the steam from the electric kettle. She's clasping her mug with both hands and he can see the veins that wind their pale green up between her knuckles and then drain it into skin a few shades more melanous than his own. He has never before had in his flat, he reminds himself, a girl whose life he might just have saved. He leans forward to kiss her.

Her tongue is warm from the tea, and then so are her fingers on the back of his neck. In this position they have to lean awkwardly into each other, as if the kiss is something heavy they're hoisting through a broken window, so he pulls his chair closer to hers in two little hops. She pivots her left leg up to rest across his knees, and when he touches the bare ankle of her dangling foot her whole body shrugs. Normally the radio by the sink is tinny, but now the bass has crawled after them into this vault they've built with their lips and eyelids, and in the limitless darkness there it seems to find room to swell until Raf feels as if he could be back at the laundrette right next to a subwoofer. Their hands squirrel up under each other's T-shirts, his fingers counting the bumps of her spine, and without thinking he starts to unhook her bra. She pulls away. 'Hey . . .' she says, not angrily.

Raf clears his throat. 'Sorry.'

Cherish is breathing fast and there's a flame in her eyes as if she's just metabolised about a double shot of rocket fuel. A single hair from her head has found its way down into the corner of her mouth. She bites her lip and looks away, weighing something up – and then at last she looks back at him, smiles, and reaches down to peel off her T-shirt. For the second time his fingers find the catch of her plain black bra, and as she shrugs off the straps he kisses her from her neck down to her nipples. 'Do you have a bed?' she murmurs.

'Yeah.' He gets up and takes her by the hand, seeing that across her upper back she has a tattoo of three songbirds: red, orange, and yellow, with black heads. Their mugs of tea are only about a quarter drunk, and he realises they can't have exchanged more than a few hundred words in total; but in a club that would never trouble him, it's only the damp daylight that's making it strange. Isaac once went home with a girl he met on a bus on a Sunday afternoon, although admittedly they were both still out from the night before.

When they get to his bedroom Cherish stops dead, and at first he's worried that it's too messy or something. 'Whoa, listen,' she says. 'I'm not that into . . .'

Raf doesn't understand. 'What?'

She is looking down at his eyemask and earmuffs. 'Isn't that, like, S&M stuff?'

He laughs. 'No. That's to help me sleep. I have a disorder.'

'And what's that thing on the pillow?'

'That's for white noise.'

'Oh! I thought maybe it was for electric shocks.'

3.50 p.m.

When Cherish climbed off Raf for the second time, he just knotted the condom and left it on the floor by the bed, which was a serious error. They're still lying there side by side when Rose scurries into the bedroom, and before Raf can stop her she has found the condom, gulped it down with an actual audible gulp, and escaped triumphantly into the hall.

'Oh my god, that is so fucking gross!' says Cherish.

'She loves used condoms. A lot of dogs do. I don't know why.'

'And you let her eat them? Like, as a treat?'

'No!' Normally he remembers to put them out of her reach.

'Is she going to be OK?'

'It'll go through her in about a day.'

'That is really fucking gross.'

'Yeah.' His penis feels, pleasantly, like a railway bridge that's been struck by a vehicle. He shifts his head on the pillow so that his eyes are only an inch from her bare shoulder, almost too close to focus, and in that position he could swear there's a phosphorescence in her skin, as if he could shut the blackout curtains and still see the shape of her. And he knows that this is probably a combination of at least three things: first of all, the light from the bedroom window skipping off her sweat; second, the persuasive impression of what she told him an hour ago about the auras you see when you swallow the right drugs; and third, the joy he now feels, as dim as this illusory light he's trying to explain, but still real joy, like he hasn't felt since his girlfriend left.

Then he remembers an article he once read about an experiment they did in Japan, where volunteers sat for three hours in a dark room, motionless and naked and very clean, as if for some purgative temple rite, and they were photographed by a camera chilled to 120 degrees below zero. Over the course of that long, long exposure, enough light trickled from the chemical reactions in their cells to make a portrait. In other words, humans really do glow, although a million times less brightly than even a baby firefly. And the researchers found that the glow has a diurnal cycle, like the sky. If you could make a film with that camera and speed it up and boost the contrast, humans would strobe. (Raf, of course, would strobe at a different rate.) He also knows that sex, like drugs, dilates your pupils. Could your pupils ever gape so wide that a naked body would disclose its light to your naked eye? Maybe if the sex was good enough.

'Do you have any vodka?' says Cherish.

'Yeah, in the kitchen. Why?'

In a typical instance, when Raf lies back to watch a girl climb out of his rumpled bed and pad across the room, it's with such unconcealed pride that you might have thought he'd assembled her himself, but this time he's still too surprised by the whole episode to feel like that. He hears the toilet flush. After a minute Cherish comes back with his half-empty bottle of supermarket vodka, sits down on the bed, and takes a swig. 'Bleh!' She wipes her mouth and looks down at him. 'Don't worry, I'm not getting the shakes or anything. It's for the oxytocin.'

'What do you mean?'

'I came a couple of times, so my brain's all full of oxytocin – plus you wouldn't leave my nipples alone, which was, you know, nice, but that means even more oxytocin – and that'll make me want to pair-bond with you and then, like, cry when you don't call. But alcohol messes with hormone release from the hypothalamus and the pituitary. So if I drink something neurotoxic right after we fuck, I don't bond with you so much. It's folk medicine, I guess, but I kind of trust it.'

'Why don't you want to bond with me?' says Raf; not forlorn, just curious.

She puts a hand on his lopsided butterfly of chest hair. 'I'm not saying I don't like you. But I don't want to like you any more than I would if you hadn't squeezed some hormones out of me with your dick. Nothing personal. It's policy.'

'Should I drink some?'

'You're a man, so you mostly just get dopamine and some prolactin, not oxytocin. Unless you're a real pussy, I guess.'

It's oxytocin, Raf recalls, that makes your pupils dilate when you're aroused, and that helps MDMA work as a truth drug. Isaac once ordered three bottles of a product called Liquid Trust, which described itself on the website as 'The world's FIRST and ONLY product to attract women by getting THEM to trust YOU'. It was just synthetic oxytocin diluted in alcohol, and you were supposed to spray it on your clothes every morning like a cologne and keep it in the fridge between uses. Isaac was going to use it in a club, a subliminal broadcast on a secret frequency. But then Raf pointed out that unless you were wearing a gas mask you'd inhale the majority of the Liquid Trust yourself, which would be like trying to date-rape someone by putting one temazepam in their drink and five in your own. So instead, Isaac sprayed some up his own nose and then spent an hour on YouTube watching conspiracy videos about the July 7th bombings to see if the oxytocin would make him more gullible, but the results were inconclusive.

The two of them have been running their continuous amateur neurochemistry seminar ever since Raf first got diagnosed with his syndrome and Isaac first took amphetamines (which happened around the same time) but it's still odd to hear words like 'hypothalamus' and 'pituitary' in conversation with a stranger. And odd, too, that she seems determined to treat her own amygdala like some lawless vertex of the Golden Triangle, purging her oxytocin with alcohol like a drug agent spraying a poppy field with glyphosate, although maybe that means she's just more advanced than Isaac or Raf. His own internal serotonin labs are up and running right now after six long weeks of downtime and he really hopes they don't get busted again. 'How long have you been into . . . brain stuff?' he says.

'There were girls at my high school in LA who'd been taking Zoloft since they were three years old and they didn't even know how it worked. If you don't educate yourself about this shit you're an idiot.' She scratches her knee. 'Do you have anything we can eat?'

He decides against a joke about the other condom. 'Not really.'

'How about a curry? I know a place near here.'

Raf sometimes thinks there is nothing in the whole world that makes him happier than spicy food soon after sex. 'Yes,' he says. 'Wow, yes.'

4.31 p.m.

Raf was considering a prawn madras, but Cherish makes him turn to the end of the laminated menu, where there's a page that says 'BURMESE SPECIALITIES': tea-leaf salad, catfish soup, peanut curry, tamarind lamb, royal noodles.

'Why do they have all this stuff?'

'It's a Burmese restaurant.'

'I always thought it was Indian.'

But in fact there were clues that it wasn't: in Raf's experience, Indian restaurants in London, even the cheap ones, usually feel a bit like funeral homes with their tinted windows and dark carpets and low lighting, whereas this place just has linoleum floors and vinyl tablecloths and a few creased posters of Buddha on the walls. On the ledge by the door are two of those battery-powered Maneki Neko cats, the white one bigger than the gold one, so their metronomic paws move in and out of phase.

'They cook Indian food here because people don't know what Burmese is. But the staff are all Burmese.'

The waiter, a short guy with a goatee, brings over their beers and takes out his notebook. Earlier, Cherish greeted him as if they knew each other.

'I don't know what to have,' says Raf.

'You want a curry?' says Cherish.

'Yeah.'

She turns to the waiter and says something in what is presumably Burmese. He nods and goes back into the kitchen.

'So that's what you are too?'

'Burmese? Kind of. At higher resolutions I'm half Danu, half American.'

'Where did you grow up?'

'In a mining town about halfway between Mandalay and the border into Yunnan.'

Cherish's earliest memory, she tells Raf as they wait for their food, is the night her Uncle Chai came back to Gandayaw after six months away in the Concession and she burst into tears because he looked so much like a monster: eyes buried alive in the gloom of their own sockets, cheeks like slack grey tarpaulins, mouth turned down in a paresis of pure despair. But he promised her he was still her Uncle Chai and he was just very tired. Years later, she would find out why. At the Lacebark mine, you got two hours a day to eat and wash and pray and play cards, and the rest of the time you were either sleeping or working. But you didn't work for fourteen hours and then sleep for eight, or even work for sixteen hours and then sleep for six. Instead, you worked for three and a quarter hours at a time, then unrolled your foam mattress wherever you stood and slept for forty-five minutes. That was the cycle. In total, you slept for only about four hours a day. When she was older, Cherish would learn that this was called polyphasic sleep, and it was used all over the world: the purpose was to maximise the productive hours of the workforce at the mine by teaching their bodies to skip straight to essential REM sleep, while also eliminating the inherent inefficiencies of the three-shift system. It was an agronomic approach to the brain, like some new method of crop rotation. And Uncle Chai had admitted that after a full month of sleeping only four continuous hours a night, he would have been passing out on his feet like a drunk, and yet even after six months of polyphasic sleep, he was still able to work. But polyphasic sleep gave you a tiredness of a different kind, a soggy tumour of exhaustion that grew heavier and heavier every sunrise, so that you could always feel it squeezed against your skull even if it hadn't yet made you sick. After Uncle Chai returned that first time, he lay down inside the house and couldn't be woken for more than a day, even to eat the welcome-back feast that Cherish's mother had been planning for weeks.

When her mother was young, Gandayaw had still been a village of only a few dozen families, so isolated that many of the locals had never seen a pair of shoes, but in 1989 the Burmese government leased a vast area of copper and ruby deposits, half a million hectares of the Shan forest at the base of the hills, to an American company. Lacebark Mining built an office on the western edge of the Concession, and Gandayaw puffed up into a boom town out of the Wild West: from China and Thailand and India and other parts of Burma came traders, pedlars, fixers, translators, builders, electricians, plumbers, doctors, drivers, hoteliers, cooks, missionaries, musicians, hairdressers, tattooists, bodyguards, extortionists, confidence tricksters, drug dealers, bootleggers, pimps, prostitutes, beggars, and government agents. Helicopters landed three times a week. A discotheque was built, with a karaoke lounge, a jacuzzi, and a sign in the foyer warning people not to bring in hand grenades or durian fruit. Uncle Chai once told Cherish that the change had come so fast that it was as if the village itself had been abducted in its sleep and then woken up somewhere entirely new.

Gandayaw was not only a boom town but also a border checkpoint, because in exchange for a forty-five per cent royalty to the government, Lacebark ran the Concession like a sovereign enclave. They couldn't patrol more than a fraction of the perimeter, but it was rumoured that if they found you 'trespassing' in the forest you might be beaten or even shot. Although some of Gandayaw's savage new prosperity came from Lacebark's executives and managers and engineers, much more came from its private security corps, who could often be seen swaggering like conquerers through the town with AK-47s strapped at their sides on their way to meetings with liaison officers from the Tatmadaw. Mine workers coming home from the Concession never seemed to want to talk much about life inside, which led to a lot of stories among the children of Gandayaw: that the Americans kept order with robotic tigers they brought to the forest in shipping containers; that when men died in accidents, which was often, they were reanimated and made to keep toiling. Even back then, Cherish had a feeling that one day she would have to see the Concession for herself.

The farthest she ever strayed into the forest as a child was one day at the end of the rainy season when she saw a fox drinking from a puddle by the ridge at the edge of town, and while her mother was distracted she followed it into the trees. The fox moved quite slowly as if it wanted to help her keep up. After a few minutes they came to a clearing where a deer was eating berries from a *longan* tree. Noticing the fox, the deer stopped eating, whereupon the fox crouched down and wiggled its hindquarters from side to side like a cat does before it pounces. Cherish was surprised at this because there was no way the fox was big enough to take down the stag, whose antlers were like a pair of crowbars. But when the fox did make its leap, it tacked too far to the right, so that the stag could easily bounce sideways out of the way. And after that the fox paid the stag no more attention. Instead, it pawed and snuffled at the ground where the stag had been standing. Cherish tiptoed close enough to see that the fox was grazing on white grubs about the size of the dung beetle grubs her uncle sometimes liked to cook in a disgusting omelette. Then she heard her mother screaming for her, and she ran back towards the ridge, resigned to a spanking.

It wasn't until she was falling asleep that night that she worked out her theory of what must have happened. The fox had deliberately made the stag lurch to the side so that it would stretch out the skin of its flank, where some sort of insect had laid its eggs. When the skin went tight over the ribs, the grubs popped out like beans from a pod, and the fox got an easy meal. Cherish did wonder why the stag couldn't have performed the same surgery on itself without the fox's help, but perhaps it was for the same reason that she couldn't scare her own hiccups away so she always had to get Zaya to do it. Years later she would still imagine hiccups as pallid larvae jumping out of her mouth.

Zaya was Cherish's half-brother, six years older than her. His father had died of a viper bite not long after Zaya was born, leaving their mother a young widow. So when dollars invaded Gandayaw, their mother had started a beauty stall selling shampoo and *thanaka* paste, from which she earned just about enough to feed her children when Cherish was growing up. In those days, her mother mostly seemed sad, her brother mostly seemed angry, and Cherish herself mostly felt puzzled and out of place: she knew she looked different from her relatives, and at a certain point she worked out that her father must have been a white man, but no one wanted to tell her anything more. Later, she would come to feel as if her personal indeterminacy was designed to click right into the general indeterminacy on which her home town ran: intelligent kids can't bear the feeling that the world is spinning and meshing all around them in ways they aren't supposed to understand yet, but because of how deals are made in a place like Gandayaw, even the canniest adult has to accept that for every three parts of the machinery she's learned to follow there are seven or eight farther back that she'll never even glimpse.

When Cherish was ten years old, however, something happened that showed her far more of the machinery of her own life than she'd ever seen before. One morning a few days after that year's lantern festival, she and Zaya were on the way to buy vegetables with their mother when a black Mercedes-Benz drove past, so slowly that perhaps one of the passengers had told the driver he wanted to get a good look at the town. Cherish had seen a lot of cars like that before, and was more interested in establishing diplomatic relations with a macaque on a chain that she could see in a bar across the road, but her mother stopped dead. Then she grabbed both her children by their arms and dragged them off into an alley. Here two crows bickered on the support struts of an air-conditioning unit.

'What are you doing?' said Zaya.

'Go back and open the stall,' said their mother.

'Why?' Zaya's friends all made fun of him when they saw him on his own behind the baskets of cosmetics, even though most of the time those boys were quite an earnest, secretive gang, muttering about politics and crowding around half-broken radios. Some of them smoked yaba tablets, sucking the fumes off heated foil through a plastic straw like a butterfly's proboscis, but not Zaya himself as far as she knew.

'Just go back and open the stall. Cherish and I have something to do. We'll be back later.'

After Zaya was gone, their mother led Cherish aimlessly from shop to shop for a while, but eventually they made for the main Lacebark building. At four concrete storeys this was the tallest structure in the town, although like a consular office it didn't really belong to Gandayaw but to the foreign territory of the Concession, and indeed a tunnel was popularly rumoured to lead from its basement all the way to the mines twelve miles away.

'Are we going inside?' said Cherish. The day was hot and she had her *longyi* folded up to her knees.

'No.' Instead, they sat down in a tea shop where all the seats were made from the top halves of old swivel chairs lashed with bamboo rope to drums of laundry detergent, weighted down with rocks. They must have waited there for at least two hours, although it seemed more like a month to Cherish, who'd never been so bored in her life. She passed the time watching an old man, hairless and hunchbacked, an animate nub of ginger root, who hobbled up and down the street selling cigarettes and flowers. Just as she counted his seventh lap, three white men in business suits walked laughing out of the Lacebark building, and her mother jumped up from her stool and hurried across the street, pulling Cherish with her. A black Mercedes-Benz was waiting for the men, perhaps the same one as before, and beside the car were four bodyguards with guns, but the approach of a woman and her young daughter must have seemed so innocuous that no one really noticed them until Cherish's mother was thrusting her towards the tallest of the white men and screeching in English, 'Your child! Your child! Your child!'

The words might have been plain enough, but at that moment it didn't occur to Cherish what they actually meant. What she did understand straight away was that her mother was doing something unbelievably dangerous. For both of them to be marched off at gunpoint and beaten up in the pit behind the disco would have taken

47

only a word, maybe only a gesture, from one of the men in suits. And indeed the bodyguards were now reaching for their pistols. But then the tall man, the object of Cherish's mother's fury, must have said something to hold them off. Cherish looked up at him, and he looked back down at her with the stunned expression of someone watching the flame from his half-smoked cigarette consume an entire heap of rubbish, a bit guilty for his carelessness but at the same time quite impressed by this reminder of his powers.

There was a pause in which no one seemed to know what to do. The tall man's two colleagues looked especially awkward. Then the tall man stepped forward and murmured something to Cherish's mother, who nodded before crouching to kiss Cherish.

'Go to your brother,' she said. 'Wait for me at home, the two of you.'

'No!'

'Go, sweetheart. I'll be back.'

So Cherish obediently crossed the street, but rather than carrying on towards the cosmetics stall she pressed herself against the wall of the tea shop so she could watch what would happen. As the other two got into the car, the tall man and one of the bodyguards led her mother around to a side door of the Lacebark building and disappeared inside. Cherish burst into tears and dropped to her knees in the dirt, certain that she would never see her mother again. On his way past, the hunchbacked pedlar drew back his lips to give her what was probably supposed to be a comforting grin, but in the darkness of his mouth there were only two brown incisors that dangled from his gums like bats from the roof of a cave.

5.49 p.m.

Raf takes a swig of beer. 'So what happened?' he says. He has that feeling of mild inadequacy he gets whenever he listens to anyone who's had a truly eventful or difficult life.

'I was wrong! That afternoon, my mom came back. My brother was about a minute from making a commando assault on the Lacebark building, but she came back. She said we were going to America. Everything was arranged. And that was the last night I ever spent in Gandayaw. The next day, a jeep took me and my mother to an airfield near this town called Kyaukme, then we got a flight to Bangkok International, then another flight to LAX. All the paperwork was already waiting for us.'

'What about your brother?'

'He wouldn't come. He said we couldn't "abandon Gandayaw to the white men and the Tatmadaw". Like the three of us were the last line of defence.'

'So you left him?'

'My mom pleaded. But he just went off into the forest with his friends. He said he wouldn't show himself in town again until we were gone. It must have torn my mom to pieces, but we were on somebody else's schedule and there wasn't a lot she could do. She knew how stubborn Zaya was. She used to tell me he'd follow us one day.'

Raf doesn't want to interrupt the story but he can't stop himself from informing Cherish that this chicken curry might be the best curry he's ever eaten.

'You don't have to tell me.'

It's fragrant like getting knocked down in the street by one of those trolleys from the flower market would be fragrant, and the hot capsaicin buzz feels as if it's seeping directly through his soft palate into his medulla oblongata, about a hundred times as good as ethyl-buphedrone. 'I wish I knew how to make one like this.'

'Me too.'

'Did you ever find out who that guy was?' Raf says. 'Your father?'

She shakes her head. 'I don't think of him as my father. He's just a genomic precursor.'

'Right, sorry.'

'He must have come to Gandayaw in 1990. Some Lacebark exec who got tanked up on Johnnie Walker one night and raped my mom. And I guess Zaya must have been there too. In the room, or watching through a doorway. He would've been six years old. That's why she sent Zaya away when she saw the guy in the car. She must have thought there was a chance Zaya might recognise the guy too, and if he did, he'd go apeshit and get himself killed. She was probably right about that.' Cherish purses her lips. 'I always used to find it weird, what that prick did. Like, if you can rape someone on a business trip, how can you also care enough to pay for a new life for your little rape kid? But now I think it was a self-esteem thing. Status. He was thinking, "I know I'm not the type of guy who has a kid growing up in this shitty town full of hookers and guns and speed. So I'd better throw some money on the ground to make sure." Or maybe he did feel genuinely guilty, too. Who knows? We never saw him again.'

Raf scoops up the last of the stir-fried beans. 'Was it weird, moving to America?'

'Was it weird? Eating macaroni cheese in the cafeteria at a middle school in Echo Park after spending my entire life up to that point in a mining town in southern Burma?'

'Sorry. Stupid question.'

Every time she smiles she puts his heart in her mouth like a wonton. 'Yeah, kind of, but then again it was definitely no weirder for me than it was for, like, the Liberian boy sitting next to me. So it's not like I won that contest.'

'Where's your brother now? Still in Gandayaw?'

'No. But my mom's still in Los Angeles.' She pushes away her plate, casting into shadow the little golden flowerbed she's cultivated beside it by picking the foil absently from the neck of her beer bottle. Her phone beeps from her pocket and she takes it out to read a text message. 'Hey, I just need to talk to the chef for a minute,' she says. Raf eats the last of her rice. When she comes back from the kitchen, she's putting something in her purse but he doesn't see what. She also has the bill. 'They're going to wrap up a couple slices of mango cake for us,' she says as she sits down. 'Do you have plans tonight?'

Yes: Isaac has a new Xbox game. 'No.'

'Well, shall we get some more booze and go back to your apartment? I'm not drinking any more of that god-awful vodka you had.'

On the way here they stopped off at the block with the Myth FM transmitter so Raf could take Rose back up to the roof. As much as he wants to climb into a dryer with this girl and never get out, there's also part of him that doesn't even want to leave the restaurant, because he knows that wherever he goes next he can't conceivably feel as much well-being as he does now. There's no clock on the wall and no other customers, and time in here only moves as fast as the Maneki Neko cats can waft it forward with their plastic paws, so why stir? But he still nods and takes out his wallet to find his share of the bill.

'What are you whistling? I think I know that tune.'

'GABBA GABBA hey!' he sings softly. 'GABBA GABBA hey!'

DAY 6

6.24 a.m.

The next morning she's gone.

The realisation is pre-empted by his hangover, which as usual waits a few seconds after he wakes up before it pounces, as if it wants to savour the expression on his face. He mews in agony at Cherish, at the assumption of her presence, already looking forward to a tactical discussion of their mutual enemy and a fried breakfast that might bring as much joy as yesterday's curry. But when he reaches out, his hand finds nothing but rucked duvet. He takes off his eyemask to look around the room, and then he takes out his earplugs to call for her. Last night, after they had sex for the third time that day, he said, 'You'll still be here in the morning, right?'

'Yes, and I will still respect you.'

'No, I mean – you have to be careful. The vans.' By this point Raf and Isaac have asked all their mutual friends about Theo, but no one seems to know anything more.

'I'll still be here.' So he lay there with his arms around her, trying to tune his breathing with hers, but couldn't get the frequency, and after a while she said, 'Are you waiting for me to fall asleep?'

'Yeah.'

'Why?'

With his ex-girlfriend, Raf didn't like to install his eyemask and earplugs while she was still awake because it felt like the first step towards a marital schedule of fortnightly sex, but she did like to fall asleep on his chest, so he used to have to wait until she dozed off and then ease out from under her so he could barricade his head. (Isaac once reported going home with a girl who wore not only an eyemask

52

and earplugs but also a retainer and an anti-congestant nasal strip, which made her look as if for some reason she were morbidly afraid of leaking cerebrospinal fluid.)

When Raf didn't answer, Cherish explained, 'We can hug for as long as you want, but I can't sleep if I can feel someone else's heartbeat. Plus spooning just doesn't work, ergonomically. Everyone knows it but no one wants to admit it.' Around this girl there were black iron railings and a neat buffer of grass. That evening, sharing a bottle of whisky at the kitchen table, she had asked him about his own parents, who moved out to Essex a few years ago, and taught him a drinking game where you had to bounce a ten-pence piece into a shot glass. In bed afterwards she was rougher and more impatient than before, and he had an enjoyable feeling of being used, but when she came it was in complete silence, like a fuse blown in a cheap speaker.

A minute ago, Raf was dreaming about those empty soundproofed warehouses, rising and multiplying until their steel roofs blocked the sun from every street. Now he rolls over to sniff the other pillow, to prove Cherish wasn't a dream too, but it's blank to him. At least the sheets do have that tired and porous quality of sheets that have been repeatedly fucked in. He wonders what Rose would be able to smell here. How would a Staffie go through a bad break-up? Reminders of your lover breathing out from every object. You'd have to move house and burn all your bedding. Which is not that different from the plan Raf recently made. The only physical object he still has of his ex-girlfriend's is a hexagon-print scarf he once bought her as a present. He could tell straight away that she didn't like it, and sure enough she didn't bother to take it with her when she was collecting the things she'd left here. But apart from the scarf, there's all the rest of London, too. Isaac keeps telling him that it's no use trying to flee the reliquary of a dead relationship. 'Statistically,' he once said when they were drunk, 'every pint of beer you ever drink for the rest of your life will contain at least a few of the same molecules of H_2O that she sweated out the first time that Brazilian cunt gave her an orgasm. So you might as well learn to live with it.'

That did not make Raf feel any better. What he hates about whisky hangovers, he thinks now, is the synthesis they achieve between the spiritual and the gastric, as if your soul needs to throw up or your stomach has realised life is meaningless. And there's more moisture between his toes than in his mouth.

He gets up naked to check the bathroom and the kitchen, but Cherish is definitely gone. Now a real anxiety begins to jostle with his headache. He goes back into the bedroom to draw the curtains, and in the early morning light, grainy and pale like an old VHS recording, he sees something that he hadn't noticed with just the lamp on: the corner of a piece of paper poking out from under his own pillow. He pulls it out and unfolds it. The script in Biro here must be Burmese – the words are made of lots of circles squashed together, so they look like ornamented caterpillars – but at the top of the page, in English, it says: 'Raf, this is really important, <u>don't show it to anyone</u>! xx Cherish.'

Raf's left shoulder begins to sting, and he sees that he has a few scratches there, as if from the claws of her songbirds. He thinks about posting an ad, like Morris. 'Did you see me get spun upside down by a half-Burmese girl? Badly smitten, not at fault. Looking for witnesses. Please call Raf.' Instead, on a hunch, he gets dressed and goes out to fetch Rose. On the way, he notices that a weed of some sort has started to spread across the lawn at the perimeter of her block, a lather of silky white blooms. When he comes back with the yawning animal and lets her into his flat, she does something she's never done before. She skids inside, looks around, and starts barking like she's trying to drive a devil out.

Someone has been here. Not Cherish, because Rose made friends with Cherish. Someone else. Not a friend.

DAY 7

10.23 a.m.

A pudgy electrician is up on a stepladder fiddling with a new CCTV camera that now hangs from the ceiling, so Raf has to squeeze past him to get to the chiller cabinet for a pint of milk. This is vexatious enough, because when you spend as much time in a place each week as he spends in this corner shop (or on the top deck of the 343) it becomes another room in your flat, an appendix stapled to the floor plan, and you don't want to find a stranger in there rearranging your furniture. But then, handing fifty pence to one of the twins at the counter, he's even more dismayed to see that they seem to be stocking only about half as many types of dog food as they did before. On that shelf instead are packets of something brown and flaky, with no English on the cardboard label, just some Arabic and a picture of a smiling prawn. Out of curiosity he picks one up, sniffs it, and asks what it is, expecting to learn that it's some sort of Iranian snack product.

'*Balachaung*,' says the twin.

'Sorry?'

'*Ba-la-chaung.*'

The last time Raf heard that word was the day before yesterday, because it was on the menu in the Burmese restaurant and he got Cherish to pronounce it for him. She said it was a prawn relish with peanut and chilli. When he takes a proper look at the label he realises that the writing on it isn't Arabic, it's Burmese, just like the note, but in a blocky typeface, and then when he digs through the other packets in the tray he does find a couple with English printed on the packets: BBQ dry snakehead fish and herbal seedless tamarind jam.

'How long have you been stocking this stuff?' he says, with a queasy sense that certain tendencies are propagating through his surroundings much too fast, as if someone has been editing the machine code on which the world runs.

'Since last week. New supplier.'

'Do you sell much of it?'

The twin shrugs. 'Not yet.'

3.50 p.m.

Raf lied on the phone to the guy he met in McDonald's, or half lied, and said he had new information about the white vans. But this time the guy didn't want to go back to McDonald's, or anywhere else public. And Raf, feeling a crackle of paranoia now, didn't really want to be on his own with the guy, so he suggested that he come to Isaac's flat. Today, the girl knitting at the table by the front door is wearing muddy skate shoes and a gabardine blazer with a lot of zips, and the girl dozing on the futon is wearing transparent stiletto heels and a dress that looks like a banana skin. As always, they are magnificent. When the guy arrives, he looks around and says to Raf, 'Who are all these people?' Raf notices that he still has that ketchup stain on his lapel, like a pin badge in support of a charitable foundation for gluttons. If he works for the British government, shouldn't he own a spare suit?

'Nothing to worry about,' says Isaac, who is growing a beard at the moment. 'Their English isn't great, and I'm involved.'

'Involved?'

'I'm another mate of Theo's. Who disappeared. Sit down.'

The guy looks around for a few seconds as if he's expecting a chair to be wheeled out for him, but at least when he finally resigns himself to Isaac's sagging sofa he flops right into it instead of perching on the edge. A folding plastic clothes airer hung with damp T-shirts blocks off one corner of the living room like some sort of ramshackle crowd-control barrier. 'So what more do you know?' he says.

'I met this girl . . .' begins Raf.

'I'm delighted for you.'

'She – they tried to kidnap her, like Theo. I saw the van. They had guns. And I stopped them once, but some time last night I think they took her from my flat. When I woke up, she was gone.' He describes Rose's reaction. 'So I know there was someone in my flat. And if they broke in and took her I might not have heard anything, because of how I have to sleep.'

'Quite audacious to snatch her from right beside you, if it's anyone but Nosferatu that we're dealing with. Do you have any other evidence?'

'She didn't drink any water.'

'What do you mean?' says Isaac.

Raf didn't mention this earlier, although Isaac did ask a lot about Cherish, excited that his best friend had finally got laid after seven weeks of dolorous chastity.

'There is no way a human being could voluntarily leave a flat the morning after drinking as much whisky as we did without drinking a glass of water first. And there was no glass on the counter.'

'Maybe she washed it up.'

'There was nothing in the drying rack. All my glasses and mugs were where I left them.'

'Maybe she drank straight from the tap.'

'You can't. The taps are too low.'

'I'm really sorry, man, but that is the shittiest "clue" I've ever heard.'

Raf knows Isaac might be right, but at the same time he feels certain, as certain as he's ever felt of anything, that right now Cherish is in the back of a white van, or somewhere even worse, with Theo. He thinks of her in a dark room, in front of a camera, motionless and naked and very clean.

'Still, congratulations on finding a girl who will spend an evening just sitting in your flat getting wasted with you for fun,' adds Isaac. 'They are the best kind.'

'Anything else whatsoever?' says the guy in the suit. 'So far this has been, once again, a total bloody waste of time. My fault, I suppose. Fool me once, and so on.'

'She left this note.' Raf passes it over.

'Do you know what this means?'

'No. But read the top. She must have needed me to keep it safe.'

The guy sighs. 'So this piece of paper is the only concrete asset you have to show me? This is truly all you have?'

'Yeah.'

He folds it up. 'I'll have to keep it, of course. I'll get it translated by one of our analysts.'

'No,' says Raf. 'I need it back.'

The guy looks at the note, looks at the front door, looks at Raf – then he jumps to his feet and tries to make a getaway.

'Hey!' shouts Isaac. And that's when his flatmate, without even looking up from her knitting, sticks out her slender right leg, and the guy topples forward and smacks his nose on the brass rim of the peephole in the front door.

'Oh, wow, Hiromi!' says Isaac. 'Wow! Cheers, darling!' With help from Raf, who now feels guilty for assuming that Isaac didn't know the names of his flatmates, he hauls the guy back to the sofa. 'Let's tie the cunt up.'

'No, that absolutely, absolutely won't be necessary,' says the guy. He hands over the note and then finds a paper napkin in his pocket to wipe a trickle of blood from his upper lip. And he does look defeated, sitting there with a red postmark stamped on the bridge of his nose. So instead Raf and Isaac just stand over him.

'Who are you really?' says Raf.

'My full name is Mark Edmund Fourpetal.'

'Do you really work for MI6 or whatever?'

'MI6?' Fourpetal laughs. 'No. Quite a long way from MI6. I'm in PR.'

'What do you know about the white vans?'

'Not much. They're kidnapping Burmese men, as I told you last time. I don't know why. But they have something to do with my former employer. An American firm called Lacebark.'

'Lacebark are a mining company,' says Raf.

'Yes, but they're vertically integrated. Everything's in-house now. Including corporate security.'

'And they're chasing you?'

'What makes you say that?'

'Outside McDonald's. That van. You were scared.'

Fourpetal nods. 'Yes. Do you know Burckhardt's *The Civilisation of the Renaissance in Italy*?' He gestures at himself. '"What a man of uncommon gifts and high position can be made by the passion of fear is here shown with what may be called a mathematical completeness."'

Fourpetal explains that it's not as if he'd dreamed since boyhood of getting a job in the mining industry. In the school playground when he was eight or nine they'd often pretended to fight the Battle of Orgreave and nobody ever wanted to be the miners. But he hadn't had any choice. After eleven years in financial PR, Fourpetal had developed a reputation as 'the most craven, two-faced, back-stabbing little wank stain that's ever sat in a fucking swivel chair', in the invigoratingly candid words of one former colleague after a night out in a strip club near Liverpool Street. And you couldn't build that sort of brand overnight.

In fact, by a certain metric, he could trace his downfall all the way back to his first job after university, when he found himself working alongside a chinless Northern boy called Drummers who seemed quite likely to get promoted above him in the near future because he spent about ninety hours a week in the office. One day, Fourpetal took Drummers aside and told him that if he really wanted to get himself noticed he should offer their boss a few lines of good coke next time they were all in a bar. Drummers thanked him warmly for the advice, unaware that their boss had taken against drugs with an almost cultic fury ever since an overdose at a New Year's Eve party had left his horsy niece with permanent brain damage. Soon afterwards, Drummers left the firm. Unfortunately, he did not leave the industry. Instead, he dragged himself, mangled and frostbitten, from the ravine and eight years later was recruited to a senior position at the company where Fourpetal now worked. On his first day, he called Fourpetal into his office and explained that in the next round of recession-related redundancies the company was going to have to wave goodbye to five trainees, two receptionists, and one account manager. That account manager was, of course, Fourpetal. Drummers said this with an expression of such tremulant ecstasy that Fourpetal genuinely wondered if he might have been masturbating under his desk.

Afterwards, looking for another job, Fourpetal found that Drummers wasn't the only one with a Fourpetal story. Everyone, evidently, had a Fourpetal story. Sometimes even Fourpetal himself wasn't sure quite how he'd found the time to fuck over that many people in little more than a decade. Nonetheless, he knew his reputation was unfair. Like a valet who beats his wife every night in loyal imitation of his master, the London financial PR industry had hurried to adopt the special ruthlessness of the investment banks it serviced even though it had none of the same salary incentives. Fourpetal didn't believe for a second he was worse than all the others. Rather, he had become a scapegoat, and that was why every door in London had been shut in his face. For a while he thought about going to America, but he knew that in a recession he'd never find a company to sponsor him for an employment visa. And he didn't like the sound of Hong Kong or Doha. So he decided he'd just have to move out of financial PR into a sector where nobody knew him. The other advantage would be that he wouldn't so often find himself in meetings with people he remembered from boarding school.

He applied for about twenty jobs, hoping to find a company that wouldn't check his references too closely. In the interview with Lacebark Mining, he had expected to talk about copper and gems, but in fact they asked him how much he knew about EBB's work for

Kazakhstan or Poxham Toller's work for Zimbabwe, so he bluffed his way through that instead. And in his first week, he discovered he wasn't really going to be doing European PR for Lacebark. He was going to be doing European PR for Burma.

In the past, the Burmese regime itself had employed several different agencies, but no one would work for them any more because they always reneged on their fees. Lacebark was willing to step in, however, because it was getting more and more awkward for the company and its investors that the landlord of its Gandayaw mine was basically perceived as a more bumbling version of Nazi Germany. A coordinated media and lobbying strategy could punch a few big airholes in the tight lid of their trading conditions. The atmosphere in the corporate communications department in London was strange, because you were obliged to make the occasional wry joke about Burma's mad generals, otherwise you seemed like a push-over, but you weren't supposed to bring up the 1988 massacres or the arrest of Aung San Suu Kyi, otherwise you got a lot of resentful looks. And of course you had to remember to say 'Myanmar' instead of 'Burma' (although for some reason never 'Myanmarese'). Fourpetal's first assignment was to find a human-rights organisation working in south-east Asia that would take a grant from Lacebark and then put out a press release about it, which took longer than it was probably worth.

One drizzly afternoon at the beginning of April, Fourpetal came back from lunch and slumped down at his desk, feeling as if all these greasy plastics that nuzzled him day after day – the grey acrylonitrile of his mouse pad, the blue polypropylene of his telephone earpiece, the black polyurethane of his (legendary) swivel chair – might as well just be stitched together into a gimp suit into which he could be zipped up for good. That morning, he'd emailed an executive called Jim Pankhead, who worked at Lacebark's headquarters in North Carolina, to see if he had the latest draft of the statement Lacebark was going to make about the environmental impact of its operations in Burma. Just as Fourpetal roused his computer, an email arrived from Pankhead with the aphasic subject line 'FW: Fw: Re:'. The environmental statement was attached, but Fourpetal also noticed that Pankhead had forgotten to delete the body of the email, which contained a long series of previous messages in the usual reverse chronological order. Pankhead and another colleague at Lacebark had been using Hotmail addresses to correspond; ever since Enron, Fourpetal knew, senior executives at a lot of American companies had moved to private email accounts for anything remotely indiscreet, just in case the Department of Justice came along one day to confiscate the corporate servers. Towards the end of their email conversation, Pankhead had asked the other executive to send him the environmental statement, and the other executive had sent it to him at his Hotmail address, so Pankhead had forwarded it to himself at his Lacebark address, and from there he'd just now passed it on to Fourpetal. After completing this uncomplex forensic reconstruction, Fourpetal scanned the conversation down to the bottom, where he found a medium-length email from Pankhead to the other executive squashed against a rampart of > signs:

I covered for you like a pro today, buddy – thank me later. The theme of the meeting was, obviously, what the fuck went wrong at Gandayaw? We had Bezant on a video link from London. He seemed like a meathead but he used to run half of Cantabrian which is apparently a big deal. He said Sweet wanted to blame it all on the cyclone but really he was botching everything way before Nargis and we should have fired him sooner. Also said he could assure us that in another few months he'd have the stable door securely nailed shut (except he didn't put it like that).

Anyway, the cripple in Chiang Mai is asking for two million dollars to keep his mouth shut, which is hilarious. CFIUS are ruling on the bond deal with Xujiabang in August, and if they read in the NYT that we supposedly tortured the wives of a bunch of guys trying to start a union, the whole thing is going to fall apart, or, worse, subpoenas are going to start pounding us like Predator drones. Then Xujiabang back out, the world finds out we can't service our debts next year, and we all get fucked in the eye sockets. The cripple would be asking for a hundred mil if he understood what he had. So, yes, we're going to pay him.

As for the other thing, Bezant claims it's under control. Harenberg keeps saying it's ten times more important than the Xujiabang deal, which is ridiculous, but that's Harenberg. No clue why Nollic trusts him with anything. OK, enough of that: still in for that fundraiser this weekend?

Fourpetal wasn't all that surprised by Pankhead's blunder because he had recently made a similar one himself: an ex-girlfriend of his friend Rich had written Rich a plaintive email about how the previous night she'd had to trudge all the way across Battersea Bridge at 4 a.m. in the rain with no pants on under her dress after bolting in tears from an imminent one-night stand because even five weeks after their split the thought of having sex with anyone else but him was still too upsetting, and Rich had forwarded it to Fourpetal with a few uncharitable comments, and Fourpetal had replied with a few more uncharitable comments, and Rich had replied with an unrelated YouTube video about a panda, and Fourpetal had forwarded the panda video to eleven people who he thought might appreciate it, including, as it happened, the ex-girlfriend in question, whose maudlin anecdote was still there at the bottom of the circular. It could happen to anyone. So to Fourpetal, a veteran, the next move was clear. But then he realised that the next move after that was clear, too, and the next move after that, and the next move after that. In fact, as soon as he read Pankhead's email, a plan had come all at once into his head, a magnificent spontaneous birth, detailed and comprehensive and with appendices and footnotes.

Part one: he played *Minesweeper* for a few minutes and then wrote back to Pankhead, 'Hi Jim, so sorry to pester you again but I really do need that enviro statement ASAP. Or if you've already sent it, many apologies – we've been having some trouble with our servers over here so a lot is getting lost.' Almost instantly, he got a second email with the statement attached, but this time with nothing else below the subject line. Fourpetal judged from the speed of the reply that Pankhead must have realised his error and had been staring at his inbox in paralytic horror the entire time. Later that afternoon, he phoned Pankhead at his office and kept him on the phone with boring questions for as long as he could, because that seemed like the exact opposite of how he would naturally be inclined to behave if he'd read Pankhead's email and was now wondering what to do about it.

Part two: he phoned a guy he knew who worked upstairs in management, and told him that he was about to give a background briefing to a sympathetic *Independent* journalist about the challenges Lacebark faced as an ethical company in an unethical industry. Which of Lacebark's competitors would have the most to gain if it failed? Which executives held the real power at those companies? Which of those executives were known for sanctioning dirty tricks?

Part three: the next morning, before he left for work, he created an anonymous Gmail address of his own and emailed Donald Flory, the Senior Vice-President and General Counsel of Kernon Whitmire Copper and Gold Incorporated. 'I work at Lacebark Mining. I have information relating to the Gandayaw Concession and the Xujiabang bond deal which could cripple or destroy the company if released. In exchange I want a job with you in New York – undemanding, high paid, lots of exotic foreign travel – and ninety thousand shares of Kernon Whitmire stock transferred to an offshore trust in my name. Are you interested?'

'we are always happy to exchange ideas with like-minded professionals at other companies,' Flory replied that afternoon, not from his Kernon Whitmire address but from yet another private account. 'are you based in nc?' he asked, meaning North Carolina.

'No, but I'm flying there in a couple of weeks for a conference. Also on the way back I have an overnight layover in Newark.'

'let me know your hotel booking in newark. someone will come to your room.'

At eleven o'clock on the night of the layover, Fourpetal stood at the window drinking whisky from the minibar and thinking about all the models he'd probably fuck in his new loft on the Lower East Side. From this distance there was something about the flat amber glare of the airport that strangled your sense of perspective, so that the jets looked like hatchbacks trundling around a supermarket car park, and farther on east all the towers of Manhattan cowered beneath the monstrous gantry cranes of Port Newark. This deal was top secret so perhaps they wouldn't come until about midnight, he thought, lying down on the bed and turning on CNN. But midnight arrived, and then one, and then two, and there was still no knock at the door. At three, now pretty drunk, he turned on his laptop and wrote an email to Donald Flory: 'Noones here what the fuck is going on. Im flying back to Londn in four hours.' Then, wondering for the first time if he might have made some sort of serious error, he Googled Donald Flory again, and on a news website he found a picture of Flory at a recent press conference. He was shaking hands with Yangmin Gao, the jowly chairman of Xujiabang Copper and Gold.

Xujiabang Copper and Gold now owned a forty-one per cent stake in Kernon Whitmire.

It wasn't even hard to find. It was in the second page of Google results. Before he sent the email to Flory, Fourpetal had only bothered to look at the first page. For the first time in his life, Fourpetal wished he actually read *The Economist* instead of just telling people he did.

So that was why nobody had come to the room. Flory must have decided that he had more to gain by warning his friends in China that some opportunist was proposing to wreck their bond deal with Lacebark than he did by making a tawdry deal with that opportunist. In fact, he must have thought Fourpetal was a total imbecile for choosing Kernon Whitmire instead of some other corporate rival who had no connection with Xujiabang. Fourpetal was still trying to think through the implications of all this when he dozed off in his clothes.

The next day, on the train back from Heathrow, he called Lacebark's headquarters in North Carolina and asked to speak to Jim Pankhead.

'Oh – I'm afraid Mr Pankhead sadly passed away last week,' said the girl on the switchboard.

'How?'

'They told us he had a very bad allergic reaction to a painkiller he was taking.'

At that moment Fourpetal felt a gauze of fear drape itself across the back of his neck, but he immediately dismissed the feeling as preposterous. 'I see. Thank you.'

The new-build block of flats in Bermondsey where Fourpetal lived had walls and floors that were about as dense as filo pastry, and at least twice a week he would be kept awake by his downstairs neighbour having parties. But she was young and fetching and single, so every time she stopped him to apologise about the previous night in the effusive and passionate tones of someone who has absolutely no intention of curtailing whatever it is they are apologising for, he just waved it off. That day, wheeling his suitcase into the entry hall downstairs, he saw her coming out of the lift.

'Hi, Mark! Will you tell your friend we're so, so sorry about last night?' she said. 'I really hope we weren't too loud.'

'What do you mean?' said Fourpetal.

'We had a few people over and it got a bit out of hand for a Tuesday.'

'But what do you mean, "my friend"?'

'You had a friend staying, right? We could hear someone walking around up there. We knew you were away for a few days so at first we almost thought it might have been a burglar but then they were still there this morning.'

Fourpetal picked up his suitcase and ran.

Outside, the sky was a triple-distilled blue with a few squiggles of cloud like someone testing a ballpoint pen. He only got as far as the building site at the end of the road before his lungs started spitting hot bacon grease, and as he stumbled panting to a halt he tried to put together what must have happened. Donald Flory had told someone at Xujiabang. Someone at Xujiabang had told someone at Lacebark. And someone at Lacebark had started an investigation. Fourpetal had been careful not to give Flory his name or even his nationality – Flory knew only his hotel booking. But if Flory had passed the hotel booking to Lacebark, then of course they could identify Fourpetal, because it was a Lacebark secretary who had booked the room. After that, they would have read through all of his emails, even the ones he'd tried to delete, and they would have found the email that started all this.

They'd murdered Pankhead, and now they were going to murder him too.

Behind him, he heard the crunch of a tyre flattening a discarded soft-drink can. He turned to see a white builder's van pulling up beside him, and as in a dream he knew at once there was something uncanny here but he couldn't identify exactly what; a minute ago he'd seen this van, or another like it, parked across the road from his flat, but it wasn't just that. The side door of the van slid open, and inside were two men dressed all in black, one holding what looked like a plastic toy gun – some sort of Taser? Fourpetal dropped his suitcase and broke into a sprint, but as he rounded the corner on to Crimscott Street the van accelerated too, ready to trap him effortlessly.

Then the van's tyres squealed, there was a second, louder crunch, and a black man with a satchel strapped across his back was twirling through the air in front of the van like something disgorged intact from empty space.

4.39 p.m.

'I met that guy!' says Raf. 'Morris.'

They've now given up treating Fourpetal as a prisoner, although Isaac did tell Hiromi to use her 'ninja skills' again if he tried to steal anything else; Raf had worried that might offend her until she replied with a sardonic karate chop.

'So you got away?' says Isaac.

'Well, I don't know if the accident with the bike was enough to make the Lacebark men turn tail,' says Fourpetal, 'or whether it just cost them the initiative, but I kept running, and I didn't look behind me for a long time, and when I finally did, I couldn't see the van. I couldn't go back to my flat, of course, and I couldn't go back for my suitcase either, but I had my passport in my pocket, so I went to a bank and took out two and a half grand. That's the most they'd let me have in cash; I haven't used any of my accounts since. Then I checked into a fleapit under a false name. I've been hiding out for nearly a fortnight.'

'Why don't you leave London?' says Isaac.

'I can't just fly the coop. Lacebark will eventually catch me. I have to buy myself out of all this for good. When all I had was that email, and no real proof of anything, no details, no documents, no photographs, the best I could really expect to get from Kernon Whitmire was a new job and a bundle of shares, yes? That was a plausible exchange if I could get them to trust me. But now that Lacebark are after me, that's not enough. I need to find a company that will give me a new name and maybe a new face, otherwise I'll be as dead as Pankhead by the autumn. I don't have the resources to disappear on my own. And no one is going to go to those lengths to protect me just for an email they can't even verify. I need a lot more to bargain with. I need something huge.'

'So what's "something huge"?' says Raf.

'I'm not sure yet. I've been looking into it for three weeks and I haven't made spectacular progress. Which is to be expected. May I remind you both that I work in PR? All I've found out so far is that, as I told you, a lot of Burmese men have been disappearing in south London. We know from the email that this chap Bezant, who runs Lacebark corporate security, he was out in Lacebark's fragrant Sulaco, and now he's in London.'

'I thought Sulaco was the spaceship from *Aliens*,' says Isaac.

'We also know from the email that he must be handling something "ten times more important than the Xujiabang deal", if this other chap Harenberg is to be believed, *contra* Pankhead. That's got to be why the Burmese men are vanishing. It's got to be Bezant doing something for Lacebark. So that's why I'm staying in London. If I can find out what Lacebark are up to here, and I can get real proof, then I can take it to one of Lacebark's competitors – not Kernon Whitmire, this time – and perhaps I can save my own skin.'

'Why don't you just go to the police?'

'And tell them what? That I'm being stalked by a Fortune 500 company? That I once saw a scary van? Furthermore, I could ask you two the same question. Why don't you tell the police about your friend Theo?'

'Theo wouldn't want the police anywhere near him.'

'Neither would either of us, to be honest,' says Isaac.

'I still don't understand why you wanted to go to McDonald's instead of Happy Fried Chicken,' says Raf.

'Lacebark have a market capitalisation of about nineteen billion dollars,' says Fourpetal. 'McDonald's have one of about ninety-four billion. My policy, so far as possible, is to confine myself to the premises of multinationals with market caps considerably greater than Lacebark's. They won't be bribed or bullied into giving up their security camera tapes. Or cleaning up after an assassination.'

Raf realises this is just the same method that he used to use at school when bigger boys were trying to bully money out of him on the street – hurry into a well-lit, fast-food place and stay there until the boys got bored and wandered off. 'Before all this started, did you know that Lacebark were . . . like this?'

'Psychopathic, you mean? I'd heard rumours about their business methods. Nothing solid, but rumours. Worse than the old days of United Fruit – that sort of timbre. It might surprise you to know how close I got to all that, working in communications.' He leans back. 'Imagine an environmental charity puts out a press release that's critical of the company. Obviously, you put out a reply. That's PR. Then you put together a file on the charity so you can respond faster next time. That's still PR. Then you send someone to a few of the charity's public events so you can add to the file. That's still PR. Then you send someone to do some work for the charity so they'll get into the private events. That's still PR. Then you send someone to lie their way into the charity's inner circle. That's still PR, essentially, but at this point the people you're using may be ex-secret service, and they clock most of their hours with corporate security. That's why "Donald Flory from Kernon Whitmire" rang a bell. Recently we sent a girl into Greenpeace who'd spent the previous six months following Flory around, probably based out of one of those white vans, or some analogous chariot of utter anonymity, depending where he lives. Still, if someone had told me they were kidnapping people, killing people . . . In Burma, perhaps. But I never would have believed they'd do it in London. Or at their own bloody headquarters.'

'So in Burma it would be fine?' says Raf.

'That's not what I said,' says Fourpetal. But he doesn't sound as if he particularly objects to the implication. 'I now begin to worry that you've misunderstood,' he adds. 'The real bombshell in that email from Pankhead wasn't that Lacebark may or may not have mistreated the wives of some union organisers out in the jungle. The real bombshell was that Lacebark are insolvent and have been trying to hide it. One is a PR problem. The other is an actual problem.'

5.22 p.m.

Walking into the restaurant, Raf sees that the Maneki Neko cats are both turned off, and for some reason he finds their stillness eerie. The waiter from last time comes out from behind the counter with an index finger held up. 'One?'

'No,' says Raf, 'I just wanted to – I was in here with Cherish the day before yesterday?'

The waiter nods.

'She left me this note. I think it might be important but it's mostly in Burmese. I was hoping you might be able to tell me what it says.' Raf feels ridiculous making the request – if you bought an anime DVD with no subtitles you wouldn't just stroll into your nearest sushi restaurant and expect them to give you a helpful recap – but neither he nor Isaac nor Fourpetal could think where else to find a Burmese speaker.

The waiter looks down at the note and then smiles. 'Cherish didn't write this. Ko write this.'

'Who's Ko?'

'Cook.' He calls out something in Burmese. A second man comes out of the kitchen. They exchange a few words then glance back at Raf and chuckle.

'You want know what this mean?' says the cook. He has bushy eyebrows and a long scar down his cheek. On the wall behind him hang two calendars, both still turned to January.

'Yes.'

Ko takes the note and begins to read. 'Three onion. Four garlic. Two spoon ginger. Two spoon cumin. One spoon coriander . . .'

And Raf remembers what he said to Cherish about wishing he knew how to make the curry they were eating. 'So it's just a recipe?'

Ko doesn't appreciate Raf's tone of disappointment. 'Yes. Best recipe!'

Raf hesitates. 'Look, I think something bad might have happened to Cherish,' he says. 'Have either of you heard from her since Wednesday?'

Both men shake their heads.

'So you friend of Cherish?' Ko says.

'Yes.'

'Want to buy some glow?'

Before Raf can respond, the waiter barks something at Ko. Raf is surprised when the uncomfortable silence that follows is broken, quite aptly, by one of those Myth FM jingles that the DJs play over and over like a nervous cough to fill space while they try to remember which advert they're supposed to cue up. After that, a pop song. Raf realises this must be Dickson's new 'community programme' playing on the radio in the kitchen. 'You listen to Myth?' he says.

'Yes,' says the waiter. 'Burmese show.'

'Do you know anything about those guys who present it?'

'They are motherfuckers,' says Ko with feeling.

'Then why do you listen to it?'

Ko shrugs. 'Who else play real Burmese music?'

When Raf gets back to Isaac's flat, he finds the other two sitting side by side on the sofa with Isaac's laptop on the table in front of them. 'Anything?' says Fourpetal.

'No. Good thing you didn't steal the note – you would've felt like an idiot. What are you looking at?'

'Watch this,' says Isaac.

The video is from the 2009 Special Operations Forces Exhibition in Marka, Jordan. The description on YouTube explains that while no video or audio recording was allowed inside the conference presentations, a Campaign Against Arms Trade activist posing as a business journalist managed to smuggle in a hidden camera. One of the speakers he filmed was Brent Hitchner, the CEO of an American company called ImPressure•. In the video Hitchner looks no older than twenty-four and he wears a baggy grey suit over a green polo shirt.

The presentation begins with a series of clips projected behind him. A British journalist reporting on CNN: 'Sources in the 82nd Airborne Division told me that for a long time Fallujah was seen as a basically pro-American city, and local sentiment didn't really begin to turn against the occupation until an influential local cleric, Abdullah al-Janabi, called for protests outside this primary school.' Shaky footage of Iraqis shooting their AK-47s in the air, this time with a female journalist speaking over the top: 'The bodies of the four Blackwater contractors were mutilated, dragged through the streets of Fallujah, and strung from a bridge.' An American army officer talking to yet another journalist: 'Public opinion here, you know – it just . . . There's a tipping point.'

Then the screen behind Hitchner cuts to a girl of about twenty-two who sits in a bare white room looking straight at the camera, and Raf thinks she must be some sort of prisoner under interrogation until somebody off-screen asks: 'How often do you drink Suspiria vodka?'

'Oh, I never drink Suspiria.'

'When we interviewed you six months ago, you said you drank Suspiria every time you went out.'

'Oh, yeah, well . . . I guess I don't any more. I prefer Ketel One?'

'Can you remember why you stopped drinking Suspiria?'

'Oh – not really.'

'Can you remember anything about the last time you ordered Suspiria?'

'Oh, well . . . I think we were at Slate? And I ordered a vodka tonic, with Suspiria, and then Ellie said something about how that guy in all the ads – the guy in that, like, hat thing? – how he's kind of a douche? And I was, like – I mean, yeah, it's funny because he is kind of a douche, so . . .'

'What does Ellie drink?'

'Oh, I don't know.'

'Does Ellie drink Ketel One?'

'Oh – I think, yeah, maybe she does?'

The video cuts to a twinkling animation of the ImPressure• logo. 'At ImPressure•, we call Ellie a "disruptor",' says Hitchner – evidently the punctuation mark in the company name is silent. As he fiddles with his lapel mic and looks out across the crowd he seems simultaneously very nervous and very cocky. 'We're the first company to do serious research into disruptors, and it showed that someone like Ellie may negate, on average, about three thousand dollars in marketing spend. And that's just offline. God forbid the bitch has a blog too! Of course, Suspiria wish they could just make Ellie disappear off the face of the earth. They can't. But maybe they can spend two thousand dollars marketing directly to Ellie until she changes her mind – net gain of one thousand, right? Or, even better, maybe they can find two of Ellie's friends – let's call them Frannie and Georgie – and Suspiria only have to spend five hundred dollars each to change their minds, and if Frannie and Georgie both change their minds, then Ellie has an eighty-five per cent chance of changing her mind too – net gain of seventeen hundred, on average. But before they can do any of that, they have to identify Ellie, and they also have to identify Frannie and Georgie, and they have to understand the relationships between them, and obviously all this has to be automated because they can't pay individual attention to every disruptor. That's where ImPressure• comes in. There are a lot of companies out there marketing on social networks. But they take the network structure as a given. That's a mistake. You can't neutralise disruptors just by browsing Facebook. We map the networks ourselves, both online and offline, using super-precise, input-agnostic flow mathematics, and then we figure out how to hit the weak points. It's like pressure-point fighting – that's where we got the name. For Suspiria, as a pilot project, we even installed cameras in five nightclubs in LA and used ImPressure•'s facial-recognition module to cross-reference the drinkers with party photos they'd already posted online. In one night we got more metadata on local vectors of influence than any conventional market research company could hope to put together in a year.

'Now, when we started ImPressure• two years ago, we thought we'd mostly be selling booze, and we were fine with that. But then we realised that what marketers call "mind share" is not that different than what you guys might call "hearts and minds". Abdullah al-Janabi is basically a disruptor like Ellie. For the first time in history, most of the world's population lives in cities, plus all the bad guys have seen pictures of the Gulf War: they know about smart bombs; they know they can't win in the open. So cities are where conflict happens now, and embodied social networks are a lot more dense and complex in cities than they are in jungles or deserts. What I'm saying is, psychological operations units have to do the same job as a lot of marketing departments. Except that PSYOPS has barely moved on since the Second World War. Our investors told us that the Pentagon wouldn't be interested in our technology. But the private sector has always been a lot more open to new ideas.

'I'm going to give you a case study. Obviously I can't name any names, so I'll just tell you that our first PMC client was handling operational security for a European company in a resource-rich region, and they were worried about volatility in the town nearby. We took their data, built an influence map of the town, and we were able to report that nearly seventy per cent of potential disruptors listened to one local FM radio station. So the client quietly purchased that radio station and gradually began to shift its coverage. At the same time, we were able to report that there were also five potential disruptors who were especially dangerous and were not going to be receptive to targeted marketing – including one old blind guy who never left his shack but had huge suction. So the client took steps to make sure those five potential disruptors couldn't do any more damage to mind share. ImPressure• facilitated all this from our offices in San Francisco. Since then, there hasn't been any trouble in the town, and that client has renewed its contract with us – and expanded it to four other locations. That's—'

Fourpetal pauses the video, leaving Hitchner standing there with his mouth open and his eyes closed. 'The client he's talking about there is an Australian private military company called Cantabrian who were working for a French oil firm in the Niger Delta – apparently that would have been common knowledge for everyone in the audience. We know from the fateful email that Cantabrian is the company that this chap Bezant ran until he was poached by Lacebark. And it was while he was still at Cantabrian that they took out their big contract with ImPressure•. If Bezant is such an admirer of ImPressure•'s product, there seems to be a good chance that he encouraged Lacebark to employ them too. Or even if he didn't, he must at least have recalled the measures they prescribed down in Africa.'

'You think Lacebark have bought out Myth FM,' says Raf.

'They probably approached Theo, and Theo said no, and they were worried he'd tell people about them,' says Isaac. 'So that's why they took him away.'

'Jesus.'

'Dickson's running the place now and he'll do anything for a bit of cash. Theo built that station from nothing. I've been playing on Myth for five years. I can't fucking believe this could happen.'

Like the Knights of Malta, Raf thinks, broadcasting is a way of having more square feet of embassies than you have square feet of sovereign territory. 'Those new DJs doing the Burmese programme . . .'

'During the Second World War, our Political Warfare Executive started a German-language jazz station,' says Fourpetal. 'The Germans knew it was all propaganda but they enjoyed the programming so much they couldn't help listening anyway.'

'Lacebark are trying to worm their way into the Burmese immigrant community in London.'

'And we have no idea why.'

'Maybe it's all about Cherish. She was born in Gandayaw. Her father was a Lacebark executive.'

'There's no reason to assume your new girlfriend is the only

Burmese immigrant in London with a connection to Lacebark. And even if she is, how can she possibly be "ten times more important than the Xujiabang deal"?'

'She's ten times more important to Raf!' says Isaac, loyally.

'Yes, well.'

After Fourpetal leaves, Isaac opens two cans of lager. 'We'll find her,' he says to Raf. 'We will. Theo, too.'

'I'm really worried they might have got hurt already.'

'Do you want a bit of DMBDB? It'll make you feel better.'

'What's DMB—?'

'DMBDB. It's a new dissociative. I got a gram from Barky yesterday. Supposed to be nice and mild. Although no drug has ever succeeded with a five-letter abbreviation. It'll need surgery on the name.'

'Isaac, seriously, where do you and Barky even hear about all this shit?'

'Mostly on Lotophage.'

'What's that?'

'I assumed you were already on it.'

Isaac passes him the laptop, Raf starts browsing, and before he knows it, more than an hour has passed. Lotophage, it turns out, is a messageboard for exceptionally dedicated and adventurous drug abusers to exchange advice and compare experiences. It's all in English but it's registered in Russia and hosted in the Netherlands; in almost every post he sees references to AFOAF or SWIM, and he wonders if those might be drugs themselves until he works out that they stand for 'a friend of a friend' and 'someone who isn't me', which is the ragged legal cloak you're supposed to wear if you're telling stories about taking controlled substances.

And these people really know their chemistry. A random post about DMBDB argues that it's not as good as MDPV 'because the heterocyclic ring doesn't allow the tertiary amine to be metabolised into a secondary amine, as it does in diethylcathinone'; another about the acetylation of opioids explains that 'adding a cinnamyl ester to the 14-hydroxyl group on oxycodone can increase potency through means other than simple lipophilicity changes by acting as additional binding moieties – the 14-cinnamyl ester on oxycodone can raise potency to over fifty times that of morphine, for instance.' Raf and Isaac might know a bit of trivia about the pituitary but they've never burrowed down this far. If anyone ever invents a cost-effective method of synthesising real MDMA without sassafras as a precursor, this is where the news will break.

The forum reminds Raf of conversations he's overheard between engineers at Myth FM (including one friend of Theo's who used to be a Communications Systems Operator in the Royal Corps of Signals before he was discharged for petty theft) about radiation patterns and capacitor rods and feedpoint impedance: the expertise is so commonplace that it should be boring to anyone with an A level in science and yet here it all feels occult, lawless, newly discovered – a pragmatic trade that does not have and has never had a theoretical or scholarly crust. And while there are sub-forums for salvia and ayahuasca and opium, the most animated discussion is about novel synthetic compounds imported from laboratories in China. Like medieval naturalists, the Lotophage users know that everything they study has been created for a purpose, but the prime intelligence is so distant and mysterious that they can only guess at its thinking.

Nonetheless, at the centre of it all, Raf feels a gap. What is absent is pleasure. In this sense Lotophage also reminds him of talking about sex with the boys at school when he was about sixteen. One of the main reasons human males have sex is because it is enjoyable to feel your penis being stimulated to ejaculation. To Raf this is not a controversial claim. But back then they always did their best to pretend otherwise. It was acceptable to talk about getting a 'good blowjob', for instance, but if you had ever been careless enough to talk about a 'good orgasm', or just 'coming really hard', everyone would probably have called you gay for weeks. Somehow there was felt to be something clammy and effete about valuing direct physical pleasure for its own sake – which is absurd, because the truth is that the supreme priority of any mammalian brain, especially a teenage boy's, is to put itself in situations where it will get the chance to bask in hedonic neurotransmitters. Lotophage is the same. They fetishise the means, but never the ends. Why do these people even take drugs? Why do they spend their money and break the law? Presumably because they want to feel pleasure. And yet you wouldn't know that from reading their posts. Pleasure is always hidden behind words like 'potency' and 'recreational dosage'. They seem ashamed of pleasure, even though really they're pleasure hobbyists. By contrast, when Raf and Isaac cut pleasure open with neurochemistry, it's not because they want to kill it – it's because they want to look deeper inside its lambent heart.

DAY 8

4.56 p.m.

Does it still count as a surveillance operation if, instead of planting a bug, you just tune your radio to the FM frequency on which your targets are voluntarily broadcasting? Raf wonders this as he sits in Isaac's car listening to the Burmese DJs come to the end of their show. Isaac isn't here, but Fourpetal is in the driver's seat beside him, and they're parked by the playground across the road from the council block where the Myth FM studio is hidden. At 17.09 by the clock on the car radio the two men come out of the exit doors and Fourpetal puts the car into gear, ready to follow.

'I think they're going on foot,' says Raf.

'So?'

'We can't just drive along slowly behind them. We'll look like we're trying to pick them up for a sex act.'

'If we get out of the car, and then they get in one, we'll lose them right away.'

'If that happens we can just try again tomorrow. They're on five days a week.'

Even on foot they have to dawdle a long way back so they don't get noticed. Raf, having never stalked anyone like this before, doesn't know any tricks; these streets are his home terrain, which ought to give him a sort of supernatural guerrilla advantage, and he feels cheated to realise that apparently it doesn't at all. (A fox would be great at this.) As the road winds up past a church, there's a box junction and a traffic island and a pelican crossing and a speed bump and a bus lane almost on top of one another as if one night the council had to dump a lot of spare infrastructure in a hurry, and that's where the Burmese DJs turn off between two squat detached houses down a path that Raf, despite all his walks with Rose, has never noticed before.

This is dangerous, because there's no visible pretext to be walking in that direction, so if they're spotted it will be obvious at once what they're doing. But they carry on anyway. The path slopes gently down, with trees and tangled undergrowth on either side; the continual yap of a dog seems to have no material point of origin but instead is immanent in the air like a rainbow. Then, as if all this weren't already enough to make Raf wonder if somehow they've been transported into the countryside, they arrive at a field of tall wild grass and flowering brambles. How can this possibly abide so close to a main road in south London? But beyond the trees three football pitches come into view, stretching off blankly towards a shed and a mobile phone mast and another row of houses bearing mullets of dead ivy on their back walls. These must be school playing fields; perhaps some administrator made a mistake annotating a map of the park, so that the ground is maintained up until a certain arbitrary border, a final touchline, but after that it's the responsibility of no one in particular, and hence this colony of wilderness. At his feet are a few chocolate wrappers that look as if they know deep down that they can't biodegrade but are doing their best anyway just to fit in. He realises it's been far too long since he last caught sight of the Burmese DJs. 'Where are they?' he says.

'They must have gone this way,' says Fourpetal, pointing into the tall grass.

This is even more dangerous, because they don't have their bearings and for all they know their quarry might still be only a few yards away, but they've gone too far to turn back. Thorns keep nipping at Raf's jeans as the two of them press cautiously on. Then they come to a tall chain-link fence so overgrown with tough vines that the woven metal of the fence itself is not much more than a vestigial splint – and beyond the fence is a derelict tennis court.

There's no net any more, although you can still see the vague white lines between which weeds are now drilling up through the asphalt, and there's even a rusty umpire's chair with broken bottles and charred wood strewn around its base like tributes before a throne. On the opposite side, several sections of the fence have been wrestled down by shrubs, leaving only the steel supports between them. There are stains on the ground, mostly black but in one corner an inexplicable violet. The yapping dog sounds no closer and no farther away. This place is sepulchral, post-apocalyptic, a *memento mori* for those complacent football pitches about the fate they too will one day face, and Raf would already be planning a birthday party here if it weren't for the four people he can see standing there in the middle of the court.

The two Burmese DJs. A balding guy who carries a sports bag. And Cherish.

Raf and Fourpetal both drop to a crouch. 'Fuck! Fuck, that's her!' Raf whispers. 'That's Cherish!' He wants to bring her a bunch of flowers. He wants to bring her a flower market.

'Not bad at all,' says Fourpetal in an appraisive tone.

Raf realises that their theory about Dickson and the 'community programme' must have been completely wrong, that somehow all these people are working together against Lacebark. They're too far away to make out any conversation, but it's obvious. He is about to shout to Cherish when Fourpetal adds, 'So the two of you have only actually met a couple of times – that's right, isn't it?'

'So?'

'I only ask because, if it should happen that she and I . . .'

'What?'

'Would you object?'

'Are you saying, would I mind if you fucked her?'

'It's just a question.'

'When would that ever happen?'

'It's just an eventuality.'

Before Raf can make any retort, he sees Cherish take two

envelopes out of her bag and pass one to each of the Burmese men. When Raf was a child he used to find it unsettling to overhear his dad make work-related calls on the phone, and that's what this is like: her demeanour here seems totally estranged from the demeanour of the girl he kissed. And it's not as if he's really any expert on body language, but when Fourpetal says, 'What are we watching? Is this a drug deal?' Raf shakes his head, because he does know the body language of drug deals, and this doesn't look to him like a drug deal. In fact, if he had to guess, he'd say she's handing over some sort of wage or stipend, like when he gets paid for walking the dog. Why would she be doing that? There is something wrong about this scene that hasn't crystallised yet, and for reasons that aren't quite conscious, he finds himself thinking back to Wednesday afternoon. Cherish with one foot on the wet tarmac and one foot in the back of the white van. Those two soldiers, each with a gloved hand on her.

The understanding hits him like two darts from a Taser. They weren't dragging her inside.

They were helping her up.

Raf finds that the only way he can calmly process the knowledge that Cherish might be working for Lacebark is by pretending he's talking it over with Isaac.

So if it seems so obvious now, Isaac would say, why didn't you notice at the time?

Because Fourpetal made me afraid of the white vans, Raf would say. But why would they have been helping her into the van?

Chivalry?

No. They were in a hurry.

You'd doubled back to get your umbrella and they didn't want you to see them.

But they were too slow, Raf would say. And then Cherish realised that there was an ambiguity in what I'd seen that she could exploit. She did a really good job of seeming shaken after I 'rescued' her.

So she wasn't kidnapped from your bed after all.

But in that case, Raf would say, why did Rose insist that someone nasty had been through my front door? When could that have happened, if not that night?

When you were both at the restaurant. The meal was her suggestion, right?

Fuck, yes, and we didn't leave until she got that text message!

She gave the Lacebark guys time to break into your flat like they broke into Fourpetal's.

So Cherish was helping Lacebark to investigate me all along?

Well, what's the alternative? Isaac would ask. That it was just a weird coincidence you ran into this girl again, right outside your flat, four days after the rave in the laundrette?

OK, yeah, that sounds stupid now. But I wanted to marry Cherish before I'd even talked to her. Wouldn't it be another weird coincidence if the girl who was helping Lacebark to investigate me was also this beauty whom I developed a big crush on as soon as I saw her?

In your whole life, how many girls have you seen at raves that you've immediately developed a big crush on?

I don't know, Raf would say.

Conservatively?

Ten to fifteen thousand. More if it weren't for the MDMA drought.

So it's statistically almost inevitable that at least one of them was going to turn out to be working undercover for an American mining company.

Fine, but I still don't understand why Lacebark would want to investigate me in the first place. I'm nobody.

We were trying to find out what happened to Theo.

But we hadn't got anywhere. We'd barely even tried. We were no threat to Lacebark. It doesn't make sense. And I really thought Cherish liked me . . .

That's as far as Raf can get with imaginary Isaac. He feels as desolate as the tennis court. But now the four figures look as if their business is concluded.

'What do we do?' says Fourpetal.

'Follow Cherish,' suggests Raf.

But the problem is that she seems to be heading off towards the football pitches. If she cuts across diagonally in the approximate direction of the mobile phone mast, they won't be able to follow her because they'd be right out in the open. They could hurry around the perimeter of the park where there's some cover, racing two sides of the triangle against a hypotenuse, but that way Cherish could lose them at the other end without even trying.

The Burmese DJs, meanwhile, are just standing there rolling a spliff. Which leaves the guy with the sports bag, who now for the first time turns far enough in their direction that they can see his face. Fourpetal jerks his head. 'Christ on a bloody cross, you have got to be joking.'

'Keep your voice down,' Raf tells him. 'What is it?'

The guy with the sports bag is going to take the same path between the street and the tennis court that they just took, in which case he'll catch them if they don't move on fast.

'It's him! It actually is.'

'Who?'

A dragonfly lunges past. 'I've seen that man's cock,' says Fourpetal.

'We really have to get going,' Raf tells him. Keeping low, they tunnel back through the wild grass, and then break into a sprint when they get to the path between the trees. There's no hope now of circling back to follow Cherish. Instead, at the other end of the path, they look around for somewhere to hide. After they've crossed the road and dropped down panting behind the wall of the churchyard, Raf finally has the chance to ask, 'What do you mean you've seen his cock?'

'Just what I said. I don't know him very well but I've seen his cock. A few months after I started at Lacebark, long before the email farrago, they put on a big staff Christmas party at a restaurant in Holborn. Afterwards a few of us carried on to a brothel. He was so drunk that at one point he came stumbling out of one of the rooms without his trousers on. He wasn't in communications so I hadn't met him before that night.'

'Is he something to do with Lacebark security?'

'If he is, he lied about it. I don't remember exactly what he said he did but I do remember it sounded tedious. Something to do with lithium? And he might have mentioned Pakistan. Not Burma, though.'

The guy whose cock Fourpetal has seen now emerges from between the detached houses and turns left up the rise in the direction of Herne Hill, so Raf and Fourpetal follow him like they followed the Burmese men and Raf explains what he now knows about Cherish.

'Well, it's very touching that it's taken you this long to realise that you can never trust women,' says Fourpetal when he's finished.

Raf thinks about his ex-girlfriend and the Brazilian techno DJ. 'I think I've just had bad luck recently.'

After about fifteen minutes' pursuit they come to a builders' merchant with a big yard at the front full of pallets of flesh-coloured bricks wrapped in a thick plastic that makes them look to Raf like stacks of human biceps. Beyond that, past a steel fence, there's a warehouse almost identical to the one that Isaac showed Raf last weekend, and when the guy they're following goes inside, he remembers that bloodstain he saw on the concrete floor. 'This must be a Lacebark building,' he says as they wait half hidden behind a bus shelter. 'Maybe they have them all over London. Fuck, I wonder what goes on in there.'

An old woman trundles by in a motorised wheelchair, Maltese between her knees, Union Jack pennant fluttering behind her, and they try not to look so furtive. Behind them, in the window of an empty shop, there are photocopied signs that read BILL POSTERS WILL BE, four words only, as if the caretaker became resigned to the futility of his job in the process of composing the warning.

'Should we wait and see who comes in and out?' says Fourpetal.

'I want a closer look,' says Raf.

'Have you forgotten that they're hunting me? I'm not going to walk in their front door.'

'Come on, we don't have to go inside.'

Reluctantly Fourpetal follows Raf past the builders' merchant to the warehouse. Here, Raf is braced to turn and flee, but he's confused by the sight of about a dozen bicycles locked to a rack by the wall, and even more so to find that the door through which the cock/sports bag guy went is made of glass and covered in stickers.

Fourpetal chuckles. 'Oh. I see. This is worse than the curry recipe.'

'What do you mean?'

Fourpetal strides forward to pull open the door, and Raf sees that this isn't a prison or a barracks or an armoury. This isn't anything to do with Lacebark. This is a climbing gym.

Inside, colourful knobbly handholds bolted to fibreglass crags simulate a mountain turned inside out. Mid-nineties jungle plays from a cheap PA system and the smell of chalk is so thick in the air that it reminds Raf of dry ice in a club; the climbers are like the couriers he saw in that pub with Morris, lots of dreadlocks and blisters and robust specialised footwear and a general perverse infatuation with egregiously hostile man-made topologies. The two of them look around for Fourpetal's former colleague, and they can't see him up on any of the walls, but then he comes out from behind a bank of lockers, still looking a bit out of place even in a T-shirt and jogging shorts. He's just started limbering up his hands on his way across the crash mats, cracking knuckles and wiggling fingers in a routine so complicated that it looks as if he's casting some sort of necromantic enchantment, when he notices Fourpetal and stops dead. Fourpetal walks over and extends a hand of his own.

But the other guy's are now paralysed in front of him so Fourpetal just grabs one and rattles it like a broken doorknob. 'Mark Fourpetal. I used to work at Lacebark. We met at the Christmas party last year. Isn't this a coincidence?'

From the guy's expression it's clear he knows exactly who Fourpetal is. 'I can't talk to you.'

'Why not? Because if you see me you're supposed to kidnap me?'

The guy looks around as if Lacebark mercenaries might suddenly come rappelling down an artificial cliff face. 'I can't talk to you.'

'Well – Martin, isn't it?'

'Yes.'

'Martin, you don't have to talk to us,' says Fourpetal. 'We can just leave. And then you can decide whether or not to call your boss and tell him we were here, and I expect you probably won't, since a meeting like this is hard to explain even if it's no fault of your own, but either way we will be gone long before one of your white vans has time to come here and gulp us down. That can happen. But considering I saved your life once, I think a reasonable code of ethics might say that you're under some obligation to help us with the answers to a few innocuous questions.'

'What do you mean, saved my life?'

'That night at the brothel in Holborn. When that bouncer pulled a knife on you because of what you made that Latvian girl do. No, Martin, I'm not saying he would have murdered you for certain, but I know you would have ended up in hospital with a lot of perforations and explaining to do if I hadn't talked him down.' Martin's mouth just hangs open. 'Bloody hell, you're not telling me you don't even remember?' Fourpetal continues. 'Were you really that pickled?' Raf has to stop himself from smiling: Fourpetal is a prick but he's really good at this. In McDonald's on Monday he didn't seem nearly so confident, and perhaps the difference here is that he finds something nourishing in Martin's obvious discomfort.

'I . . . don't remember any of that.'

'Well, that might be for the best, actually. But, Martin, the main thing is, you have a chance to return the favour now. Just help us understand what we've got ourselves into.'

'If they found out I've told you anything . . .'

'They won't. How would they?'

Martin sighs and then walks over to a row of wooden bleachers.

Raf and Fourpetal sit down beside him. 'I honestly don't even know that much,' he says.

'Fine. But maybe you can start by telling us why you're involved in all this. Aren't you a lithium man? There's no lithium in Burma.'

'There is, actually,' Martin says. 'A bit. But this isn't about that.' He didn't realise it at the time, he explains, but his career in the lithium sector came to an end one day in January about twenty-five thousand feet above the southern hallux of the Hindu Kush. Martin was on his laptop but all three of the bodyguards were at the Cessna's windows watching the dawn enfire the snow like paraffin sluicing through the valleys. In a little while they would cross the border from Afghanistan into Pakistan and by seven o'clock local time they were supposed to have landed in Quetta, where Martin was going to make a last, urgent, probably hopeless attempt to convince officials from the Balochistan provincial government that the exploration licence for lithium deposits north of the city should go to Lacebark instead of a newly established Kernon Whitmire subsidiary called Adosh Mining Corporation.

He hadn't slept or eaten since they stopped in Odessa to refuel, so by now he was hungry and bored and could already feel against his eyeballs the first crinkly touch of the hundred-metre roll of cling film that jet lag was going to wrap around his head today. All his life he'd carried an alarm clock in his belly like the crocodile in *Peter Pan* – boring about bedtimes, incapable of staying up late, clicking awake at six every day even back when he was at Oxford – but like an idiot he'd let himself take a job that obliged him to fly thousands of miles a year, and he was convinced it was wearing out his heart. In London it would only be coming up to two in the morning. Supposedly his jet lag would get even worse if he thought about that too much. But it was impossible to keep London out of his mind. Back at City Airport, when the plane was already gaining speed on the runway, he had got a call from his wife about his stepson.

'You have to come home,' she'd said, damp-voiced.

'What's wrong?'

'Dylan's at the police station.'

At first Martin charitably assumed that the sixteen-year-old had been in a bicycle accident or something. 'Is he hurt?'

'No, no, they came to the house and took him away.'

'Jesus, why?'

'It's so awful! Where are you?'

He felt the Cessna lift into the air. 'On the plane. I'm going to lose you in a second.'

'. . . have to . . . home!' Already the signal was dropping as they soared out of reception range.

'Darling, I'm sure it's all a mistake – I'll talk to you when I land!'

Actually, Martin wasn't sure it was all a mistake. For a while now, in fact, he'd been firmly expecting to find out one way or another that Dylan was up to something criminal. Almost every day of the recent school holidays he had got up at six to see light still creeping out from under the door of the boy's bedroom. That light always made him uneasy. Sometimes he wanted to knock but he knew it would start an argument. He paid the mortgage on this house every month and yet here inside it was this shady separatist zone where he couldn't set foot, like one of the semi-autonomous Third World slums that were too dangerous even for the riot squads; his own fault for falling in love with a woman who was already a divorced mother by the time she was twenty-seven. Most likely, he decided, Dylan was involved somehow in selling drugs. He'd read in the paper recently about new pills coming in from China. When they landed in Odessa he couldn't get a GSM connection, so by the time they were over Afghanistan he was desperate to get back on the ground and have a chance to talk to his wife again.

But then one of the pilots, a Frenchman, came out from the cockpit. 'We're changing course.'

'Is there a problem?'

'Instructions from London.' Martin's employer, unlike his wife, had the privilege of contacting the plane in flight.

'Where are we going?'

'Sukkur.'

'Where's that?'

'About four hundred kilometres south-east of Quetta.'

'But my meeting with the MMD is at lunchtime.' And Lacebark were spending a ludicrous amount of money to haul his mouth to that meeting. There wouldn't be another chance: strictly speaking the committee was supposed to have concluded its deliberations the previous day.

The pilot shrugged. 'They say they'll call you to explain as soon as you have reception on the ground.'

'Don't we have a flight plan we have to keep to?'

'They'll pay someone off.'

They descended towards Sukkur's single short runway over bland fields of cotton and rice and jute. On their right was the Indus, which new Indian dams and a cold winter had shrunk down inside its grey banks like a consumptive in a baggy old suit. As the Cessna's wheels hit the tarmac, Martin turned his phone back on, waited for it to negotiate a connection to a Pakistani provider called Telenor, and called his boss in London. He didn't want to speak to his wife until he could tell her for certain how soon he'd be back.

'Can you please tell me what I'm doing here?'

'Harenberg needs someone in Khairpur right away and no one could get a flight in time. Luckily you were already in the air.'

'What about the MMD?'

'We weren't going to get that licence anyway. And Harenberg is saying this is bigger than your MMD meeting.'

'What does he mean?'

'There's a five-seater van and a driver waiting for you at the terminal. You need to get to the police station on Faujdari Road in Khairpur – it's about twenty miles south of Sukkur. They're expecting you. There's a guy in a holding cell there. They're going to release him into your custody. Lock him in the back of the van and don't let him out of your sight until Bezant can get there.'

'What? Holding cell?' The plane slowed to a halt and Martin

stood up to get his suitcase down from the locker. 'How long is that going to take?'

'Maybe twenty-four hours.'

'I need to get back to London.'

'We'll take care of everything at this end.'

'No, I've got a . . . family thing. I really need to get back.'

'Look, Martin, we didn't divert the plane because Bezant needed you in Khairpur, all right? We diverted the plane because Bezant needed three trained security guys in Khairpur and you happened to be on the plane with them. But at least you'll be there to make sure nothing gets ballsed up too badly. Twenty-four hours maximum, then you can go back.'

'So who's the guy in the holding cell?'

'It doesn't matter. You won't talk to him, he won't talk to you.'

'Is he Pakistani?'

'He's Myanmar.'

'How did he end up in Khairpur?'

'Apparently there are lots of Muslims from Myanmar in southeast Pakistan. Whoever he is, he has friends there. He was hiding out for a few nights on his way to the coast. The house got raided for something completely unrelated and the police picked him up. Unlucky sod. That's all I know.'

Even on the short walk to the terminal building the three bodyguards formed a protective triangle around Martin and the pilots. Grateful that in small planes and small airports they didn't find it necessary to shout at you about your mobile phone every thirty seconds, Martin finally had a chance to call his wife when they were queuing to get their passports checked. She started sobbing again when she heard his voice but after a while he got her to explain it all. 'The police told me Dylan put up this website where . . . Apparently there are these companies in Brazil . . . You pay them three hundred pounds and they'll make a film for you with two girls. And you can have extra girls in it for another hundred pounds each on top of that. You can tell them exactly what you want the girls to do. Dylan commissioned one of the films and then sold downloads on his website. And he sold so many he commissioned three more films. But the police say some of the girls don't look like they're eighteen.'

'But he didn't make the films?'

'No, but he was selling them from his own server, so legally—'

'There's lots of glossy porn for free on the internet – I don't understand how he was making any money.'

'It's because of what the girls did.'

'What do you mean?'

'I could only watch about a minute of the video before I . . .'

Martin waited for her to continue, but she didn't. There was something about the long silence on the line, like a redacted memory, that made him recall that grim night at the brothel after the Christmas party, and that blonde girl from Eastern Europe. He knew his wife's mother would tell her that this never would have happened if the man of the house hadn't been away on Lacebark trips so often, and perhaps that was right, but then by what mechanism, exactly, would Martin's presence have imprinted on his stepson a virtuous code of behaviour towards young foreign women? From a business point of view, he had to admit that the boy's model was pretty shrewd. You could make a lot of money from the arbitrage of sexual dignity. If it was any other type of service for which Dylan had established himself as a middleman or outsourcer he probably would have been nominated for some sort of Young Entrepreneur of the Year award. Martin thought again of that seditious glow under the door. The police would have gone into the boy's little *favela* to take away his computer, he realised.

'You have to come back,' his wife said. 'I can't handle this on my own.'

'Darling, as soon as I can. Lacebark won't take me home until this time tomorrow.'

'Can't you just get on a commercial flight?'

'They don't fly to London from here.'

'Martin, for God's sake, our son is in prison! They're holding him for twenty-four hours and after that he'll get out on police bail and then something about a magistrate . . .' She broke down. He told her he'd talk to her in the morning and that he loved her and that she should get some sleep.

Outside the terminal, the pilots hailed a taxi to take them to a cheap hotel in town, while Martin and the bodyguards looked around for the van they'd been promised. After several minutes it dawned on them that it had been parked right in front of them all along and the bearded driver had even been waving from the front seat, but they hadn't taken any notice because they were expecting something in dirty white or perhaps metallic black. Instead, every inch of this van was painted like the world's gaudiest Victorian fairground carousel in turquoise and red and orange and gold, with a mural on the side of Hercules fighting a lion inside a spiral of butterflies and flowers and Arabic calligraphy, as well as heart-shaped cutouts over the tail lights and beaded whirligigs on the hubcaps and tinselly fringes hanging from the mudguards and a panelled mosaic across the rear doors. For a moment Martin wondered if one of Lacebark's local fixers had made a comical error, and then realised that on the roads of southern Pakistan this would be a lot less conspicuous than a well-maintained American SUV. Nonetheless, when all four of them got inside and the driver set off for the highway, he thought they must look as if they were performing in some sort of West End musical about a gay psychedelic pop band touring with their guru. On the narrow barrage bridge over the Indus they dodged past scooters and rickshaws and two-wheeled donkey carts, and the driver remarked in his laboured English that if you watched the water you could often see dolphins, which then led him by word association to a long unsolicited account of the recent triumphs of the Karachi Dolphins cricket team.

After they pulled up to the gate of the police station in Khairpur they were directed around to the car park at the back of the building, and the prisoner was brought out to them in a blindfold and handcuffs by two policemen. He did look as if he might be Burmese, but Martin could still hardly believe that this was the man that Lacebark had gone to all this effort to scoop up. You wouldn't need three trained security men to hold him captive, you'd just need a length of fishing twine knotted around his ankle. He might have been as young as twenty-five, but he was as shrunken as the Indus, with a rime of red sores on his lips, and he stumbled along as if he were on the point of dropping to his hands and knees. Even so, Martin's bodyguards jumped down out of the van, took the man from the policemen after a short parley, and loaded him into the back. Then they drove to a hotel around the corner, where Martin, improvising as best he could, pretending it was a creative leadership exercise, dismissed the Pakistani driver and told his bodyguards to organise themselves into eight-hour shifts until Bezant arrived: one resting, one in the hotel keeping Martin safe, and one guarding the magical mystery bus and tending occasionally to the prisoner. It wasn't until Martin had sat down on the bed that he had a chance to think about how strange it was that at dinner parties he often refused to explain his job to people because he found it so boring and now here he was, apparently participating in some sort of covert operation. Had the scrofulous Burmese guy really committed a crime, he wondered? And if he had, how might its contribution to the net total of human misery compare to Dylan's porn site if you could analyse them on a spreadsheet? It was probably much worse, Martin guessed, but of course he couldn't be certain.

For nearly two days they heard nothing from Lacebark. Martin fell asleep around lunchtime on the first afternoon, which didn't make sense even according to GMT, and woke up at dusk, if you could really call it waking up, to the sound of the fifth call to prayer. He'd read once that some Muslims got over jet lag faster because they were used to going to bed at odd times during Ramadan, but he didn't find it plausible that a religion with circadian rhythms built into its compulsory schedule of worship could loosen you up in that respect. After sending his current sentry out for kebabs and bottled water, he called his wife and she told him that Dylan had come home with her from the police station, but, predictably, was refusing to get on the phone. She wasn't crying so much any more but he still felt monstrous when he had to tell her that he didn't know yet when he'd be back. For the rest of the night he worked on his laptop and napped at random, and the next morning he was so sick of the room that he went out, accompanied, to get a shave from one of the barbers who worked in the square at the end of the street. As he was being towelled off he watched a donkey cart trundle past with a huge cumulus cloud of empty plastic milk jugs lashed behind the driver, but then one cartwheel slotted into a pothole, the cart tipped, a rope broke, and the avalanche buried the donkey up to his cartoon-ishly perky ears.

Finally, as the bodyguards were starting their sixth uneventful shift, he got a call from his boss. 'Bezant's landing in Sukkur in half an hour. Drive back up there and meet him for the handover.'

Before they left, Martin opened the back of the van to check on the Burmese guy, which he regretted at once: the prisoner lay there on his side in the shadows, warm debris, twitching a little, smelling of piss, and Martin knew he'd never be able to tell his wife what had happened on this trip. But what would a good man, that notional creature, have done? Or an upright stepfather? Just let the guy walk free – limp free – having no idea who he was? Even if he'd tried, the Lacebark bodyguards wouldn't have let him, and if he'd defied them he would have been imperilling not only his job but also his only means of safe transport back to Europe. Perhaps in other circum-stances he might still have been capable of taking a moral stand. But not submerged in his jet lag. So instead he just told the bodyguards to put the handcuffs back on the prisoner and lock up the back of the van.

They met Bezant at a dusty margin of vacant land between the Airport Road and the canal, shaded on one side by palm trees. Above, the sky was lithium white; the naked sun hadn't shown itself since Martin landed in Sukkur. The Australian arrived in a dented tan rental car but he showed no bemusement at the lurid van. Even compared to the three big bodyguards this man was a pillar of tungsten and steaks, and he would have made any normal product of the human genotype feel like a fiddly new model that had been miniaturised by some clever Japanese company to fit better into the handbags of teenage girls.

'Let's have a look, then.'

Martin took the keys from one of the bodyguards. He unlocked the van, swung open the doors, and braced himself for his third sight of the prisoner.

But there was no one in the back of the van. The prisoner was gone.

'Right, so where have you put him?' said Bezant. Then he saw the horrified expression on Martin's face. 'Are you telling me he was in here?'

'Yes.'

'Is this a joke?'

'No.'

A puff of small pinkish pigeons leaped up from a telephone wire beside the canal. 'When did you last set eyes on the cunt?' said Bezant.

'Before we set off from Khairpur.'

'Have you stopped since?'

'No. Not even in traffic.'

'There was nothing in the back of the van? No tools? No handy set of screwdrivers?'

'No,' said Martin. He'd seen that for himself.

'I assume someone had the common dog fuck to give him a cavity search?'

One of the bodyguards nodded. 'They tell us they give him one at the police station. We give him another one anyhow.'

Bezant turned back to Martin. 'How long were they alone with him at a stretch?'

'Eight hours.'

'I was looking for something along the lines of "six minutes". Eight hours at a stretch? Whose brilliant idea was that?'

'He looked so frail, I didn't think . . .'

'Didn't anyone bother to warn you who this wanker was?'

'No.'

'Right. Of course they didn't.' Bezant ran a hand over his shaven scalp and spat contemplatively on the ground. 'What has happened here, to the best of my estimation, is that our man in the van talked one of these oxygen thieves into slipping him some sort of widget, and on your drive over here he used it to get out of his handcuffs and then out of the door. The reason I say this is because it's happened before. He's got a very special tongue on him.'

'I didn't even know he spoke English,' said Martin.

'He speaks enough. Which one of them was it?'

'Sorry?'

'You've spent the last few days with the Three Musketeers over there. If you had to take a punt, which one would you say has the benevolent heart?'

'I don't know,' replied Martin without even thinking about it. Because how could he know?

But then he glanced at Riquinho, the tallest of the three body-guards, a loose-limbed Brazilian. (A lot of the Lacebark security corps were Brazilian, Ecuadorian, Fijian, Nigerian, Jordanian, Serbian. If they came from countries like that you didn't have to pay them so much.) On the plane, Riquinho had carried on watching the sun rise over the mountains long after the other two had lost inter-est; and in the van, he'd welded himself to the window as soon as the driver mentioned the dolphins; and in the square, he'd flinched as if he'd wanted to rush over to help the donkey, though it wasn't even hurt. He seemed far more porous than the other two, more open to the surge of the world. In 2006 there had been a damaging leak to a journalist from the American *Harper's* about some bribes that Lacebark had supposedly attempted to pass to government officials in Bolivia (which had millions of tons of lithium under the salt flats).

Martin's boss, ruling him out straight away, had asked him to write short loyalty evaluations on all his colleagues in the department. He enjoyed the task enormously, and he felt more powerful around the office for months afterwards, as if he had a dagger at his hip, even though no one else knew he was writing the reports and the culprit was never actually identified. That was how he felt now, thinking about Riquinho.

'Come on,' said Bezant. 'I can tell you've got an opinion. Spit it out. Which one?'

But it was also possible, thought Martin, that the recent vindication of his suspicions about Dylan's criminality had made him over-confident. His 'evidence' here was ineffable even compared to a trickle of light under a bedroom door. Who wouldn't want to see some dolphins? In any case, he didn't know quite what use Bezant would make of his answer, but he assumed it would be unpleasant. 'I'm sorry, I don't know,' he said.

Now Bezant and all three of the bodyguards were staring at Martin and he could feel a cold sweat kissing the back of his neck. When his phone vibrated in his pocket it made his whole leg spasm. His wife was calling. As he fumbled to turn it off Bezant screamed, 'Which fucking one?'

The phone slipped from Martin's hands. 'Riquinho,' he blurted, pointing.

Bezant walked right up to Riquinho and stared him in the face for a while. Then he said, 'I think you might be right.'

'I didn't say a word to the *cuzão*!' said Riquinho.

'Fair enough,' said Bezant. 'We'll establish that one way or another. You two: cuff him.'

The other two bodyguards didn't hesitate. 'No! Fuck this!' shouted Riquinho.

'Wait – it was just a guess,' said Martin, who didn't want to be responsible for trapping a second human being in the back of that van.

'You should learn to trust your judgement, mate,' said Bezant. As

Riquinho was hauled inside the van the heels of his boots knocked half a dozen tin stars from the rim of the number plate.

'What are you going to do with him?' said Martin.

'Not your problem. Anyway, you can take my car back to the airport. The plane's waiting.'

This was enough to distract Martin from the fate of Riquinho for a moment, although at this point he felt as if he couldn't even bend down to pick up his phone without asking for permission. 'You mean I can go back to London?' he said.

Bezant smiled. 'Probably better. You'll want to be seeing your kid, eh? Big time in a boy's life. First visit from the blue heelers.'

7.03 p.m.

'How did he know about your stepson and the police?' says Raf.

'Bezant always seems to know everything,' says Martin. 'Anyway, I think he stayed in Pakistan for a while after that to see if he could track down the Burmese guy we lost. And I don't know whether he caught him in Karachi or whether the trail went cold or what, but when he got back to London, he called me. He said Riquinho had confessed to slipping the Burmese guy a pin or something so he could pick his handcuffs. I'd been right, and I think Bezant was impressed. And somehow he'd got hold of those reports I wrote about the leak in 2006. He told me they were some of the most detailed he'd ever seen and I had an aptitude for sniffing people out and I was wasted in lithium and he had a gap on his team here. He didn't really give me a choice. And at least this job keeps me in London – well, not that they ever would've sent me back to Khairpur, most of it's underwater at the moment. So my wife's happy, even though I have to lie to her about what I'm doing.'

By now the climbing gym is starting to empty out, although there are still quite a few parents and nannies watching kids who move over the walls like spiders because of their weight-to-muscle ratios. Martin has been talking for so long that Fourpetal has bought him a box of apple juice from the vending machine. Nearby is a vacuum unit with a sign that says 'PLEASE DO NOT BLOCK THE CHALK EATER', thick foam filters worn away to raggedness like aeolian caves.

'And what are you doing really?' says Raf.

'Technically I'm in personnel. But it's a kind of counter-intelligence. Bezant has me looking for security leaks.'

'Isn't that ironic?' says Fourpetal.

'And what were you up to just now?'

'Mostly I work with Lacebark security men. But also sometimes with the Burmese who Bezant is paying. Those two guys from earlier

– they think I'm just another liaison from Lacebark – but actually I'm supposed to tell Bezant whether he can trust them.'

'What about Cherish?' says Raf.

'The girl? Oh, she's solid,' says Martin, and Raf's heart sinks. He'd still been holding out some hope that they might have got everything backwards. If Cherish was working for Lacebark, maybe that was the real reason she didn't take that nasty fake glow he gave her. If only Raf had been so careful about what he was willing to swallow from a stranger he met in a club. On Friday, after Cherish vanished, he had felt so sure that she was under guard in a white van or a warehouse somewhere, and he realises now that he was probably right about that. He was just wrong about the details.

'If you don't mind me saying,' says Fourpetal, 'I hoped you might be candid but I never expected you to be this candid.'

Martin kneads his cheek with the heel of his hand. 'A few weeks ago, Bezant said he wanted to try me on something new. He said I could be good at interrogations. They do a lot of those. I went to a warehouse and inside they had a guy in a cell with a hood over his head. They had all these different ways of disorienting him. They'd keep the lights on for thirty-six hours and then turn them off for four hours and feed him in the dark and then feed him again forty minutes later and then put the lights on for ten hours and then leave them off again for twenty hours without feeding him and then finally feed him again and so on and so on, so he never had any idea how much time had passed or when he was supposed to sleep. And they had the floor of the cell on springs and they blasted him with all these low-frequency sound waves to make him feel sick.' Raf remembers the speaker cable on the floor of that warehouse. 'I had to watch while they questioned him. I can't even make myself talk about what I saw them do. And I don't know what they wanted from him but I think he's probably dead now. I never asked to be part of that. I had to tell Bezant I didn't have the constitution for it. He laughed at me. You know, I've heard stories about him from the soldiers. In the Niger Delta there's a cult called the Egbesu Boys. They fight the oil companies in the name of the local god of war. They say Egbesu gives them special powers. In particular, they like to brag that they can drink battery acid. Well, when Bezant was still down there working for Cantabrian, he once caught this kid who'd shot a few of his men in the swamp. The kid was defiant. He told Bezant all about Egbesu. And apparently Bezant told the kid to "prove it". He made him drink battery acid. Made him do shots of it like tequila. With lemon and salt.'

The chances that Lacebark are holding Theo alive and well somewhere, the chances that Raf and Isaac will ever see Theo again, seem pitifully small. This inference has been scratching at Raf's mind for a few days now, and he's been trying as hard as he can to ignore it, but after Martin's stories that isn't going to work any longer. Still, he can put off thinking about it properly for one more hour. 'Why don't you go to the papers or something?' he says.

'I'm not going to ruin my whole life over it. I have a family. Bezant got Lacebark to pay for a lawyer for Dylan. In the end he only got a referral order.'

'You still haven't explained what exactly Lacebark are doing in London,' says Fourpetal. 'Is it something to do with the Shan forest Concession?'

'Yes. Some of the Burmese that Bezant is looking for – the town near there is where they come from. But I think there's a lot more to it than that. I still haven't got the whole story. I haven't been given the clearance.'

'Probably wise,' says Fourpetal.

'All I know is that they have something big planned for the first day of June. I overheard a Fijian guy talking about it. Then of course I had to tell Bezant he was being indiscreet, so he's gone now.'

'But what were they asking the guy in the cell about?'

'They have this software—'

'ImPressure•.'

'Yes. Mostly, they were just looking for more information to plug into their ImPressure• database. They're still trying to map the "vectors of influence" among the Burmese community in south London. And they keep talking about a book by a guy called "Villepinte". I don't know why.'

Could it be because of Lacebark that the Iranian corner shop has started stocking *balachaung*, Raf thinks? To tempt Burmese people inside and then catch them on security camera so they can be added to the ImPressure• database? Obviously one shop couldn't be much use on its own, but if they're doing the same with a couple of dozen others they might sweep up some data, although even then it seems to Raf like a silly idea. Meanwhile, the name Villepinte is familiar but he can't remember why. 'So what next?' he says. 'Should we carry on following those DJs?'

'You won't get anywhere. Bezant's keeping them at a distance.'

'So we're at another dead end,' says Fourpetal.

'There is one other thing.' Lacebark's usual method, Martin explains, is to put up a warehouse in a few hours, use it for a day, and then abandon it like a husk. But there's an old disused freight depot near the Bricklayers' Arms junction that he's seen again and again on logistical documents since he started working in south London for Bezant. He doesn't know what's inside, but it must be something that takes up too much space for the normal prefabricated warehouses, and in the last few weeks there's been more chatter about the location than ever.

'I get the sense they're trying to get something finished there by the beginning of June and it's running behind schedule.' Martin looks at his watch. 'Shit, and so am I. I'm meant to be taking Dylan to some Shakespeare.' He gets up and flexes his shoulders as if to shake off the ichor of the story he's just been telling: Raf can see that it must have been a relief to confess the worst of it for the first time. 'Before I go . . . The Latvian girl.'

'What about her?'

'Was she all right, after I . . .'

Fourpetal pauses to consider this. 'I expect if she takes her vitamins it will grow back eventually.'

DAY 9

6.47 p.m.

When Raf comes into the kitchen, Isaac is bending to put a muffin pan in the oven. 'What are you making?'

'*Takoyaki*,' says Isaac after shutting the oven door. 'They're baked octopus dumplings with dashi. I also put in some squid and some cuttlefish. Fumiko gave me the recipe. I'm going on an all-tentacle diet for a week.'

'Why?' This doesn't surprise Raf very much because the only times Isaac bothers to cook anything other than curry or pasta are when he's making advances in outsider neuroscience. That doomed false false-morel omelette was most likely the first and last omelette ever produced in this kitchen (although you couldn't absolutely rule out a Burmese omelette with dung beetle grubs at some point in the future). Today, the girl winding a pocket watch at the table by the front door is wearing snakeskin brogues and a poncho that looks like a church bell, and the girl dozing on the futon is wearing pink ballet slippers and about half a wedding dress. As always, they are magnificent.

'Imagine that most of your body was made of fingers,' commands Isaac, 'and those fingers could bend and twist and squeeze in any direction, and they had suckers at the ends, and they were full of sensory fibres. Then imagine the synaptic density you'd need to keep all that under control.' The theory he's testing, he explains, is that if you want to repair the damage from taking a lot of neurotoxic drugs like ketamine, you should eat a lot of synapse-dense food. 'I'm talking to a Canadian guy on the internet who says he can sell me some star-nosed mole meat made into jerky.' Raf looks puzzled.

'Star-nosed moles are the only mammals with tentacles,' Isaac adds. 'They have face tentacles. They can smell underwater.'

'Oh, fuck off.'

'Seriously!'

'If you want synaptic density, shouldn't you just eat poached lamb's brains or something?' says Raf. 'I ordered that by accident in a Turkish place once.'

'Too much cortisol. Cephalopods are healthier. Anyway, these won't be ready for a while – do you want some ice cream?'

'Are you allowed ice cream on the Tentacle Diet?'

'Cows have udders – close enough, right? Anyway, Fumiko knows where to get octopus ice cream.' Raf takes a step back from the tub on the counter. 'But that one's just green tea.'

Raf smiles and yawns. Last night he was about to put on his eyemask and earplugs and acoustic earmuffs as usual, but then he remembered Martin's account of Lacebark's prisons, a fear in a brain in a head in a hood in a cell in a warehouse in a city that doesn't know that you're there, seven Matryoshka dolls of impenetrable blackness, and it jarred him so badly that for the first time in months he had to try to sleep with bare sense organs. The Hittites, he once saw on a documentary, used to bury their dead wearing earplugs of beaten gold, although no one knows whether they were to keep something out or to keep something in. At the moment he's at a conventionally nocturnal stage of his cycle, so he went to bed at midnight when the sun was down and the street was quiet, but he's so used to his bulkheads that it still took him a couple of hours to doze off. Then this morning he awoke from a fluttery dream retaining such a definite sense of the jut of Cherish's naked hip bone against his belly that when he looked down he almost expected to see a little indentation in the skin.

Raf goes back into the living room, and that's when he realises to his surprise why the name Villepinte was familiar: because a fat paperback called *Lacunosities* by René Villepinte has been lying around here for weeks. But that doesn't make sense, because surely there's no way that any book that's on the Japanese girls' syllabus at fashion college could also be of interest to Lacebark's ImPressure• operators.

He waves at the girl winding her watch. 'Hey, is this any good?' She shrugs. He turns it over to look at the blurb. 'The most consequential contribution to postmodern critical theory since Deleuze and Guattari's *A Thousand Plateaus*,' declares someone at Penn State University. He opens it at random but it looks like gibberish. So, instead, he sits down on the arm of the sofa with Isaac's laptop to check his email, because he's waiting for a contract extension from the Polish 3D modelling company, and he finds that it hasn't arrived yet, but he does have a message from someone calling themselves 'Horologium Florae'. The body of the message is empty apart from a link to a YouTube video which was posted last night and so far has only four views. Raf watches it twice and then calls Isaac over to watch it a third time.

There's no audio track, and because the video is shot at night on a mobile phone camera it's churning and cindery, but you can still recognise the grid of white blobs that trembles in the background as a five-storey council block with a fluorescent security light over every front door. Closer at hand, a van is parked beside one of those communal lawns that Raf has always found so pointless, and two men stand on the lawn dressed just like the Lacebark soldiers he saw on Wednesday near his flat, except that they both wear anti-pollution masks over their mouths and one of them has a small plastic tank strapped to his back with a hose leading from the bottom of the tank to a long nozzle. For a while he just walks back and forth to move the nozzle over different patches of grass, diligent as a stag beetle, presumably spraying a liquid that doesn't show up on camera. The other man, who has no tank or nozzle, might be a lookout. Twice the whole screen goes black as the person with the mobile phone ducks out of sight behind a wall or maybe a car, but in all other respects it's pretty boring to watch.

Then, at seventy-two seconds, five foxes rip into view so fast they look like corrupted sectors in the video file. Raf has to pause it just to count them. And what happens after that is impossible to follow, a riffle shuffle of melty and almost abstract frames, but it ends with three foxes dead on the ground and both Lacebark men stumbling back towards the van, silenced pistols drawn, foreheads painted with blood, one clutching his leg and the other his throat.

'Christ! Have you ever seen a fox attack like that?' says Isaac.

'No.' To Raf there's something especially creepy about silent amateur footage like this, when the camera becomes your own two lidless eyes forced up against a thick glass wall, so it's all happening right there in front of you but you can't hear and you can't intervene and you can't turn away.

'I think foxes can get rabies, though.'

'Yeah, but rabid foxes don't run in packs.'

'Normal foxes don't either,' says Raf. 'I've never seen more than two at a time.'

'We should send this to *Animals Do the Funniest Things*.'

'What do you think the Lacebark guy is spraying?'

'It's got to be pesticide or herbicide.'

'Lacebark didn't come to London to do covert gardening. Except, oh, look up "Horologium Florae".'

Isaac types and clicks. ' "The flower clock . . ." ' he reads. ' "Invention of the Swedish botanist, physician and zoologist Carl Linnaeus . . . A garden plan that can tell the time of day using plants that open or close their flowers at particular times . . . From *Tragopogon pratensis*, the meadow salsify, also known as Jack-go-to-bed-at-noon or showy goat's-beard" – showy goat's-beard, that is brilliant! – "which flowers at 3 a.m., to *Hemerocallis lilio* . . ." – um, sorry – "*lilioasphodelus*, the lemon day lily, which flowers at nearly 9 p.m." Anyway, Carl Linnaeus died in 1778. So I'm not sure how helpful this is.' Isaac sniffs the air. 'Dumplings!' He rushes back to the kitchen.

Raf stays there on the sofa, a sudden darkness settling over him. He's been delaying it since his conversation with Martin, but at some point tonight he has to tell Isaac that he's almost sure Theo is dead.

DAY 10

11.08 a.m.

The five old men in the corner look as if their game of cards has been going on for so long that even if they've been playing for penny stakes their total wins and losses could bring down the international banking system. Like copper on rooftops, the tattoos on their forearms have discoloured with age, in this case black to dark blue. Raf and Fourpetal are the only other customers in the café, which is no surprise – there's almost nothing this side of the main road but warehouses and car parks and other null zones. The problem is, Raf does not find this a good place to sit by the window staking out the freight depot Martin told them about, because it's so much the sort of café he'd normally come to with a hangover or a serotonin deficit that all the departments of his brain capable of concentrating on anything serious even for a second automatically shut down for maintenance as soon as he got through the door half an hour ago and smelled the eggs scrambling. Still, he's doing his best.

The old depot, a long building of weathered brown brick, is tall enough for about two storeys, but Raf assumes it's just one giant open space inside, and around it is a high fence topped with barbed wire and a lot of conspicuous security cameras. On the other side it rubs up against a stretch of railway viaduct that now only carries overground passenger trains but must once have been connected to some sidings here. So far, the most dramatic thing that has happened is that two white vans have driven inside and three white vans have driven out.

The waiter comes over and asks if they want anything else. He's a startlingly pretty boy of nineteen or twenty with a black quiff and eyes so big and liquid that in his irises you can see the same subtle rainbows that swim in the film of grease on a puddle.

'Another coffee,' says Fourpetal.

'What's *salep*?' says Raf, looking at the laminated menu.

'Orchid tea,' says the waiter. 'It's really sweet.'

'Has it got any caffeine?'

'No.'

'I'll have one of those.'

'Are you Turkish?' says Fourpetal.

'We're Serbian.'

As the waiter goes back to the counter, Raf passes *Lacunosities* to Fourpetal. 'Apparently Lacebark are really into this book but I don't understand how that can be.'

Fourpetal flips through it. 'Well, the IDF read Tschumi on deconstruction. All the young generals are mad for this kind of thing now – supplementing their tactical manuals with postmodern conceptual schemes.'

'We should read it to see if there are any clues about how Lacebark operate.'

'Yes, perhaps one of us should, but why me?'

'You went to university.'

Fourpetal harrumphs. At that moment a man in a black suit walks out of the depot's side entrance and carries on past the gate. 'Do you recognise him?' says Raf.

'I haven't seen his cock yet, if that's what you mean. But he could still be with Lacebark.'

Fourpetal throws down a tenner for the drinks and they hurry out of the café. It's one of those May mornings when you can stand in the sun and it might already be summer but the slightest breeze will peel all the warmth from your skin. Hanging back at a cautious distance like they did with the Burmese DJs, they follow the man as he turns left at the self-storage facility on the corner. Doing this kind of thing with Fourpetal has started to feel surprisingly normal.

'He must be walking up to the Tube,' says Raf. 'Otherwise why wouldn't he have taken a car?'

'You know my flat's about ten minutes from here?'

'He's not going to your flat.'

Even though there's not much traffic at the next junction the man still pauses at the crossing and presses the button on the panel. The traffic lights around here wear tiaras of spikes to stop kids from climbing them. While the man waits for the green hieroglyph to appear he takes his BlackBerry out of his pocket and starts thumbing through his messages.

Without permitting himself the chance to think it through, Raf flips his hood up and breaks into a sprint.

The man doesn't look up until Raf's almost upon him, and Raf doesn't slow down, he just snatches for the BlackBerry and drops his head and charges on up the road before he's even certain that the thing itself is there in his hand instead of just the anticipation of its weight. Veering off behind a row of semi-detached houses, he can't hear feet behind him, and he hopes the man was too surprised to react in time, but he can't be sure, so he carries on running until his lungs are crumbling into powdery white ash and then finally stops to catch his breath. Behind him an old dub track lollops out of someone's open bedroom window. He pulls off his hoodie to stuff it underneath a hedge just in case it might be recognised, and down there already is a child's discarded glove, damp and blotchy like the carcass of a small blind mammal with a body made mostly of fingers.

1.06 p.m.

'Just to confirm your appointment to tour the south London facility at 9.30 a.m. on Monday. Looking forward to showing you round – I think you'll be very impressed. Best wishes, Denise.'

That's the only email of any relevance that Raf and Fourpetal can find on the BlackBerry when they meet at a McDonald's to look through its folders. They do discover, at least, that the man in the black suit works for a South African company called Nostrand Discovery, and he's visiting London specifically to take this tour, but there are no hints about what might actually be inside the freight depot. When Raf was fifteen he wanted so much to know what sex felt like that he thought his brain was going to pop with the frustration, but he still didn't want to know that as much as he now wants to know what Lacebark are doing in there.

'How are we going to get in without getting caught?' he says.

'Well, if you're really that eager, there is a means.'

'What?'

Fourpetal drafts an email on the BlackBerry and shows it to Raf. 'Hi Denise. One of my colleagues has just had to change his travel plans and he's going be in London for a couple of days this week. I'd love him to be able to see what you showed me this morning. Sorry for the short notice but is there any way we could set up another tour? I'm going to be out of contact for a while, so if this does turn out to be practical, please call my colleague directly on the UK number below.'

'Do you think that will work?' says Raf.

'Yes. After we send it we delete the sent message from the email server. The Nostrand chap may never find out he's been impersonated.'

'So I'm just going to walk in there pretending to be South African?'

'All you really have to worry about is ImPressure•.'

'What do you mean?'

'You remember that presentation video we enjoyed so much? ImPressure• has a facial-recognition system built into it. If you're in their database – and you presumably are if they've been in your flat – it won't matter how well we disguise you. The system will notice the match.'

'And then I'm fucked?'

'Not necessarily. All those facial-recognition systems spit out plenty of false positives. Someone will look at their screen and say, "ImPressure• is telling us that this important executive from

Nostrand Discovery is actually a carefree young Londoner called Raf whom we already happen to have on our watch list. But that's absurd. ImPressure• must have made another blunder. Cancel the alert." Have you ever bumped into a close friend but the context was wrong and you had no idea who they were?'

Nearby a teenage boy in a uniform is trying to mop up a spilled strawberry milkshake but the milkshake is trying to ooze away to safety. 'So the only thing that's going to keep me from getting hand-cuffed is that they don't trust their own computer systems?'

'I know you've never had a real job, so take it from me: it doesn't matter what industry you're in – nobody trusts their own computer systems. Anyway, you'd better make your mind up. We don't know how soon your mugging victim will remember to change the pass-word on his email account.'

'Would you do this?'

'Honestly?' says Fourpetal. 'No.'

Would Raf do it? Would he risk his life against Lacebark like those foxes did? It horrifies him to think that Theo, the born rescuer, might be beyond rescue. But if that's true, he wouldn't want Raf to hurl himself down the same bottomless hole. There's nothing left to do for his friend now but mourn. He also has no reason to think he can even do anything useful for any of the Burmese people who've been snatched by the vans, and he certainly can't 'save' Cherish. In any case, whatever quiet war Lacebark is waging here, whatever toxin may be gushing from their nozzles, he's supposed to be leaving for good in a fortnight. The city isn't his problem any more. None of this is.

But then he thinks about the reason he's given himself for going away, his sense that he had to make a physical escape from the site of his heartbreak because this cold termite hollow wasn't just in him, it was out there, objectively, in things, in all of them, down to the waltzing fall of a cigarette paper when it slips from your fingers, down to the VOID VOID VOID VOID that the ticket machine at an overground station prints on the orange chit when it cancels a sale.

Now Lacebark are in south London, infiltrating it, altering it, coughing this mist of dread over the streets that once meant so much to him. When his girlfriend left, everything here went to shit for a while, and all he could do was sit there and suffer. Seven weeks later, everything is going to shit again, but this time he has a chance to try to stop it.

DAY 11

11.58 a.m.

While he's waiting at the gate of the depot, Raf happens to reach into his left trouser pocket and discovers for the first time a sheet of paper crumpled up in there. He takes it out, uncrumples it, and realises that it's the order of service sheet from his grandmother's funeral in 2007, which was the last time he took this suit off its hanger.

'Mr Rose?'

Raf looks up. A woman in wireframe glasses is striding towards him across the concrete. He stuffs the sheet back in his pocket as fast as he can. 'Yes,' he says, pronouncing it 'Yiss,' because yesterday he watched a lot of South African accent tutorial videos on YouTube, and now he's trying to keep his premolars pressed against the thighs of his tongue.

This woman's accent, on the other hand, is American. 'Great to meet you. I'm Denise Belasco. We spoke on the phone.' They shake hands. 'How much did Mr Jacobs tell you about the facility?'

'We didn't have a chance to speak for very long. But he told me he found it very impressive.' Raf reminds himself he needs to ride like Fourpetal, high in the saddle of his lies. Two Lacebark security guards stand like bouncers outside the side door of the depot and as he passes them he thinks of how he felt the first time he brought pills into a club in the toe of his shoe. Inside there's a windowless ante-room where a third guard sits at a desk behind a bank of screens. A fridge in the corner is filled with mineral water and energy drinks. There are no clues here. For all he knows it could be a gate to the underworld.

'We'll just need a scan of your passport,' says Belasco. 'Sorry for the hassle but as you can imagine we take a lot of precautions at a facility like this.'

'I'm afraid my passport's in the safe at my hotel. But I've got my driver's licence.' Raf takes it out of his wallet. Fourpetal had warned him this might happen so last night he went over to Jonk's flat with Isaac and the three of them spent the evening forging this card. Because Jonk once tried to start a side business selling fake IDs, he already had a pirate copy of Photoshop, a second-hand inkjet printer, and a box of those butterfly laminate pouches that you can seal with a clothes iron. The only problem was, Jonk had ordered the pouches from a website that specialised in supplying the 'novelty' ID market, so they were all printed in advance with generic foil holograms, but South African driver's licences don't actually have holograms on them, just pink watermarks, with the result that Raf's fake licence has more 'security features' than a real one. In most circumstances this wouldn't matter, but Fourpetal also warned him that quite a lot of Lacebark's goons are hired from South Africa.

So Raf's as nervous now watching the guard run his card through the scanner as he was earlier when a security camera first swivelled its head towards him like a carrion bird as he waited outside the gate of the depot. Then he realises that if he just stares across the desk in silence it's going to make him look even more unnatural, so he turns back to Belasco and tries to think of something to say, but his mind is suddenly an empty trough. To his enormous relief, it's Belasco who asks, 'And you work with Mr Jacobs in Tanzania?'

'That's right.' ('Thitt's hroitte.')

'He told me he was in the Nostrand office in Fehedou at the time of the truck bombing. That must have been a really nasty thing to experience.'

'Yes, it really was.'

On the heavy steel door that presumably leads through into the main section of the depot, there is a sign that says AUTHORISED

PERSONNEL ONLY, which to Raf seems hilariously mundane and redundant in this context. (He's relieved that the security measures here don't extend to a fingerprint or iris scanner, and he remembers Isaac's proposal for a biometric identification system which required the user to perform thirty seconds of oral sex on an androgynous piezo-electric tubercle, on the basis that any given individual's precise oral sex technique is both unique and impossible to teach or imitate.) The guard at the desk hands back Raf's driver's licence without meeting his eye. Since he seems to be safe for the moment, he scrapes together his courage to take a small risk. 'I must say, Ms Belasco—'

'Denise.'

'I must say, Denise, until recently I only really thought of Lacebark as a mining company.' This remark will make sense as long as Raf is about to get a tour of something that is not a mine, and that seems like a good bet, unless Isaac is correct in his speculation that Lacebark's big secret is the diamond mine they have dug under the streets of London with its entrance hidden in this depot. (Isaac has never believed that the true explanation for why south London doesn't have a proper Tube network is that its subsurface geology makes tunnelling impossible – he has a selection of mutually contradictory conspiracy theories to propose instead – and in a sense an urban mine would prove him correct.)

'Oh, sure,' says Belasco. 'You're by no means alone there. The vast majority of Lacebark's business is and always has been resource extraction. That's what we're known for. But over the last twenty years we've faced a lot of the same problems in Myanmar that you and your colleagues at Nostrand are now facing in Tanzania. One of Lacebark's basic corporate values is that we never outsource when we can insource. So we've pumped major resources into developing skills that lie quite a long way outside our core competencies. And the best way to begin to defray an investment like that is to offer some of those skills on the open market. It's much the same approach that San Miguel took with Sentinel back in the 1960s, for instance, if you're familiar with Sentinel. If we build you a facility like this in Tanzania, you can be confident it will do the job, because we rely on facilities of exactly the same kind. We are our own most demanding customers.'

Raf tries to translate all this in his head. He knows from the Pankhead email that Lacebark are in financial trouble. By now they must be aching for cash so badly that they'll accept contracts from other companies for services that have nothing to do with mining. Nostrand Discovery is a potential client. In that case 'Mr Rose' can probably afford to play it a bit more aloof.

'Shall we head on through?' says Belasco.

After the security guard presses a button on a panel, the steel door in front of them emits a buzz and then a clunk. Belasco holds it open for Raf. And Raf steps out, somehow, into the open air.

Many times in his life, Raf has carelessly said, 'I thought I was dreaming' or 'I had to pinch myself' or 'It was a total nightmare'. But he won't say those things again after this. Because never, ever before has he had any experience which made him feel so much like a drowsy and gullible consciousness floating through its own depthless improvisation.

He stands in a London street. Above his head, there is a sun, but the sun is both weak and very close, as if the world is ending. On his left there is a post office, followed by a laundrette, a mobile phone shop, a fried chicken shop, a pound shop, a pawnbroker, and a pub, and on his right there is a Chinese takeaway, followed by a green-grocer, a charity shop, a butcher, a hairdresser, a kebab shop, a bookie, and a chemist; and all these are easy to identify even at a distance because their signs just say POST OFFICE, LAUNDRETTE, MOBILE PHONES, and so on, in an invariant sans-serif typeface. Most of the road has white zigzag lines on either side, but farther on, past a bus stop, a few cars and vans are parked. And about two hundred metres away, blocking the end of the street in a way that you would never see in real life, is an orthogonal pair of two-storey council blocks overlooking a small park with swings and a tree. Everything is a bit too bright and concentrated, sickening, like undiluted orange squash. Raf can hear radios and car horns and the rumble of an overground train, and he can smell chip fat and bus exhaust and fishmonger's ice melting in the gutter, but there isn't enough bustle here to generate any of those harmonies, just a few men and women walking up and down the street, nearly all of them Burmese, dressed in cheap sportswear, pretending to have somewhere to go. And there's no chewing gum on the pavement, no stickers on the lamp-posts, no paint flaking from the windowsills of the flats above the shops – none of the scurf and sebum that distinguishes a body from a mannequin. He's rendered architectural models on his computer with more texture than this.

Of course, if you put everything together rationally, it becomes apparent that Lacebark have built some sort of film set or theme park here inside the freight depot, but at first sight, before he understood what he was looking at, it seemed more like a dip in the band-width of reality itself. When at last the trance breaks, he walks over to the greengrocer and picks up a delicious-looking plastic mango from a cardboard box at the front. Underneath the top layer of mangoes there are chunks of styrofoam to bulk up the pile. If that climbing gym was a mountain, this is the village at the foot of the slopes. Perhaps in some way the tacky fake hologram on his driver's licence was the visa that got him across the border.

'Our team can build one of these for you in less than three weeks,' says Belasco behind him.

Raf turns. 'My colleague was right. This is . . . very impressive.' He tries to imagine what this place would look like if it were abandoned for a while like that tennis court, and how its progress would compare to a real street that was abandoned at the same time. At first, dilapidation would reveal the differences, but later it would begin to elide them: the two worlds would diverge and then converge, in the same way that two half-siblings might look the same as kids and different as adults and the same again as skeletons. Belasco politely takes the mango from him and puts it back in the box.

'Maybe I shouldn't say this, but some of our higher-ups do wonder why we need our own MOUT facility like this. They find it hard to imagine London being exotic to anyone. After all, it's just London, isn't it? But if you did your training in Lagos, for instance, terrain like this is going to seem really sparse and exposed. And we also have guys accustomed to desert or mountain operations for whom the opposite is true. They can learn so much in just a few days of exercises here. It justifies the cost even before we start running any of the more specific tactical simulations.'

'The people who designed all this – were they Londoners themselves?'

'No,' says Belasco. 'We find that natives of the simuland have a tendency to introduce unconscious distortions into their models.'

At this, Raf feels oddly indignant. How can these tourists think they're qualified to author a précis of a city they can't possibly understand? Anyway, they can't really be that concerned with accuracy if they've decided to populate their south London microcosm mostly with Burmese extras, one of whom has just strolled into the 'laundrette', making Raf wonder how you get recruited for this sort of work, and what the wages are.

'Let's take a look at the control room,' says Belasco.

Behind another steel door up the back stairs of the 'pub', two white guys of about Raf's age sit in voluptuously ergonomic office chairs before a wall of monitors that alternate video feeds with digital control panels. The room is dark except for the shifting diode light that falls across their bodies like crepuscular rays through a stained-glass window. One of them, Raf notices, was just in the middle of eating a supermarket chicken wrap, and there's a certain stale quality to this control room that reminds him of the fourth hour of an Xbox session at Isaac's flat. On the floor is a copy of Villepinte's *Lacunosities*.

'From here we can observe and communicate with anyone in the facility,' says Belasco. 'And it's also where we set ambience, climate, time of day. The default is a three-hour day/night cycle with seasonally appropriate weather but of course we can alter that as we like.'

Raf can't stop himself asking, 'So instead of three hours you could set it to about twenty-five hours?'

Belasco looks at him quizzically. 'Sure. Now, Max, give us 4 a.m., heavy rain, please.'

The guy on the left types a few commands on his keyboard, and as darkness falls outside, the screens all switch over to night-vision emerald.

'It doesn't look like much from up here,' says Belasco. 'You might want to see for yourself.'

Raf wouldn't have believed he could possibly be enough of a mug to get bewitched twice in a row. But when he goes back downstairs, he can feel grudging tears of wonder in his eyes, like when you're watching a Hollywood romance that you know is cynical factory product but by the end you just can't help yourself. Because when he sees the pavement dragging worms of dappled amber out of the reflections of the street lights in its wet rough stone, he could be walking home from a rave in the rain, serotonin still trickling through the gutters of his head. It's as fake and as real as Cherish's kiss. The water must be coming from a few hundred sprinklers in the roof, but there's such a depth to the sound of it, and he wonders if Max upstairs is playing a tape of a real downpour to give the impression of clouds stretching off for miles overhead, the same way a video game will enclose the player in a cuboid called a skybox to suggest a deep horizon when it's really just a sort of frescoed ceiling. As he looks across at the two council estates lit up like docked spaceships, there is an orange spark in his peripheral vision, and when he turns his head he sees something he can't possibly have seen – but before he can get a proper look, the 'sun' comes back on, and in the time it takes his eyes to adjust, the anomaly has scurried out of view. The rain carries on for a few seconds and then sputters off like a garden hose, leaving the street puddled but bright, and some small stupid part of him wants to search the sky for a rainbow. He realises Belasco has come down the stairs behind him.

'You know, I wouldn't like to work in a dark control room all day,' she confides. 'But for Max it's the perfect job. He has a condition called solar urticaria. His skin is very sensitive to sunlight. He gets a rash.'

Raf wonders how the solar urticaria messageboards compare to the non-24-hour sleep/wake syndrome messageboards. Someone should organise a football league for all these different disorders. 'Denise, is it possible that I saw . . .'

'What?'

He doesn't want to say any more. If he's wrong, it will make her suspicious. A real Nostrand executive wouldn't be so impressionable that this training facility would make him hallucinate. But he has to know.

'I expect it was just a trick of the light . . . but is it possible that I saw an animal?' He clears his throat. 'A fox?'

Belasco nods. 'You've got sharp eyes, Mr Rose. When the US military was setting up its first simulated Iraqi villages, the soldiers told them it wouldn't be realistic without the animals. Donkeys, goats, dogs . . . They even got camels, I heard. We try to match that standard. So, yes, we have, uh, we have foxes, and we're in the process of sourcing some pigeons.'

Raf has spent only about twenty minutes with Belasco, so it's not as if he knows her very well, but there was something about how she stumbled over her words just now that made him wonder if she was telling a lie of her own. 'Now, if I may, I'm going to show you an example of a core scenario installation that we have up and running at the moment.'

This turns out to be one of the flats on the second floor of the council block on the left. As they follow the open walkway down to number 14, a smell reaches Raf that is surely too vigorous in its tang to have been pumped out of an artificial scent machine. He looks at Belasco, and she's wrinkling her nose, but also staring rigidly ahead, almost as if it's a bodily odour that she's too embarrassed to acknowledge. She unlocks the front door of the flat, and once inside

Raf realises that somewhere in the swirl of the stench is that toothy peat musk he remembers from the fox on the night bus the weekend before last – but there's also tamarind and bleach and dung and a lot more, which makes it almost the only stimulus he's encountered since he set foot in this depot that has the same sensory complexity as real things have out there in the unbounded world.

'Our associate here is playing the role of a high-value target,' Belasco says, leading him through to the kitchen. A slender Burmese guy stands at the sink soaping his hands, and it feels strange to walk in like this without even nodding hello, but Raf isn't sure whether it's like a theatre and the actors have to pretend you're not there. This 'core scenario installation' has been arranged to look like a makeshift laboratory: cluttering the counters are flasks, beakers, burettes, and funnels – many of them clamped upside down to steel ring stands and interconnected by loops of tubing, like the renal system of an android – as well as plastic tubs, latex gloves, rubber stoppers, paper towels, cotton wool, coffee filters, a couple of electric hotplates, and all sorts of other props. On the table is a laptop; on top of the fridge is the exact same brand of cheap radio that Raf has in his own kitchen, tuned to a station that in the circumstances seems pretty likely to be Myth FM; and on the windowsill is a sort of DIY incense burner made from two empty cans of Rubicon guava juice that have been glued end to end with extra holes drilled in the lids and half the sides cut off. It seems as if the set of a 'core scenario installation' is dressed with an especially close attention to detail – if you're trying to evoke a believable world it's natural that you spend more time on the sections that people are going to pay attention to – but that still doesn't quite explain Belasco's weird reaction to the odour.

'This apartment has even more cameras per hundred square feet than the rest of the facility,' she says, 'but they're all concealed, for realism. We can analyse every tactical simulation with incredible specificity. The action couldn't be clearer if it was in chess notation.'

Now the Burmese guy is filling an electric kettle from the tap. The linoleum tiles on the floor have a hexagon pattern.

'So what's he supposed to be making here?' says Raf. 'Explosives?' If this is how Lacebark have chosen to array their simulated high-value target, then presumably at least one of their real high-value targets is believed to be hiding out in a real laboratory somewhere.

'For the purposes of the tactical exercises, all that matters is that there may be volatile chemicals in the apartment.'

Raf rehearses his next question in his head a few times before he voices it. 'I'm curious to know how much evidence you have that a tactical exercise in a controlled environment like this can translate to concrete results out on the street.'

'Do you mean from our own experience? I don't have direct access to a lot of that information. But based on what I've heard from Lacebark personnel in London, it's hard to overestimate how helpful this facility has been to prepare for their recent operations.'

How far can he push this? 'Those operations . . .'

'Obviously I'm not at liberty . . .'

'Right. Sure.'

'Is there anything else you'd like to see?'

Raf shakes his head. 'This is already a lot to take in,' he says, truthfully.

As they leave the kitchen, Raf turns back for one last look, and by accident he makes eye contact with the Burmese guy, who is standing there watching them go while the kettle boils. For an uncomfortable second they have both broken character, although if any coded signal passed between them, Raf wouldn't be able to say what it was. He follows Belasco back down the stairs and out into the 'street'. Rain is still trickling from the trees.

'How long are you staying in London?' she says.

Raf begins to relax. The tour has reached its epilogue of rote small talk. Now all he has to do is get to the exit. 'Just until tomorrow morning.'

'And then more travel?'

Raf remembers that town she mentioned earlier. 'No,' he says. 'Straight back to Fehedou.'

Belasco frowns. 'But I understood that Nostrand pulled out of Fehedou right after the truck bomb.'

A puff of liquid nitrogen in Raf's guts. How bad was that slip? He can't tell. But now Belasco is looking straight at him, and he knows that just because he's got this far without fucking up, it won't necessarily keep her from leaving him with a security guard while she calls Nostrand to check his credentials. He thinks of the order of service sheet in his pocket. 'Yes,' he says. 'We did.' If he tries to explain away the mistake he'll just make another one. But Belasco has a fontanelle of her own, and Raf's best option is to put his thumb on it. 'By the way, Denise, the core scenario installation you showed me: I was wondering about the smell. Is that all artificial too?'

His guess is that if he'd asked any other question, Fehedou would still have been on Belasco's mind. But instead she looks as if now she just wants this conversation to conclude as fast as possible.

'Sure,' she says. 'All artificial. We use the latest Biopac Scent Delivery System, with sixteen cartridge slots. I guess it might have been a little, uh, a little too thick in the air today!'

She smiles, and Raf smiles warmly back. Inside his polished black shoes all ten of his toes are clenched so hard they feel as if they might snap off.

4.15 p.m.

It's about glow. It's got to be about glow. This is what Raf says to himself as he unclips Rose's leash after a trip to the Iranian corner shop for booze and dog food. Back at Lacebark's doll's house, when Belasco showed him the fake laboratory, the reason he asked about bombs in particular was that news footage from the War on Terror was looping in his head, satellite maps riddled with 'black sites' like tumours on a CT scan. But Belasco didn't confirm that and he shouldn't have jumped to conclusions. Instead, he needs to get to his computer and do some homework to batten his new hunch. He's trying not to think too hard about the risk he took today, because now that the adrenaline's turned to vinegar and he's safely back in his flat, there's some chance he might start whimpering to himself. And it's funny that for comfort he's turned instinctively to a bottle of whisky and a faithful hound, which makes him feel like some sort of red-faced country squire. But no one has invented a pill yet that does the job so well.

A laboratory is like a radio transmitter: if you have one in your flat you might just be a hobbyist but you are more likely a criminal. Most of the laws you can break with a glass pipette involve either drugs or weaponry. Once in a while the two coincide. There's a synthetic opioid called 3-methylfentanyl that's about six thousand times as strong as morphine and has its own small population of addicts dispersed across the Baltic States like an obscure and wretched religious sect, but which was also the basis of the aerosol spray that killed over a hundred hostages when the Spetsnaz pumped it into the air-conditioning system of that theatre in Moscow in 2002. In principle, an entrepreneurial terrorist planning an attack on the London Underground could wholesale half his 3-methylfentanyl to drug pushers in order to subsidise the production of the other half. But what rules out 3-methylfentanyl here, along with sarin and acetone peroxide and every other high explosive and nerve agent that Raf can find listed on the internet, is that none of them has organic precursors. If Lacebark are using herbicides against something that's blossoming outside council estates, it must be for the same reason that Thai customs officers confiscate sassafras oil: they're trying to scotch one of the ingredients in a drug recipe. And in this case it's not going to be coca shrubs or opium poppies or sassafras trees. So what is it?

At first, Raf tries reasoning forward from the precursor to the drug. Thinking of that anonymous email, he wonders if the precursor might be one of the forty-three plants that Linnaeus listed for his flower clock. But none of them is known to have narcotic derivatives. The best he can do is the Icelandic poppy (7 p.m.), which has some of the same alkaloids as the opium poppy but not nearly enough to be useful, and the dandelion (5 a.m.), which makes dandelion wine. Raf feels pretty confident that Lacebark haven't come to London for dandelion wine. He's leaning too hard on a rickety clue. Perhaps the precursor is just some other plant with the potential to fill a slot in the *Horologium Florae* but that wasn't necessarily known to Linnaeus. That could be any one of a few hundred thousand species.

So he tries reasoning backwards from the drug to the precursor. With real ecstasy so scarce, London is a salon of avant-garde compounds at the moment: ethylbuphedrone and DMBDB and MDPV and a lot of other pretenders. But there's one that stands out. Glow. Cherish asked him about it at the rave. Ko offered to sell him some a few days later. That's why he was wondering about it even before he started this research.

Fourpetal has estimated that Lacebark came to London around January. And Raf didn't hear about glow for the first time until last week. But when he searches on Lotophage for the earliest mention of glow, it's in a post from 28 October 2009. 'Anyone heard anything about this new stuff "glow"? Haven't been able to track any down yet but apparently it's a very potent entactogenic :)'. (An emoticon like that is the closest anyone on Lotophage ever gets to a moan of anticipation.) In another post in a different thread, the same user happens to mention that he lives in London. The timing is exactly right.

Still, it can only be glow if glow does have a botanical precursor. As Rose dozes at his feet like a small black hole on loan from a particle accelerator, Raf reads through every single forum post about glow in chronological order to see what he can find out. Most of them are no help. Everyone wants to try glow, but almost no one can get hold of any, and no one knows for sure where it comes from. However, even though scholars at the University of Lotophage don't usually have much tolerance for speculation, there's something about glow that seems to give rise to a lot of competing tattle. One user says that all extant glow comes from a single batch of experimental medication that was stolen from a hospital in South Wales where the Ministry of Defence were using it to treat post-traumatic stress disorder in Iraq War veterans. Another says that glow is rare but not new and he tried it for the first time in Ibiza in 1995. And another says that all this hype about glow is just more evidence of how the placebo effect is getting stronger every year in the feeble-minded populations of the developed world.

But there is one Lotophage user who seems to know a lot more than anyone else.

His username is 'Fitch', and rather than showing off his expertise, he steps in only when he wants to correct a misconception that he finds particularly irritating. In one thread, for instance, people are speculating that part of the difference in the respective effects of glow and ecstasy might result from a faster enzymatic conversion of dopamine to noradrenaline.

'you think glow might feel like that "because" the dopamine/noradrenaline balance different???' writes Fitch. 'what the fuck you think you mean by "because"?! all you bitches need to read *L'Amour Médecin* by Molière. one doctor says "Most learned bachelor, whom I esteem and honor, I would like to ask you the cause and reason why opium makes one sleep." the other doctor says "The reason is that in opium resides a *dormitive virtue* of which it is the nature to stupefy the senses." nothing changes in three hundred years except the terminology. "Most learned bachelor, whom I esteem and honor, I would like to ask you the cause and reason why MDMA makes one dance." "The reason is that through the brain gushes a *catecholic neurotransmitter* of which it is the nature to inflame the senses." no explanatory power, no predictive power, no falsifiability . . . no real theory. there are >100 neurotransmitters in the brain. we don't know shit about what most of them do. dopamine used to get all the research funding. now oxytocin. soon octopamine/enkephalin/substance P/something else. when we still so ignorant, none of this has any meaning!! anyone who uses an individual neurotransmitter to support an explanation of human emotion or behaviour is talking out of his ass. we all be old or dead before anyone get a handle on how subjective experience supervenes on brain activity . . . and, by the way, it's obvious that anything with an N-methylyhio-tetrazole functional group gonna have an indirect inhibitory effect on dopamine β-hydroxylase, so your whole bullshit chain of causation backwards.' There follows a GIF of a sailor in a tricorne hat looking the wrong way down a telescope.

It's the final sentences of these posts that are especially intriguing to Raf – Fitch insists that these debates are pointless and yet he can't resist winning them anyway. Compile the whole lot, and it becomes clear that Fitch is an expert on glow. He also makes occasional contributions to threads about some of the more esoteric new chemicals from China, concluding one dense post about the possible neurotoxicity of halogenated amphetamines with 'so, yeah, all you guys playing russian roulette with your brain tissue.' But he never mentions taking any drugs himself. As Raf sees it, there are two obverse reasons you might talk a lot about drugs without ever indulging in them: either you're very distant from the drug world, or you're deep inside it. Fitch might just be some pharmacology graduate student at a rural college in the US who enjoys making Lotophage users look stupid. Or he might be directly involved in the manufacture and distribution of glow.

So Raf makes a list of the exact times of every one of Fitch's posts, hoping to triangulate him not in space but in time. This is going to be fuzzy at best, since most Lotophage users keep odd schedules. But Raf can't find any statistical tendency whatsoever. Fitch has posted at least once at every different time of day. Could he have non-24-hour sleep/wake syndrome? Could he work in a corner shop?

Rose, meanwhile, is up and yawning. Raf leans down to knuckle her under the chin. 'All right, girl, what do we know?' he says to her. 'Lacebark's "high-value target" is a Burmese chemist making something shady in his kitchen. That might be glow. Fitch might have something to do with making glow. So Fitch might be a Burmese chemist. Fitch might be Lacebark's "high-value target". Bark if you think that makes any sense at all.' In that case, would Fitch's written English be quite so good? Would he be quoting French playwrights? Cherish is fluent, but that's because she moved to America when she was ten.

The only way to get any further is to contact Fitch directly.

But if Fitch is on the run from Lacebark, and he gets a message groping behind his alias, then of course he's going to suspect Lacebark of sending it. They could have found him through Lotophage just like Raf did. And there's nothing Raf can put in the message that will prove otherwise. Any collateral he offers for his identity could just be another meticulous Lacebark creation like the plastic fruit outside the 'greengrocer'. Also, that goes in both directions. Even if Fitch says, 'Yes, you're right, I am a Burmese drug chemist, a thousand congratulations for finding me,' it might still be a ruse. In fact, for all Raf knows, Fitch is a Lacebark operative himself, sitting in an office somewhere with carpal tunnel braces on his wrists, writing well-researched posts to win the trust of some other 'high-value target'. Raf could ask Fitch to tell him something that only a Burmese drug chemist would know. But for any given datum that only a Burmese drug chemist would know, there will, by definition, be no means for Raf to confirm it.

For a moment he feels frustrated that most of the internet is only mutters in the dark, but then he thinks of Cherish and all her pretence. What difference do screens and keyboards make? You can be skin to scalding skin with a naked human being, you can feel them squirm in what you assume at the time is total abandon, without any inkling of who they really are. And every powder Raf has ever taken at a rave has been white and bitter like rat poison. You learn nothing from the surfaces of things. An anonymous email address, a pill capsule, a padlocked warehouse door, a joyful look in a girl's eyes – you just have to push blindly through to the space behind them and hope there's no void there to trap you.

'Lacebark killed my friend. I don't know what they're going to do next, but I want to stop them. Can you help me?' That's the message Raf sends to Fitch through the Lotophage private message system. He finishes his whisky. Rose has fallen asleep again in that disconcerting way she sometimes does with her eyes half open and her pupils rolled back like someone having a 3-methylfentanyl overdose. He's still in his funeral suit and he decides to take a long shower. When he returns in his dressing gown, he finds that Fitch has already replied.

His heart's thumping as he opens the message. 'sorry about your friend,' it says. 'but how you think I could help you?'

Raf writes: 'Does glow have an organic precursor or not?'

This time the reply takes less than a minute to arrive. Fitch is still online. 'meaningless question. any alkaloid can be made from laboratory chemicals without pestling shrubs. just an issue of whether the yield from known methods large enough to make it cost-effective. for glow, it ain't.'

Raf: 'Are Lacebark here because of glow? Why would they need to come all the way to London for that?'

Fitch: 'maybe they heard about that big UKG night in Elephant & Castle next week.'

Raf: 'If they're looking for you, wouldn't it be dangerous for you to talk to me? You don't know who I am.'

Fitch: 'doesn't matter who you are!! even if you could make Lotophage turn over their IP records, I access the site through a proxy. I could be right behind you on the sofa typing this on a laptop. no way you could trace me.'

After Raf instinctively turns to look, he feels like an idiot. 'Are you Burmese?'

Fitch: 'why all these questions about glow? you buy drugs?'

Raf: 'Sometimes. Why?'

Fitch: 'the government say when you buy drugs you funding terrorism.'

Raf: 'Was it you that sent me that video on Sunday? Are you Horologium Florae?'

For the next twenty minutes Raf sits there refreshing his Lotophage inbox and reading a long news story about a vet who nearly died after she induced vomiting in a dog that had eaten rat poison without knowing that the zinc phosphide in the rat poison had turned into phosphine gas upon contact with the water and hydrochloric acid in the dog's stomach. But Fitch stays silent. Raf is excited, but when he looks back over the exchange, he realises Fitch didn't say anything to confirm he'd ever even heard of Lacebark before Raf started asking questions. If you set aside that reference to Elephant and Castle, Fitch still might very well be a college student in Wisconsin.

He gets dressed, fills up Rose's water bowl, and leaves the flat. The sky is a mess of sagging aeroplane contrails, and by this stage of the spring the street lamps come on long before the sun is down, hanging around awkwardly like guests early to a party. When he gets to the Burmese restaurant, it's the same waiter as usual, but one of the Maneki Neko cats seems to have run away. Raf wasn't actually planning to eat here but when he smells the food it occurs to him that he's ravenous.

'I'll just have the same curry I had last time,' he says after he's been seated. 'And sticky rice, and some of those stir-fried beans, and a beer. But I need to speak to Ko first.'

'Ko cooking,' says the waiter.

'Just for a minute. Please.'

The waiter purses his lips. 'OK.'

Raf gets up again and follows him around the counter to the kitchen. Ko is torturing something in a wok flame while a second chef is peeling a butternut squash faster than a normal person can shuck the foil off an Easter egg. The waiter says something in Burmese, and Ko looks up. 'Yes?'

'Can I talk to you?' Raf says. 'Outside?'

The second chef takes over the wok and Raf goes with Ko out to the alley at the back of the kitchen, a bit surprised that this didn't take more persuasion. Empty drums of cooking oil are piled against the wall beside the wheelie bins and three canisters of butane lie around like circus animals inside a locked metal cage. Ko takes out a packet of cigarettes and lights one. 'So?' he says.

'Last time I was here you said you could sell me some glow,' Raf says. 'I need to know where you're getting it from.'

Ko blows out a smoke ring. 'Want to see something?'

'OK.'

After pausing to balance his cigarette on the edge of a wheelie bin, Ko takes something dark out of his pocket and holds it out at chest level. As Raf looks down to see what it is, his forearms are grabbed from behind, and Ko flips the black hood neatly over his head.

Before he has any idea what's happening, Raf feels something tightening around his wrists, and he's hauled sideways down the alley. He struggles as hard as he can, and shouts for help, but then his feet are off the ground, and four hands lower him on to the floor of what must be a van because he can feel the vibration of the idling engine through the rubber mat on which his cheek now comes to rest. The doors slam and the van drives off. They've got him.

The inside of the hood smells of damp socks, and the loop around Raf's wrists feels as if it might be one of those cheap plastic zip ties with ratchets at the ends. He is fucking terrified. Sitting there already in his head is a proposition, one that has substantial mass but that he doesn't yet know how to approach or interpret, like a non-Euclidean cadmium sculpture that just appears in your kitchen one morning, and the proposition is that he is going to die tonight. Ten days trying to find out what happened to Theo and now he'll see for himself up close. Perhaps it took Lacebark a few hours to be absolutely sure that their facial-recognition system hadn't registered a false positive after all, and by that time he'd left the training facility, so they had to snatch him at their next opportunity. Or perhaps it was his message to Fitch. 'Lacebark killed my friend. I don't know what they're going to do next, but I want to stop them.' He might as well have filled out an application form to get kidnapped and interrogated.

Isaac will take good care of Rose.

He can hear a scooter engine, and dance-hall burping from some-one's car stereo, so they must be out in traffic now, and he wonders if he can work out where they're going by paying attention to the turns they make, but he decides there's no way his vestibular gyroscope is sensitive enough. Then brusque hands are under his armpits again as he's pulled into a different position – a more comfortable one, in fact, sitting up against the side of the van with his knees half bent.

'Ko?' he says.

'Don't worry,' Ko says.

'What do you mean, "don't worry"?'

'Don't worry,' Ko says again.

'Ko, do you work for Lacebark?'

Ko doesn't reply.

After ten minutes – or maybe five, or maybe fifteen – Raf feels the van pulling up to a kerb. As Ko helps him down out of the back, he can hear a dog barking, which is odd, because that means they must still be out in the open, whereas both the Lacebark warehouses he's seen have sliding garage doors so that vans can drive inside, out of sight, before they unload. But then Ko prods him impatiently in the back, and he walks a few steps forward, nearly tripping on the threshold of what feels like a front door. Behind him, he hears the van drive off.

'Stairs,' warns Ko, and puts his hand on Raf's shoulder to guide him. Awkwardly, Raf makes his way up three flights. On the first landing he can smell bacon frying, and he begins to consider the possibility that, for the second time in one day, he has entered what he expected to be a sterile Lacebark dungeon and has found himself instead inside a block of flats – except that, to judge by the creaking yield of the wooden stair treads under his feet, this block of flats seems to be genuine.

Ko knocks at a door and shouts something in Burmese. The door opens, and once Raf has shuffled through, Ko finally pulls the hood from his head.

The first thing Raf sees is Cherish standing there with her hand on the shoulder of an emaciated Burmese guy in a wheelchair.

As Ko snips the zip tie off his wrists with a small pair of pliers, Raf looks around. He's in the living room of a two- or three-bedroom flat, part of an old converted house rather than a council estate. Just now, when he heard those two heavy bolts sliding back, he was reminded of the Myth FM studio, and he sees now that the comparison was pretty apt: this is another of those small pressurised containers you sometimes find in London that are put to such a brutally demanding and urgent and contradictory selection of uses that every organic or inorganic body within them, and perhaps also the local fabric of space itself, will before long find itself scoured and mulched into a sort of ragged black kimchi. There are bin bags taped over the windows and cardboard boxes stacked in the corner next to a folding futon. Up on the wall there's a map of London, a faded poster of a huge pyramidal temple somewhere in the jungle, and a one-page advertorial torn from a magazine announcing Lacebark's new annual human rights grant. The table by the doorway through to the rest of the flat has been converted into a sort of workstation whose purpose is clear to Raf because he's seen others like it, with latex gloves, spoons, tinfoil, small resealable plastic bags, a few tubs of lactose, a vacuum brush, and a set of microgram digital scales.

'What is this?' says Raf. 'What the fuck is going on?' If he'd been thinking more clearly when he was in the van, maybe it would have occurred to him sooner that the van's engine wasn't silent.

'We had to get you away from the restaurant before Lacebark worked out what we were doing,' says Cherish. 'But we also had to make sure you didn't see the route here. Ko's English isn't that good and there wasn't going to be time for him to coax you into putting the hood on. So he did what he had to.'

The guy in the wheelchair murmurs something in Burmese. He's so deathly in appearance that Raf is almost too squeamish to look straight at him – cheekbones and eye sockets way too big for the rest of his face, glossy lesions swarming around his mouth, skin greyish and almost translucent in places like undercooked prawns – and yet there's something in his gaze and in the set of his shoulders that gives the impression of real strength.

'Also, it won't have done you any harm to see what it would be like if Lacebark really got to you,' adds Cherish, apparently translating. 'It's happened to a lot of our friends. We all need to learn to be grateful for our good luck so far. Incidentally, don't go back to the restaurant for a while after this, OK? Lacebark aren't going to believe you like *mohinga* that much.'

Raf starts rubbing his wrists where they're sore from the plastic cuff but then he remembers how often he's seen the gesture in films and feels so self-conscious about it he has to stop. 'I thought you were working for them.'

'Yeah. That's my day job.' She gestures at the sofa. 'Sit down. There's a lot to tell you.' She's wearing a black rayon zip-up shift dress with no tights, and the dress shows nothing off, it's tersely functional, but this is still the first time he's seen her in anything girlier than jeans and a T-shirt, and the contrast would be enough to staple his gaze to her hemlines if he weren't so unnerved by what's happening.

'Who is this?' he says.

'Raf, I want you to meet my brother Zaya.' The guy in the wheelchair nods at Raf. 'By the way, he can understand us fine. His English is good. But he's really sick at the moment. Even though he's barely taking any pain meds, he has to work really hard just to keep his mind clear. It's too tiring for him to speak English. So I'm going to translate for him.' She says something in Burmese. And then, through Cherish, Zaya starts telling the story of the day the two of them met for the first time in eight years.

Living in the hotel during the monsoon, Zaya explains, was like being half blind and half deaf: the site was surrounded by jungle, a warm mist blurred the air, and the rain drowned out nearly every sound, so that nothing broke through into the swaddled pinhole of your awareness until it was close enough to toss a pebble at your feet. He didn't mind this too much, because it liberated you from the delusion of vigilance – in December, as you tried to fall asleep, you still listened for every hornbill squawk, convinced that somehow you would be able to pick out the one that warned of an attack from the jungle, but in June, you just learned to accept that there might be a noose of fifty soldiers tightening around your base and you wouldn't know it until the first shot was fired.

However, today, it also meant he didn't hear the truck until it was almost at the top of the slope. He hurried out from the lobby to the verandah and watched as the old grey Toyota shuddered to a halt like a mule forced home with too much on its back. Mae Sot, where Kham had gone to pick up Cherish, was only about forty miles east, across the border into Thailand, but if you were trying to avoid checkpoints the drive through the muddy hills took five or six hours that left you numb and boneless and shaky. From this distance he couldn't make out through the streaming windscreen whether there was anyone in the passenger seat, and he knew it was still possible that Cherish had refused to come here with Kham, or that something else had happened to pull her out of their reach in the three days since they'd got word of her arrival in Mae Sot. But then the passenger-side door opened, and the girl who got down was his half-sister. She saw him and her eyes widened.

He tried to take in her height, her beauty, her tourist clothes. As his heart swelled in his chest, he forced himself to recall that almost half this girl's life was unknown to him, that she was an American of untested loyalties, that for all he knew she had Lacebark money in her bank account and a GPS tracker in one of her body cavities. But then their arms were tight around each other and for a while none of that was in his mind. He waited until the motor of her sobs had slowed before he said, 'Come in out of the rain,' and led her by the arm back to the shelter of the verandah, the bank of the vertical river. Behind them, Kham was fixing a tarpaulin over the van.

After she put her rucksack down she stood there wiping her face and wringing out the hem of her vest. 'Where are we? What the hell is this place?'

At first, you might have taken it for the overgrown ruins of an old British governor's mansion. But if the building lacked an east wing or a rear elevation, it wasn't because they'd been shelled by the Japanese, it was because they'd never been built. Back in the eighties, Zaya explained, an Indonesian company had come to this site to begin construction on a colonial-style hotel. They had plenty of investment from the Burmese government, who also planned to build a road here from Kawkareik; on the other side of the slope there was a gorgeous natural waterfall, and the aim had presumably been to tempt a few travellers across from northern Thailand during the dry season. But the Ministry of Hotels and Tourism didn't put up the rest of the stake it had promised, and the Indonesians pulled out.

This was such a reliable pattern whenever the Burmese government had any dealings with a foreign business that it began to resemble a kind of bureaucratic derangement, this uncontrollable compulsion towards starting projects and then reneging halfway through so that all the money that had already been spent was squandered. Today, even the few completed rooms were often so wretched with moss and rats' nests and leaky ceilings that sleeping there felt only a little bit milder than sleeping out in the jungle, and Zaya and his seven comrades didn't really live in the hotel so much as they lived in a camp that happened to use the hotel for scaffolding. At the back of this monument to waste and stupidity there was still a stagnant midden full of all the plastic debris that the builders hadn't bothered to take away with them when they left, and under a half-completed stairwell Zaya had found a stash of Thai porn magazines, fused by twenty years of monsoon damp into a greenish loaf of nipples.

'In a sense, it's exciting that you're here,' Zaya said. 'After all this time, an American tourist finally comes to stay. By the way, can you understand me all right?' He was speaking a mixture of Danu and Burmese.

'Yeah. This is how I talk to Mom most of the time.' She was still dripping like a banyan tree. 'Are you OK, Zaya?'

'Don't I look OK?'

'You look like Uncle Chai the day he came back from the Concession.'

'Cherish, I have Aids.'

She was silent for a while. At last, quietly, she said, 'For how long?'

'Since 2004. Only a few years after you left. But until recently it wasn't so noticeable.'

He told her about the night he had gone into the Concession with Sam and Chao to plant bombs on three of Lacebark's diesel generators. They moved through the darkness past the smelter, the crusher, the water tower, the engine workshop, the kitchens, the clinic, all three of them knowing the layout by heart because they'd done their time as workers at the mine, and it was so easy, they had so much good luck, that Zaya's fear turned to exhilaration and he began to feel as if he had superpowers. He wanted to stay in the Concession for ever, flitting around like a vengeful ghost, disassembling it bolt by bolt, breaking into the foremen's dormitories to piss in their yawning mouths. Then, when they were almost back at the hole in the fence, the emergency floodlights came on and the shooting started.

Zaya took a rifle bullet in the back of his thigh, and the other two had to half carry him for nearly a mile before they felt safe enough to stop and rest. While they made a tourniquet, all Zaya could think about was that he hadn't heard any explosions. The bombs hadn't even gone off. They'd failed. He passed out.

When he woke up, he was lying on a mat in a hut, and his tourniquet was being untied by a man he recognised as the stuttering doctor from Gandayaw. Zaya could see the doctor's instruments laid out on a cloth, and on their blades were flecks of rust or dried blood or perhaps both. The last thing he remembered before he passed out again was a fly crawling out of the doctor's open mouth, but he realised afterwards that he must have been delirious.

'I didn't notice anything for about a year after that. Then I started getting weaker, and after a while I started to suspect what must have happened. That doctor treats plenty of hookers in Gandayaw. Sam and Chao probably hustled him out of town without giving him time to get a clean set of instruments together.' While he was recuperating he read a paperback anthology of Karl Marx's writings in Burmese translation from the eighties, the spine repaired with duct tape. Marx's creed seemed to be that material things had more power over people than people had over material things, which struck Zaya as not all that different from the animism of his grandparents, with its tribe spirits and crop spirits and weather spirits. His wound would heal up without even leaving a scar, as if the virus were so cunning that it wanted to scrub all evidence of its ingress.

'Have you ever taken a test?' Cherish said.

'No.'

'So you're not sure?'

'I'm sure. You'd be sure too if you saw me with my clothes off.'

'Don't they have drugs for it now? I know a couple of older guys in LA who've had it for years and they don't even look sick.'

'Did you pass a dispensary on your way here?' Zaya said. 'No. It's only going to get worse. I live in the jungle, for fuck's sake. Even the air is sick here. Living in the jungle with Aids is like having Aids twice over. But it's not going to kill me for a long while. I'm sure of that too.'

'Do you want me to tell Mom when I get home?'

'No. Because you can't tell her, or anyone else, that you saw me. How is she, though?'

'She's fine. She likes her new job. But we argue a lot. She couldn't understand why I'd want to go partying in Thailand a few months after a cyclone. What was that like, anyway?'

'What was it like?' Zaya looked at his sister and for the first time he was aware of her not as a potential ally or a potential infiltrator

142

but merely as a young woman who had seen almost nothing of life since she left Burma. He remembered the two days he'd spent travelling south in that boat, when he learned that the best way to shunt a floating corpse out of your way without slowing yourself down was to jam the oar in its armpit and wheel it past you. Except that sometimes you'd notice too late that it was tied by the wrist to the corpse next to it, probably to help the two of them stay up in a palm tree during the winds, and just at that moment you'd feel the second corpse knock its heels imploringly against your bow. 'It was bad, Sis,' he said. 'It still is.'

'What was it like in Gandayaw?'

'Gandayaw was too far north for the worst of the flooding. But the Concession was in chaos for a while.'

'So that's what you do now? You go into the Concession and blow stuff up? In that case, why are you here? Isn't Gandayaw a hundred miles away?'

'Nearly four hundred miles. Yes. But at the moment we need to be near the border.'

Cherish slapped at a mosquito on her wrist, but not fast enough, so it left behind a jewel of her own blood. 'For what? Zaya, why'd you bring me here now after all this time? What's all this about? Are you fighting the regime?'

'No,' Zaya said. 'Not the regime.' He gave the generals only about five more years, he told her. Between Cyclone Nargis and the Shan State Army and the Karen State Army and the monks in Mandalay and the punks in Yangon, and the sheer complexity, for men with no geopolitical competence whatsoever, of playing China off against the West year after year, they were starting to lose their grip. He believed that the instant a despot took power the date of his humiliation and death was in some sense carved in the stars, or if not his own humiliation and death then his successor's. A tyranny grew old and tired and palsied just like any other beast. But if killing a tyranny was like killing an elephant, killing a corporation was like killing a colony of sentient fungus. Lacebark was founded in North Carolina in 1919. Only one government in Asia was older than that, in the sense of surviving continuously without a destructive transfer of power, and that was the constitutional monarchy of Bhutan. Anyway, Lacebark, at eighty-nine, still wasn't even that long-lived, relatively speaking. Freeport was ninety-five. United Fruit was a hundred and eight. Chevron was a hundred and eighteen. De Beers was a hundred and twenty. Unlike governments, corporations endured: deathless, efficient, self-renewing. And whoever replaced the generals in Burma, whether it was Aung San Suu Kyi or Maha Sammata back from the dead, Zaya was sure that they would let Lacebark keep their Concession so that they could carry on slurping up the royalties from the mine.

Back in the mid-eighties, when Lacebark prospectors first arrived in Gandayaw, they probably assumed that the local tribes had been there since the Stone Age. But even six or seven generations earlier, Zaya and Cherish's ancestors had been down in the valleys, tending rice paddies and trading with Mandalay. In Burma, though, when a king asked for too much rice in tribute or too many sons for his army, he would often have to watch as his subjects flew away like skittish doves, into the forest or up to the hills, far beyond his control. In the process, they might abandon their written language, their genealogy, their folk stories, because all those things made you dangerously intelligible to the valley powers, and even to be included in a statistical table was a submission too far. That willingness to leave everything behind in the mud was why no government had ever had real control over the entire nation and why no government ever would.

Still, the people of Gandayaw and the neighbouring villages might have returned to the valleys in the long run. They'd moved back and forth several times before. But only in their own good time. And when Lacebark came to Gandayaw, the locals should have made the same sort of escape they used to make from all the old kings and conquerors. They should have gone far enough away that they wouldn't even have been tempted to sell their souls for a few dollars in the Concession. If Zaya had been old enough for leadership by then, perhaps that's what would have happened. But they were all just too awed by what the Americans brought.

'You know the best thing that Burma ever got from America, really?' Zaya said. 'Cassava. You plant it in the ground. You leave it there as long as you need to. Then you come back and eat it when you get a chance. It won't be noticed. It can't be burned. It's not worth the effort of confiscating. It doesn't need tending. It won't rot or dry out. It will grow where nothing else will grow. For a free people, it's the best food in the world. But we're not a free people any more. We eat Lacebark rations.' He scratched at the rash on his hip.

'If you have cassava, there's only one real problem with going up into the hills when the king starts asking too much of you. How do you get anything back down to market? If it's timber or bamboo or cattle or potatoes, you can't lug that all the way down into the valleys. You can only really stray from the towns if you have something to sell that you can carry for a day on your back. So that's what the tribes in the hills started trading. Elephant tusks, peacock feathers, sappanwood, rubies . . . For a while, the best was pepper. A few hundred years ago, peppercorns were more valuable than anything in the world except silver and gold, and you could pluck the drupes right off the vine. If you have pepper to trade and cassava to eat, you are truly free.'

'Is that an old proverb?'

'No, it's an anachronism. Back when pepper was still expensive, there was no cassava in Asia yet. But you understand what I mean.'

'I guess.'

'Are you hungry?'

'Yes,' said Cherish. 'What's for dinner? My guess is . . . cassava? Right? Cassava with lots of pepper?'

Zaya smiled. 'Maybe some of that. But it's your first night here. We should celebrate. Let's go out and get something tasty while it's still light.'

'Go out and get something?'

'Yeah. It's not raining so hard now.'

Zaya went inside to tell Kham where they were going. When he came back out he brought with him a machete, a catapult, and a nylon bag full of rusty half-inch nuts. He handed the catapult to Cherish and said, 'Do you remember how to use one of these?'

'I think so.'

'You used to be really good at it.'

While Cherish practised shooting into the trees, Zaya searched for truth behind the concentration in her face. At this stage he could still get one of the others to drive her back to Mae Sot, and even if really she were working for Lacebark she couldn't do any damage. They were moving on from the hotel soon and he hadn't told her anything important yet. But a few sentences could change that. If he took her past a certain boundary and only realised afterwards that she wasn't on his side, he would have to make sure she disappeared from the world for at least as long as their plans in London were still a secret. It wasn't that he wanted to believe she could betray him. The thought made his stomach twist. But in 2008 it had taken him weeks longer than it should have to realise that Chao had switched sides, and he'd nearly died in a raid as a result. He wasn't going to make that mistake again. Also, Cherish was an American now, and he knew that every American had a price.

Thankfully, it was still just about plausible to suppose that Lacebark didn't know enough about Cherish to have considered approaching her. Back when her father had organised her hasty emigration, there wouldn't have been any obvious reason for the company to bother keeping track of her afterwards. In that case, they would no longer have any means of connecting this eighteen-year-old from LA with either Zaya or Gandayaw. That was what he hoped. Today she didn't look to him half Burmese and half white but rather fully, emphatically both.

'I'm so bad at this now,' said Cherish, looking down at the catapult.

'You can practise some more on the banana blossoms,' said Zaya as they set out through the trees. They were following a path that the men in the camp often used when they went hunting, although the vegetation was still so dense in front of them that if you weren't used to the jungle you wouldn't have recognised it as a path at all. These days he couldn't use the machete for very long before his arm started to ache.

'What are we looking for?' said Cherish.

'Probably grouse or quail. Keep the catapult ready.' They paused for a moment while Cherish untangled her foot from a dead vine. 'Have you ever been to London?' Zaya said.

'No.'

'When you get home you'll need to tell Mom that you're moving there in a few months.'

'Are you kidding?'

'No.'

'Zaya, I'm going to college in September.'

'You'll move to London and work for Lacebark. You'll be a resourceful American girl who speaks Burmese – they'll think they're lucky to have found you. I'll follow you there in about a year.'

'What's happening in London?'

'Pepper,' said Zaya. Noticing a baby leech on his forearm, he plucked it off and threw it into the trees.

'What do you mean?'

'Sis, this is really big now. It's bigger than you or me. It's bigger than Gandayaw. It's bigger than Burma.'

'I just graduated from high school. I live in Echo Park with our mom. I still don't really understand what you want from me, but I'm not a freedom fighter.'

'You're my sister and I know how strong you are.'

'From when I was ten?' said Cherish.

'You can't have forgotten that talk we had the night before you left. I was going to stay and fight. You were going to come back and fight when you were old enough. We both swore to it. And now it's time.'

147

Then he saw the snake.

It was a hognose, about four feet long, pale yellow with hexagonal brown blotches, and it was slithering out from behind a mango tree. Dead leaves didn't even quiver as it passed, as if it existed at a slight physical remove from the rotting muddle around it. He pointed, and Cherish gave a little gasp. 'Is it dangerous?'

'Yes. Shoot it in the head.'

'What?'

'Quick – shoot it in the head.'

But Cherish aimed too fast and her hands were shaking, so the nut whished through a fern beside the snake. Hissing angrily, it lifted its head and flattened out its hood.

'Again.' This time the nut hit the hognose just below its right eye and its head dropped back to the ground.

'Is it dead?' said Cherish.

'No, of course not, it's just stunned. Pick it up by the tail.'

'Zaya, use your machete!'

'There isn't time to argue – just pick it up.'

Cherish bent over, trying to stretch out for the snake without putting her feet anywhere near it, but Zaya knew that was no good so he shoved her forward. Cringing, she reached for the tip of its tail.

'No, about two thirds of the way down. Both hands. Just don't let its head near you.'

Slippery in the rain, the snake flexed hard as Cherish lifted it off the ground, and from the way she jerked her shoulders around you would have thought she was wrestling an opponent of twice her own weight. No one ever gripped a big snake in their hands for the first time without feeling badly unnerved by the strange autogenous torque of it, this lever with no fulcrum.

'Swing it against the tree to break its skull,' Zaya said. Cherish faltered, and the hognose, hanging upside down, made a lunge at the flesh of her thigh just below her shorts. 'Sis, don't freeze up! Listen to me: do Lacebark know you're here?'

148

'Lacebark?'

'You may want to whirl it around your head a couple of times to build up speed. Did Lacebark come to you? Did they offer you money?'

Cherish hadn't got the motion right yet and she was just flopping the snake around. 'How the fuck would Lacebark even know who I am?'

'Tell me the truth!' Zaya watched her face, knowing that for the first time today he'd be able to see all the way through to her bloody core, like holding a snake's jaws open to look down the tunnel of its body.

'I am telling you the truth!' she screamed. And Zaya, with relief, felt certain that she was. Now that Cherish had raised her arms higher she could finally build up some momentum, hurling spiral ripples out through the downpour. After a couple of spins she dropped her arms again and let the snake's head meet the mango tree. There was a gristly thud and for an instant the whole length of it went stiff.

'Good. Again, to be sure.'

This time, more confident, Cherish put all her fury into it, grunting with exertion, and hit so hard that wet bark shrapnel jumped from the tree. Afterwards, Zaya could see that part of the skull had caved in. 'All right. You can drop it.' The hognose landed in the dirt and a last couple of shivers fled down its tail.

'I could have fucking died just now! What was that? A cobra?'

'It was just a hognose. The bite hurts but all you get afterwards is a nasty swelling. You wouldn't have been scared of one of those when you were eight.'

'You said it was dangerous, you prick!' She was panting.

'It is, if you're a frog.' He thought about making her skin and gut the snake as well, but he decided the kill had been enough to make his point. So he carried it over to a tree stump and hacked off its head with two strokes of his machete. A weak gargle of blood soaked into the wood.

'Why the fuck did you make me do that?' Cherish said. 'And why the fuck were you asking me about Lacebark? I hope you choke to death on a chicken bone.' She was swearing in a mixture of Danu and English, alternating like a boxer's two fists, but then for the second time that day she started to cry. She sat down heavily on the ground.

With the tip of the machete Zaya made a slit all the way down the snake's belly. The skin was so tough and elastic that it peeled off in one long rag like a split condom, and the innards could be ripped from their binding almost as neatly, leaving a long pink tube of meat which the scales had stained with that same faint imbricated pattern that you sometimes saw inside fish. Only when he was finished with the hognose did Zaya get up and go back over to Cherish. He squatted down and tried to put his arms around her but she pulled away. 'Don't touch me with your disgusting snake hands,' she said.

He knew how proud of herself she'd feel later. 'You're just like I remember, Sis. If you stayed for a week I'd probably come out here and find you knocking mangoes out of the tree with three pythons in each hand. You're going to go to London and you're going to win this fight for us before I even get there.'

She sniffed and glanced over at the coil of hognose meat, like a pork loin forced through an exhaust pipe. 'Is that what we're cooking later?'

'Of course.'

'Is it nice?'

'Didn't you ever eat snake when we were kids?'

'No.'

'It's horrible. But it's good for your heart. Come on. Let's wrap it up and take it home.'

9.04 p.m.

Perhaps it makes Cherish uncomfortable that her brother is almost powerless to speak except through her, and that was why she made sure to tell this story about herself precisely as Zaya wanted it told, not adding a word of her own commentary, as if she were reading out a long confession that someone else had typed up on her behalf. While they were talking, Ko made dinner; he'd explained apologetically that he couldn't really cook because the stove in the kitchen was out of use, so instead he sat at the table by the door chopping up mangoes and carrots for a dried shrimp salad.

'I was in London for about a year before Lacebark started their operation here,' Cherish adds. 'They recruited me right away.'

'What did you say to them about why you were in London?'

'I said I'd come for the parties because there's nowhere to dance in LA. Which is true. Then Zaya arrived in February. He nearly got caught on his way through Pakistan.'

'Oh my god, that was you!' says Raf, who still has a damp paper plate on his lap and peanut crumbs stuck in his teeth. 'I heard about this! How did you talk that Brazilian guy into letting you out of the van?'

Translating again, Cherish says, 'The type of guys who carry guns for Lacebark have a lot more in common with us than they have with their bosses. If you talk to them for long enough, you can often make them see that. Most of them are basically good guys. Although it wasn't the Brazilian who gave him the pin to get out of his handcuffs, he says. The Brazilian wouldn't listen to him.'

Raf wonders what Martin would say if he knew that. 'But if Zaya wasn't in London until February, why were Lacebark already here last year?'

'Getting revenge on Zaya for causing five years of mayhem in the Concession is secondary. They're here because they want to get glow back.' This is just Cherish talking now.

'Get it back?'

'To make glow in significant quantities, you need an organic precursor. You understand what that means, right?'

Raf nods.

'The precursor is a flower. In Danu it's called *glo*. And until we brought it to London there was only one place in the world where it grew. You can guess this part.'

'Inside the Concession?'

'Yeah. But now it's all over south London. We've been planting it since I got here.'

Lacebark arrived at the Shan forest in 1989, Cherish explains, far too recently to change the course of *glo*'s evolution, so it can only be an accident that the species has certain genes that help it thrive in anthropogenic environments. Most flowers that open and close do so at regular times of day and prefer the high-colour temperature of real sunshine. (Raf knows all about colour temperature from his freelance 3D rendering jobs, because property developers like it high, too.) *Glo*, on the other hand, is both nourished and seduced by the wavelengths of artificial light. If you plant *glo* near a light that shines twenty-four hours a day – such as any security light outside an estate – the flower's photonastic rhythm will run faster and faster until it's opening and closing every eight or nine hours. Somehow, the constancy of the light seems to compensate for the deficiencies of the local climate, so that *glo* will happily bloom at latitudes with average temperatures several degrees colder than the Burmese jungle, as long as it never has to endure the dark. There's even a condemned council block in Stockwell where the housing office put big concrete flowerboxes on all the balconies to beautify the wreck a little bit but all the plants died last summer and now *glo* has found a home there instead. Linnaeus wasted years trying to find a way to acclimatise tea plants to northern winters so that European nations wouldn't have to spend so much of their South American silver on Chinese imports, but *glo* would have been a better proof of concept.

'And you know what else we brought here from Gandayaw?'

Cherish adds. 'The one guy in the world who knows how to make glow, the drug, from *glo*, the plant.'

'Nobody else knows the process?'

'Nobody.'

'But why should Lacebark care?' says Raf. 'They mine copper and rubies.'

'Yeah, but they're not very good at it any more. They want a new business. You know what 3M stands for? The Minnesota Mining and Manufacturing Company. They used to mine aluminium oxide. They make a lot more money now selling Post-its and Scotch tape and stuff. That's why Lacebark want to start manufacturing and selling glow. If no one else had the plant or the process, they'd have a monopoly over it, like the British East India Company had over opium in China. The wholesale ecstasy market is worth about twenty billion dollars a year worldwide. It's impossible to find out Lacebark's real annual revenues because they pull a lot of Enron shit to keep people from finding out that they're fucked, but by now the number might be about seven billion and dropping fast. If Lacebark could get glow to the point where it was even half as popular as ecstasy, then they could forget about mining. They'd be profitable for ever, and no one would ever have to find out how close to the edge they came, and none of them would have to go to jail.'

'But they're a legitimate company.'

'Those laboratories in China that make mephedrone and ethyl-buphedrone are legitimate companies too. Soon they'll all be part of conglomerates. That's the way it's going.'

Isaac has a theory that drugs like mephedrone are a sort of delayed act of revenge for the Opium Wars: two hundred years later, the Chinese finally get to sell a debilitating narcotic back to the British.

'Lacebark are accountable in America, though,' Raf says. 'They'd have to start laundering money.'

'Are you kidding? They already do. Most of the money Lacebark makes from the Concession goes through banks in Macau to dodge corporate taxes. If things worked out with glow, they'd probably keep the Concession open, but by then it would just be another step in the money-laundering process. The fabric softener or whatever. That's one thing Lacebark and the tribes of Burma have in common. We both love dodging taxes.'

'So Lacebark are paying you to help them find Zaya and this chemist.'

Translating for Zaya, Cherish says: 'Our people don't have a lot of legends, but there's one from about eight hundred years ago that's very important to us. When we lived farther down in the valleys, there was this jumped-up local king who tried to take a census. No one had ever tried to take a census before. We dragged him off the throne and cut off his head.'

'That's the whole legend?'

'Yeah. The point is we don't like people trying to make lists of our names.'

'And that's what Lacebark are doing right now?'

'Yeah. They know glow is being produced and distributed through the Burmese community in south London. So they think if they map what they call our "vectors of influence", they can eventually trace the supply of glow back to its source. That's what I'm meant to be helping them with. But obviously most of the information I'm feeding them is false. You know, every time I go to that tennis court to talk to those assholes from your radio station, it reminds me of the old hotel.'

This is so much information to absorb that Raf begins to wish he was on Isaac's tentacular neuroplasticity diet himself. He realises he still hasn't told them about going into Lacebark's training facility. 'I've seen some of this from the inside now,' he says.

'What do you mean?'

When Raf explains, he can see that Cherish and Zaya are as astonished as if he'd told them he'd challenged Bezant to a fistfight. 'You're a brave man,' Zaya says. It's the first time Raf has heard him speak English.

'Well, yeah, it was really scary, but now I'm wondering what the point was. The only thing I found out that's any use is that Lacebark are looking for a chemist. And if I'd just waited a few hours you would have told me that anyway.'

Translating for Zaya, Cherish says: 'Anything that's a big "fuck you" to Lacebark is worth doing. As long as it doesn't get anyone killed.'

'So what happens next?'

'At the end of this month, Lacebark are going to change tactics.'

'Oh right, yeah, the Lacebark guy I met said that they had something big planned for the first day of June.'

'So far, we think Lacebark have kidnapped, interrogated, and murdered around eight or nine people since they got to London . . . including your friend Theo. I'm really sorry, Raf,' she adds when she sees the expression on his face. 'But, anyway, it's not getting them results. And Bezant's getting impatient. If they haven't got what they want by the end of this month, they're going to come down really hard. Simultaneous raids across the city. A lot more people are going to die in one night.'

'But this is London,' says Raf weakly.

'Oh, because this is a First World city with good tapas bars, nothing really bad can ever happen here? None of the soldiers working for Bezant have ever been here before. London is just another foreign battlefield to them. They might as well be in Yangon or Mogadishu. They don't give a shit. And neither do we. This is a war between two stateless peoples that happens to be taking place inside a state.'

Zaya adds something. 'This is nothing new for us. In the sixteenth century Bayinnaung held on to his empire only because he hired mercenaries from Portugal with better weapons.'

Raf has always felt vaguely stateless because of his syndrome. Arizona observes daylight saving time, but inside Arizona there's a Navajo reservation that doesn't, and inside the Navajo reservation there's a Hopi reservation that does, two assertions of autonomy that cancel each other out. No enclave except the Concession, however, has yet had the courage to abandon the quotidian clock completely. Or perhaps it's not right to say that Raf has declared independence from the world, but rather that his suprachiasmatic nucleus has declared independence from Raf: those old-fashioned, dotted-line diagrams of the brain have always reminded him of territorial maps, and his SCN might be a microscopic Gandayaw, refusing to submit to his government. For the first time he wonders whether one reason he's let himself get pulled so deep into this – even after he realised how dangerous it might be, even after he pretty much gave up hope of rescuing Theo, even when he thought the girl he wanted so much was working for the wrong side – was that in some way he feels suited to it: this ghost conflict detached from everybody else's London.

'So how are you going to stop them?' he says.

Cherish glances at her brother. 'At this point we have no fucking idea. Short of giving ourselves up. Which we are not going to do.'

'Couldn't we call the police with an anonymous tip that the freight depot's a big cannabis farm or something?'

'It wouldn't work. And even if it did, you saw how many Burmese they have there, right? The actors? We're not going to do anything to fuck those people over.'

'But they're working for Lacebark.'

'You lose your family in the cyclone. You spend six months in a refugee camp on the Thai border. You find a way to get to London. And then you get offered a job wandering around a warehouse for three times what you'd make as a janitor on a night shift. What are you supposed to do? We don't blame them for working for Lacebark. They're not in this fight yet. The last thing we want to do is get them arrested or deported as collateral damage.'

'Well, isn't there anything I can do to help?'

'We may have a job for you soon. Until then, we just wanted you to understand what's going on.' She gets up. 'Also, there's someone I want you to meet.'

As Raf is following her down the corridor, it's as if the refractive index of the air fluctuates just for an instant, and he finds himself looking around and wondering if any of this is real. When Ko let him out of the van he heard that dog bark and he felt a breeze tickle the back of his neck but a sound-effect tape and an electric fan could have done just the same job. For all he knows, he might be back in the freight depot and Cherish might be loyal to Lacebark and Zaya might be an actor and the bin bags over the windows might conceal a steel partition all the way around the flat. The depot was only two storeys tall, and he climbed three flights of stairs to get here, but he's suddenly so antsy now that he asks himself if the 'ground floor' could have been sunk two storeys underground or if they could have put him on some sort of imperceptible treadmill. So he forces himself to look hard at the old goitres of Blu-tack on the walls and the dead wasps sunbathing around the bottom rim of the paper lampshade, all this fractal detail of reality like the foil threads in a banknote, far beyond Lacebark's power to forge.

They get to the kitchen. 'Raf, this is Win,' says Cherish.

And as if Raf weren't feeling unstable enough, he sees that he's already rehearsed this scene. Once again, a Burmese guy is standing there by the sink, and once again, the worktops are overcrowded with laboratory instruments, except that this time the laboratory instruments are presumably functional and the Burmese guy presumably knows something about drug chemistry. What it does prove is that Lacebark did quite a good job with their imitation. The feel of the room is almost the same. But, if anything, the equipment here looks even more shabby and mismatched, and there isn't that inexplicable stink, and there's no ultrasonic trill of tension when he looks the Burmese guy in the eye.

'Win developed the process for refining *glo* into glow when he was still in Gandayaw,' says Cherish. 'Every gram of glow that anyone's ever taken, Win has made. He doesn't speak much English, though.'

This proves that Win can't be Fitch from Lotophage, which makes Raf glad that he didn't bring up Fitch earlier, because he would have felt stupid for getting so excited about some anonymous messageboard user who probably has nothing to do with any of this. Although there is a laptop here, it sits unplugged next to the stove with the screen shut and the power cable wrapped a couple of times around the AC adaptor. Raf raises his hand in greeting and Win raises a hand back. That's when Raf notices the incense burner on the windowsill, and a shiver beetles down his spine. It's exactly like the one he saw in Lacebark's core scenario installation, except that instead of two pink cans of guava juice this one is built out of two purple cans of passionfruit juice. He tells Cherish.

'And?' she says.

'I can understand that Lacebark could work out for themselves what a kitchen drug lab might basically look like, but how could they know that exact detail unless they'd seen inside this flat? Doesn't that mean you might already be under surveillance?'

'If we were they would've snatched us days ago.' She says something in Burmese and Win says something back. 'Win used to make those same incense burners when he was back in Gandayaw,' she says. 'He didn't invent them in this apartment.'

Raf doesn't understand why Cherish isn't more concerned about this. 'Yeah, but it's the same brand of juice.'

'It's a coincidence, Raf. Chill out.'

Raf is reminded of Isaac's reaction when he insisted that Cherish must have been abducted by Lacebark because he couldn't find a used glass of water on his kitchen counter. So he asks her about it.

'You had some OJ in your refrigerator,' she tells him. 'I drank some straight from the carton and then I put it back.'

'Oh.' Raf realises Isaac was right – it was an idiotic 'clue'. Now he doesn't feel so sure about the incense burner. The lesson here seems to be that fruit juice is always a bit of a rogue element.

Cherish cocks her head. 'Why do you look disappointed all of a sudden? Are you worried about getting my germs?'

One of the unrealistic qualities of Lacebark's simulation was that their 'chemist' showed no signs of personalising the space in which his character was supposedly toiling for at least two hours of every three-hour day. But Raf notices there are two pictures of a smiling, shirtless guy up on the fridge here, and although they're even more sallow and grainy than the average print from a cheap disposable camera with the flash on, there's something unmistakably intimate about them. In one, the guy's been lipsticked with red marker.

'Hey,' says Raf. 'I recognise him from somewhere.'

And then he remembers. It's that young waiter from the Serbian café opposite the freight depot. Which doesn't make any sense.

'That's Win's boyfriend Jesnik,' says Cherish.

'Boyfriend?'

'We wanted to keep the depot under surveillance, but we all had other things to do, and also it seemed kind of risky to hang around the neighbourhood that much. We started paying Jesnik to do it instead. He came over here a few times to talk to us about what he saw, and the first time we happened to leave him alone in the flat with Win . . . They don't have a language in common, so I don't know how it happened, but, I mean, good for Win – Jesnik's a cutie, right? OK, "boyfriend" might be a little bit of a stretch but I think they really like each other.'

'If you don't want Lacebark to bring down the hammer, couldn't you just move Win out of London? Make sure Lacebark know he's a long way away, so they have to start the hunt from the beginning again?'

'Yeah. That's what we want to do in the long run. But it's too dangerous to move him at the moment. Lacebark have too many eyes. Until we can find some way of making them blink . . . Anyway, there's one last thing we have to deal with before you go.'

He follows her back down the corridor and off to the left into what turns out to be a bathroom. Even here there's a bin bag over the window opposite the toilet. The bath's enamel is so stained that it looks as if it's been dredged up out of a lagoon, an old rubber non-slip bathmat lying damply on the bottom like two and a half feet of tripe. 'We only have, like, ten minutes,' she says. 'Ko has to drive you home.'

Raf looks at his digital watch: 9.51. He's been here for nearly two hours. 'Ten minutes for what?'

She wets her lips with her tongue and pushes him up against the wall.

'Now?' This is the kind of amazing thing that normally only happens to Isaac.

She nods. 'Why should Win be the only one to get laid in this apartment?'

'You brought me here in handcuffs and a hood,' he says.

'Yeah, and it'll be the same when you leave. You can't know where we are right now.'

'But last week you told me you weren't into bondage.' She laughs and puts a hand in his hair to force his mouth down to hers. He can taste mango on her upper lip like joy itself. Between kisses, he adds, 'For a few days I really thought you were working for Lacebark. I really thought you were on the other side.'

'There's still a little bit you don't know about me.' She starts efficiently unbuttoning his jeans.

'Wait, just promise me . . .'

'Promise you what?'

He looks down. 'Promise me you're not going to shoot at it with a catapult and then whack it against a tree.'

'Enough jokes, OK? Just shut up for a minute.'

With her left hand she reaches down past the waistband of his boxer shorts to cup his balls and with her right hand she doesn't just cover his mouth to stop him talking but actually jams three fingers inside like dental instruments. This renders Raf both physically and intellectually incapable of speech. When she's satisfied that he's got the message, she drops to her knees and takes his cock in her own mouth for just long enough to light up all its nerve endings brighter than a maritime distress flare. She rises again and he turns her around to pull her against him so that he can lift the hem of her dress and slip a hand into her pants while he grazes on the back of her neck. After a while, Cherish moves over to the low tiled windowsill, clears off a couple of empty shampoo bottles, and perches on it with her thighs parted and her dress bunched up at her waist. Raf puts on a condom from his wallet and he's about to do something about her underwear but she shakes her head impatiently so instead he just stretches the crotch to one side, which makes what follows awkward but not impossible. She's been so much in control up until now that when Raf pushes inside her he almost expects her to show no reaction at all, but in fact she gives a lung-filling gasp and they look into each other's wide eyes in that way people do in the first few seconds of sex as if the two of them have just uncovered something phenomenally surprising and important that no one else has ever suspected before. Then as he starts thrusting she bites her lip and lolls her head back against the covered window. And that's when Raf first notices that, as a result of a strip of Sellotape peeling halfway off, the top right corner of the folded bin bag has flopped down on itself, revealing a small triangle of windowglass and a tight view of the street outside.

His consciousness is distilled instantly into two volumes, one melted and the other frozen: below, the hug of Cherish's interior and the sting of her fingernails; above, the awareness that he really isn't supposed to be seeing this and the question of whether to mention it. Fortunately, it isn't that serious an oversight on Cherish's part, because from this angle he can't see a street sign or a pub or anything else that could lead Lacebark back to this flat if they interrogated him about it – this peep-show is just a bin and a tree and the awning of a noodle buffet. And at least he knows for sure now that he's not back inside the freight depot.

Then, as Cherish locks her ankles across the backs of his calves, he realises it's not a noodle buffet. It's a noodel buffet. It's Noodels City, the most conspicuous misspelling in all of south London. He sees the illuminated red sign with its two endoscopic ovals of chow mein every time he goes past Camberwell Green on the bus. Which means he now knows approximately where he is, and if he needed to locate this flat, he could just stand outside Noodels City and look around for the blacked-out windows on the third floor of a building opposite. Without even trying, he has found out precisely what he wasn't supposed to find out. And somehow he already feels certain that it would have been a lot better if he hadn't. Cherish murmurs to him to go faster. Caught between these two narrow apertures like the laser beam in the experiment proving that light is both a particle and a wave, interference patterns rippling across the goosebumps on his forearms, Raf wishes that for the last few minutes he could have been struck blind.

DAY 12

Last night, before he fell into bed like a corpse into a gulch, Raf could just about whip his fingers into sending one more message to Fitch: 'I know you're not the chemist who's making all the glow. So who are you?' By this stage in his cycle the vanguard of his slumber has overrun most of morning, and when he wakes up he can see that it rained while he was still asleep – except he doesn't feel as if he missed the rain, he feels as if he was there watching it, in the freight depot and then in Zaya's story and then in a frenetic dream of which he can't remember any other details – three unreal rains that coagulated into one real one.

Raf goes back to his computer. Fitch's reply – 'how you know I'm not him?' – came in only seventeen minutes ago, which means he might still be online.

Raf writes, 'Because I met the chemist yesterday. He didn't speak English, and you do.'

As he was hoping, the next message arrives within a few minutes. 'oh you that confused-looking white guy? early 20s, blue eyes? actually, my English is fine, you can see that, but it's not like she gave us much of a chance to chat when she showed you around.'

Raf is so stunned that he doesn't stop to think about his next question. 'So it was you that I met in the kitchen when I was with Cherish?'

The final message comes back right away like a slap. 'no names. fucking moron'

Raf tries to send another reply, but the Lotophage message system won't allow it.

Fitch has blocked him.

When you're having an anonymous conversation with no way to visualise the opposite end, the internet's strange acoustics can give you the illusion that the other voice comes from some cluster of points very nearby, so that when it stops you feel disproportionately spooked and bereft, as if the birds outside your window have fallen silent all at once. Raf could just register for a new account and send Fitch/Win a message from that one, but it doesn't seem as if he'd have any hope of getting a reply. So he's left with a puzzle: why would Cherish want him to think that Win didn't speak English? Whatever the reason, Win himself must be willing to go along with the lie, because he didn't intervene to correct it back at the flat. Assuming he wasn't just lockjawed with shyness, the best explanation Raf can think of is that, on the contrary, Cherish believes Win to be so dangerously indiscreet that he can't be trusted to have even a casual conversation with an outsider in case classified information starts leaking out of him like yolk out of a poached egg. And, on one hand, maybe she's right to be worried, since Win keeps showing off his expertise on the internet for no useful reason; Cherish probably doesn't even know that Win posts about glow on Lotophage, otherwise it seems certain she would have stopped him by now. On the other hand, Win can't really be that careless if he brought down the guillotine on this latest correspondence the moment Raf was stupid enough to mention Cherish's name.

While he's getting ready to take Rose for an overdue walk, hoping it will rinse his head clear, an ad comes on Myth FM for the rave that Isaac is putting on at the empty Lacebark warehouse in Walworth on Friday. There's a mobile phone number for people to call on the day of the rave to find out the location, which the ad repeats about nine times. He sends Isaac a text message: 'You're still buying ads on Myth??' Raf feels guilty enough just for listening, but the problem is there's no other station that plays so much of the music he likes.

Isaac texts back: 'Dickson keeps the cash. Anyway, if I don't get a decent crowd, that means we've let Lacebark win!!!'

DAY 13

12.33 p.m.

Fourpetal passes across the table an article torn from last night's *Evening Standard*. Most of the headline is missing so Raf reads from the first paragraph.

Rock singer Matty Wilton is due back in court today to face charges connected to his noisy parties.

The twenty-four-year-old Calmatives frontman, who was recently given a suspended sentence for cocaine possession, will appear at Southwark Magistrates' Court charged with breaching a noise abatement order. Wilton was first served the order in March after neighbours complained to the police, but council officials claim the all-night parties have continued.

Local resident Latimer Nollic said: 'My wife and I have two young daughters and they can't sleep when the music is coming through the wall into their bedrooms. Sometimes it's four or five nights a week.'

Guests including TV presenter Tabitha Derby and model Lizzy Kyeremateng have been photographed leaving Wilton's home in the early hours. The five-bedroom house on Camberwell Grove, south London, is believed to belong to Wilton's parents.

The photograph above the article has the caption 'Matty Wilton's party house', with a margin of blue sky clouded only by Fourpetal's greasy fingerprints, and an inset of Wilton himself wearing a straw hat and aviator shades.

'What has this got to do with anything?' says Raf. Yet again, they're sitting in McDonald's; sometimes it feels as if they're having an affair and this is their favourite discreet rendezvous.

'Latimer Nollic is Lacebark's Chief Operating Officer. His wife is English – Old Bedalian, I think – so they spend about half the year in London and half the year in North Carolina. I saw him give a speech at a conference once.'

'How do you know it's the same guy?'

'How many people do you think there are in London called Latimer Nollic?'

'OK, but what does the Chief Operating Officer of a company like Lacebark make a year?'

'Maybe two to three million dollars, including bonuses, stock options, and pension contributions.'

'And you're saying he decided to live in Camberwell?' says Raf. 'Half a mile from Noodels City?'

'Have you seen all those Georgian mansions at the south end of Camberwell Grove? It doesn't look much like the rest of Camberwell. Still, you do have a point. Perhaps his wife has a sentimental attachment to the area. Anyway, if we go down there, we can work out from the photo which house belongs to this pop singer's parents, and then we'll know that Nollic lives in one of the houses either side.'

'And how does that help us?'

'This is our chance to get to Nollic when he's not at the Lacebark offices surrounded by security. We go down there, pull him into the bushes the next time he goes jogging or something, and hold him hostage until Lacebark agrees to withdraw their troops from south London.'

'Are you serious?' Although Fourpetal's bunker of misanthropy probably makes him better prepared than most people for living on the run with nobody to trust, Raf doesn't get the sense that it's been very good for his state of mind: even in the ten days since they met, the guy seems to have frayed and crinkled, as if the ketchup stain on his lapel was just the first surface indication of a deeper haemorrhage. Raf is alarmed by the thought that at this point he might be Fourpetal's best friend.

'Utterly serious. You said yourself, things are going to get very gory around here before long, and your freedom fighter pals have no idea what to do about it. We have to take extreme measures. In any case, kidnapping is apparently all the rage at the moment. I'm almost embarrassed that I've still never kidnapped anyone myself. It's like being the last person in your year at school to finger a girl.'

'No. This is a bad idea.'

'Look, I'm going to go down there and find Nollic's house whether you come with me or not. Anyway, Harenberg reports to Nollic. Pankhead mentioned him in that email. For all we know Nollic is the real power behind everything that's happened. Wouldn't you at least like to see his face?'

Raf fiddles with his straw, herding the ice around the bottom of his cup. Last night, just before he got chauffeured home with a hood over his head, he asked Ko how he got involved in all this. 'Lacebark kill my friends in Gandayaw,' Ko said.

'So what now?' Raf said. 'What's the mission?'

Ko shrugged. 'No more kill.' That seemed sensible. And seeing Nollic isn't going to save anyone's life. But Raf has to admit that he's curious.

6.25 p.m.

Fourpetal was right about Camberwell Grove: it doesn't look anything like the rest of Camberwell. With the sycamores leaning protectively over the narrow roadbed and the semi-detached houses set back at a haughty remove from the pavement, it's impossible to imagine any sort of fuss or flurry ever being permitted here, which makes it an example of a paradox Raf's noticed about certain posh segments of the city: the quieter and more secluded the street, the more likely its architects are to have topologised the zone between the kerb and the homes on either side with such a pedantic and well-proportioned bagatelle of gates, railings, trees, hedges, bollards, and low stone walls that you might have guessed they were expecting twice-daily inundations of people, livestock, ball bearings, ginger syrup, or some other rushing matter whose complex fluid dynamics could be disciplined only by the most meticulous advance planning.

'You know, it was John Coakley Lettsome who planted the gardens behind these houses,' says Fourpetal. 'Quite appropriate in the circumstances.'

'Who's that?' says Raf.

'Like most of the characters in our present narrative, he was a collector of rare plants and experimental herbs. He moved here in the 1780s when Camberwell was still just a village with a serious hedgehog problem and an actual well.'

Raf shrugs. He's always felt that if you have to research what was going on before you were born to find London interesting or magical, you don't really deserve to live there. Right now the two of them are hiding behind a turreted pink Wendy house in the garden across the road from Latimer Nollic's villa. If they get caught, they're planning to pretend to be obsessive Calmatives fans. They know which address is Nollic's because half an hour ago an SUV pulled up to the right of Matty Wilton's alleged sin palace and Fourpetal recognised Nollic as he went inside. Raf has passed the time since then giving Fourpetal a few more specifics of what happened to him the day before yesterday, both at the freight depot and at the flat on Camberwell Green. He explained the basics back in McDonald's but there was such an overwhelming amount to tell that he was too impatient to go into detail.

'So the Lacebark woman called it an "installation"?' says Fourpetal. 'The flat with the unconvincing chemist in it?'

'Yes.'

'That's funny. Normally you only hear about a person being "installed" in furnished lodgings when it's some aristocrat's mistress in a biography. "He installed her at the Dorchester." "He installed her in a fashionable apartment in the Marais." As if it's not a human being but an appliance. Accurate, perhaps, in both contexts.'

'How are you getting on with *Lacunosities*?'

'After several hours with it I now know that warfare, like tailoring, is all about transversality, aporia, and endopolitics.'

'What does that mean?'

Fourpetal exhales. 'Yes, well . . . The thing is, I read some Kant at Cambridge, and I understood most of that. But I can't understand any of this. Which I suppose demonstrates beyond question that this Villepinte fellow must be a lot cleverer than Kant was.'

Nollic's front door opens, and the two of them crouch lower. A girl of about seven years old comes down the steps under the pediment, followed by a second, almost identical girl, then a tan Pomeranian on a leash and finally Nollic himself, who was wearing a suit before but has now changed into khakis and a loose checked shirt. They look like a TV ad for expensive private health insurance. As they pass, one of the girls says, 'Daddy, are you taking us to the climbing wall on Saturday?'

'No, Alicja is taking you, but your mum and I will both be at your soccer game on Sunday.'

'You mean football.'

'Soccer.'

'Football.'

'Soccer.'

'Football!' both girls shout happily.

They pass out of earshot. 'Come on,' says Fourpetal.

Raf points out that he's chaperoned by twins and a small dog. 'I don't think this is a good time to follow him.'

'What else are we going to do?'

They set off. The incongruous council block at the top of the hill has a gabled roof with omelettes of yellow moss at the edges and below that satellite dishes roosting between the drainpipes. When Nollic and his kids cut across the playground at its edge, it becomes obvious that they're on their way to the big supermarket on the other side. Raf and Fourpetal dawdle in the car park for a couple of minutes and then carry on through the automatic doors.

'It's hard to believe this is all about something as trivial as a party drug,' mutters Fourpetal. 'I do have some respect for good coke, but on the whole I always assumed drugs were something invented by film directors to densify value after inflation rendered big suitcases of cash obsolete.'

'Why did they let him take his dog in? No one ever lets me take Rose into shops.'

'People like him get what they want. They understand the congenital deference of the working classes.'

Remembering Zaya's story, Raf initially hopes they'll be able to move around in here unnoticed 'like vengeful ghosts', but when a supermarket worker lunges out of nowhere to force a free sample of marshmallow chocolate brownie on him, he realises they are going to need a different approach. He picks up a basket.

'What are we supposed to be cooking?' says Fourpetal.

They might as well get at least some use out of Ko's curry recipe. 'Let's get onions, garlic, ginger. Um, coconut milk. That kind of thing.' Raf's noticed that in chain supermarkets like this the coconut milk, next to the sweet chilli sauce and poppadoms in the Asian section (which stocks Asian ingredients for non-Asian people), is at least double the price of the coconut milk next to the ackee and kidney beans in the much smaller West Indian section (which stocks West Indian ingredients for actual West Indian people), demonstrating that, as many skunk dealers in gentrifying areas will assure you, there is money to be made selling the same product at different prices to different ethnic groups according to their willingness to pay.

'Are we a gay couple?' says Fourpetal.

'We're flatmates.'

Fourpetal frowns. 'You and me? Really? How did we become friends?'

'I genuinely have no idea.'

They find Nollic in the baking supplies aisle, and for a while they just stand there watching him from a distance. He's carrying the Pomeranian under his arm while his daughters swing one shopping basket between the two of them. Maybe they're going to make pancakes or something. Raf thinks about what Lacebark has done: all the troublemakers executed inside the Concession; all the union organisers' wives tortured in Gandayaw; all the friends of Zaya – and one friend of Raf – kidnapped and interrogated and then deleted from existence no more than a few miles from here. Somebody above Bezant had to order or at least approve all that horror, and it's not as if Raf was expecting to see talons and hooves instead of hands and feet – he knew it was just going to be some normal-looking guy in a suit. But he just can't make himself believe it was Nollic. Perhaps it's not so much his loving manner with his daughters as his obvious affection for their silly candyfloss dog.

A few hundred million dollars a year in royalties to help prop up a military dictatorship: Nollic could probably live with that. Rivers running black from all the mine tailings dumped upstream: Nollic could probably live with that, too. But not dozens of murders. That was what Raf learned listening to Martin: yes, every one of these men has a price, like Zaya said, but every one of them also has a limit, even if they don't know that they have one until suddenly it locks them in place like the clutch in a seatbelt. And it doesn't necessarily mean they're moral. It just means they want to look at themselves in the mirror and feel like nice guys.

Raf strides forward. 'What are you doing?' hisses Fourpetal.

'Latimer Nollic?' Raf says when he's almost at the white sugar.

Nollic turns. 'Yes?'

'You work at Lacebark.'

'Sure. Did we meet at . . .?'

Fourpetal catches up with Raf and starts yanking at his arm in panic, but Raf ignores him. 'You have a guy called Bezant working for you in London. You know that, right? You've heard of him?'

Nollic sighs. 'You're journalists? Guys, honestly, I'm with my kids here. This isn't how you do this.' He has dark grey hair and one of those wealthy physiques that isn't all that tanned or muscular but for some reason still seems unusually well tailored and resilient, as if he's reinforced by a fine mesh of platinum filament just under the skin.

'We're not journalists. Men working for your company killed my friend.'

'Is this for a documentary?'

Raf takes a deep breath. He can make this work. 'You must know what's happening in London right now. And you must be in a position to do something to stop it. I know you want glow. But, trust me, you're not even close, OK? The other side are running rings around you. If you carry on with what you're planning, then, yeah, I bet you'll succeed in killing plenty more people. But that's all. So why don't you just end it now? Maybe I can put you in touch with the people you're chasing. Maybe you can even negotiate. Maybe you can still get something out of this.'

'Oh, I get it, you're activists. You're activists for Myanmar. Guys, we release reports on the human rights situation every six months.'

'Yes,' says Fourpetal, 'I used to write them.'

Nollic gives him a quizzical look. 'I've been to Myanmar,' he says. 'I can tell you, it's not great, but it's getting better every day. We're doing everything we can. But this isn't the place to talk about it.'

'Have you ever been to Gandayaw?' says Raf.

'Yes, of course. Once in 2001 and once before that . . . I think it was 1990.'

This sets a pinion turning in the back of Raf's mind. The Pomeranian's long tongue hangs out of its mouth like a cord to be pulled in an emergency. Then Fourpetal blurts, 'Take me back.'

'Pardon me?' says Nollic.

'Take me back. I know more about all this than anyone at Lacebark. I can tell you everything.'

Raf looks at Fourpetal in disbelief. 'What the fuck is this?' he says. One of the girls giggles at the swear word.

'With what I know, you can catch them all tomorrow,' says

Fourpetal. 'Just promise me I'll be safe. Please. Let's make à deal.'

If Raf had to guess he'd say Fourpetal didn't make the decision to do this until the moment the words flopped out of him. Hurriedly Raf starts indexing what he told Fourpetal earlier today. Fourpetal knows about Cherish tricking Lacebark. He knows how to find Zaya's flat. He knows about Ko working for Zaya. He knows about the boy from the Serbian café sleeping with Win. And, of course, he knows about Raf lying his way into the training facility. If Fourpetal talks, everyone on that list who can't get away in time is going to die in a Lacebark warehouse.

Nollic's expression has changed, and now the box cutters of contempt in his gaze warn that he's bored with pretending not to understand what this conversation is about. 'Let me be clear, Mr . . .'

'Mark Fourpetal. I was at the conference in North Carolina in April. I very much enjoyed your speech.'

'Mr Fourpetal, even if I could make any sense of what you're saying right now – and even if I would ever be willing to consider "making a deal" under these circumstances – I don't need to make a deal with you or your friend. Understand? Right now nothing could interest me less. I have full confidence in all of Lacebark's employees and I already feel sure that we will meet every one of our targets and objectives this quarter.' From the way he says it, his meaning couldn't be clearer: 'We are going to win this war.'

Raf realises he was wrong before. If Nollic has a limit, he isn't anywhere near it. Maybe it shouldn't be possible for anyone to be scary with a Pomeranian nestled in the crook of his arm, but Nollic is scary, and mostly it's because of his confidence: he doesn't seem shaken in the least that the pathogenic reality behind his strategic calculations has invaded his life like this. That's how certain he is that nothing can touch him. Raf and Fourpetal are no more of a threat than the foxes out in his garden.

'You do need me,' says Fourpetal. 'Once you've heard what I know . . . You do need me.'

'No, Mr Fourpetal. I don't. Are we finished here?'

Raf recognises the trout-eyed expression on Fourpetal's face because he's seen it once before, in Isaac's flat. So he knows, a useless semiquaver before it actually happens, that Fourpetal is about to make a run for it.

This time, unfortunately, Hiromi isn't here to trip him up. Leaving Nollic to his pancakes, Raf drops his basket and sets off after Fourpetal, who is going in the wrong direction, away from the supermarket entrance, and will at some point have to double back down another aisle if he wants to get out. The chase that follows is like a badly edited tap-dance routine in a second-rate old musical, as the two of them dodge past pushchairs, shopping trolleys, and yellow WET FLOOR signs, swerving awkwardly every few seconds and never working up any real pace. Before long, Raf is growling in frustration, and he wants to grab a can of coconut milk from a shelf to hurl at Fourpetal's head but he's too afraid of hitting the wrong person. Still, his reactions are generally quicker, so that by the time their squeaky dash has circled back around to the fruit and vegetables at the front of the supermarket he's almost close enough to reach out and hook Fourpetal by the neck.

Then he feels a hand on his upper arm. 'Sir!' A tubby security guard stands in his way, glaring at him from beneath a mucoid crest of gelled orange hair. 'Would you mind emptying your pockets, sir?'

Raf points indignantly at Fourpetal, who is now at the automatic doors. 'What about that guy? Stop him too!'

'We can go into the office if you'd rather, sir.'

As fast as he can, Raf proves to the guard that he hasn't stolen anything, and finally he's sent off with a warning that there's no running allowed 'within the store'. So he hurries out to the busy car park, with its tall halide lamps like spindles twisting the last flax of gold out of the dusk. But Fourpetal is nowhere to be seen.

8.19 p.m.

The dentist's surgery here has a window display consisting of two overgrown pot plants and about a dozen maxillary dentures scattered at random across the tiles like vermin lying there dead after a fumigation. Reflected in the glass, the traffic lights and box junctions of Camberwell Green are a parcel-sorting machine sending bus after bus off south or east or north or west according to the address written on the label. Raf stands at the entry door on the left-hand side of the dentist's window, harassing the buzzer of the third-floor flat where he's now determined that Zaya lives.

He's not looking forward to explaining to Cherish why he didn't tell her sooner about seeing Noodels City through the window. What excuse is he going to give her? 'I didn't want you to stop having sex with me.' Not good enough. 'I thought I might get in trouble with you, even though it wasn't really my fault that it happened.' Not good enough either. Whatever he says, she'll probably be so angry that he'll never get to see her naked again, so he might as well just unwrap the deeper truth: that despite all she revealed that evening, he still had an inchoate suspicion that she was holding something important back from him – a suspicion backed up the next day when he found out about Fitch/Win's perfect English – and so, for reasons that were either strategic or merely childish, he felt as if he ought to hold something back from her too.

This is going to be an uncomfortable conversation. But he doesn't have any choice. Raf doesn't think Fourpetal would be such a moron that he'd try to make a deal with Lacebark a second time after having been turned down so humiliatingly the first time. But there are a lot of other ways he might be reckless enough to get himself caught. Today, even before he lost his only ally, he was talking about kidnapping an adult man in broad daylight; tomorrow, maybe he'll strap on a water pistol and launch a commando raid on Lacebark's offices. To an extent it's Raf's fault that Fourpetal is such an urgent liability now, since the cunt might never have made that destructive gamble if Raf hadn't tugged him into the moonless gravity well of Nollic's dominance, and it's also Raf's fault that Fourpetal is pregnant with data about the Burmese underground. He has to warn Cherish and Zaya.

But no one is answering the buzzer.

Raf isn't sure if the intercom upstairs is even connected, and he can't stay out here with his hood up for too long in case he attracts attention to the flats, which is the last thing he wants to do. The handwritten indicators next to each button are lit from behind with a weak electric amber like windowblinds hiding their own formic tenements. Hoping he can at least get into the building, Raf tries the second floor, but the button must be broken because it drops back with no resistance and no bleep. Next, he tries the first floor, and after a few seconds a woman says, 'Yes?'

'I've got a pizza delivery for the third floor but they're not answering.' Seven eighths of the sky is clouded over, which makes the sun setting in the west look even brighter by contrast, like someone pushing open the door of your darkened bedroom to let in the glare from out in the corridor.

'I don't let strangers in,' she says, her Irish accent shredded by the speaker.

Just then, Raf is perplexed to see what looks like a small waffle taped up over the lintel of the door. But then he remembers Cherish explaining that her Uncle Chai used to keep honeycomb as a charm because for some reason the Danu believe that ghosts can understand only right angles and so are confused by hexagons. Zaya must be more superstitious than Raf realised. Then again, part of Cherish's job is to supply Lacebark with information that won't be any use to their ImPressure• network: inputting hexagons when it's compatible only with squares.

On the way home, Raf wonders what to do. He doesn't have Cherish's phone number, and she specifically told him not to go back to the Burmese restaurant, and he can't just wait for her to get in touch with him. The only mode of contact he has left for anyone in Zaya's network is Lotophage. Until tonight, it didn't seem worthwhile to register for a second account, since Fitch/Win could block that one too, or even ask the forum administrators to ban Raf's IP address. But this is too urgent for Win to ignore. The only trouble is, if Win passes on Raf's warning, then Cherish will learn that the two of them have been communicating without her knowledge. Win might not want that. On the other hand, he might not care.

Sitting down at his computer when he gets home, Raf looks through Fitch's last few posts to get a sense of whether Win is likely to check his messages soon. He's discouraged to find that Fitch hasn't shown himself on Lotophage for about a day: his last activity was a quarrel with two other users about the possible interactions of pramexipole and aminopropyl, which started at 6.11 p.m. BST and tailed off around 11 p.m. Raf isn't sure what to do, and to put off deciding he switches over to the problem of how to find Fourpetal. He knows Fourpetal doesn't have much money to spend, so he must be living in a cheap hotel or hostel somewhere in south London. If he was following the McDonald's principle, he might have chosen a Premier Inn, because apparently the InterContinental Hotels Group has a market capitalisation of about four and a half billion dollars, which is much less than Lacebark and much, much less than McDonald's but still more than Whitbread or Travelodge. The problem is, there are Premier Inns in both Greenwich and Southwark, and Raf can't stake out two hotels at once. He's still clicking around when he's distracted by the thought that something is wrong with what he just read on Lotophage.

Fitch made short, flippant posts at 9.38, 9.45, 9.49, and 9.56 on Tuesday. When Raf saw Win's laptop in the kitchen, the screen was shut and the power cable was unplugged and coiled around the AC adaptor, as if Win hadn't used it for hours. Right after that, when Raf checked his watch in the bathroom, it was 9.51.

This doesn't actually prove anything. Raf has already surmised that Win would want to keep it a secret from Cherish that he was posting on Lotophage. So in theory it's possible that he hastily stowed the laptop away as soon as he heard Cherish coming and then took it out again as soon as she was gone. But it's enough to make Raf wonder.

He goes back to the spreadsheet he made that sorted into chronological order the exact times of every single one of Fitch's posts on Lotophage. Tonight, instead of just scanning the list by eye, he adapts it into a format that he can load into the program he bodged together a couple of years ago to chart his own sleep/wake cycle. The program begins by rounding off every time stamp to the nearest fifteen minutes and then drawing a line graph of the results, with the X axis as the twenty-four-hour clock divided into ninety-six increments of fifteen minutes and the Y axis as the total number of posts in each increment. At first, he can't make out anything meaningful. The frequency distribution looks densely random, like a musical score for the white noise machine in his bedroom. There's certainly no hint of a longitudinal time zone, British Summer Time or otherwise.

He's just about to start work on the more intricate polyphasic calculation he'll need to refute his own ridiculous fancy that Fitch might also have non-24-hour sleep/wake syndrome. But before that, to be sure, he triples the height of the Y axis on his screen and then gradually lowers the periodicity to see what will happen to the graph. And before the periodicity gets to zero, the pattern shows itself. For a moment he has a sense of petals opening, legs spreading, black bin liner curling away from a window, and he pities the ImPressure• algorithms that could make a thousand of these determinations a second and yet never feel this tremor of discovery.

He's looking at a reverse sawtooth wave with a phase of exactly one hundred and eighty minutes, like the deepest synthesiser tone in the world. Fitch is most likely to post at 12.15, 3.15, 6.15, etc., and he's least likely to post at 3.00, 6.00, 9.00, etc., and in between there's a gentle 165-minute decline. This is Raf's best explanation: every three hours, on the hour, something happens to draw Fitch back to his computer; it takes him about ten minutes to catch up on the rubbish people have been offering in his absence; he soon starts posting himself; and then at some point over the next three hours he drifts away from his computer again. This isn't happening in every three-hour period, or even in most of them – the wave is shallow and foamy, and Fitch sometimes does post at 3.00 and 6.00 and 9.00. But the pattern is too regular to be an accident.

What it looks like to Raf is that Fitch is a guy who likes to nap when it's dark, but every three hours he gets woken up because the lights come back on.

2.46 a.m.

If Raf was right and Belasco was lying about Lacebark deliberately introducing foxes into their training facility, then maybe the only reason they're still there is that Lacebark can't get rid of them. Therefore the foxes can't have set up home inside the freight depot, because in that case it would have been easy for Lacebark to find their dens and throttle their young, which is probably one of Bezant's favourite ways to spend a lazy Friday afternoon. Instead, the foxes must live somewhere nearby, but they must have some way of getting in and out that Lacebark don't know about yet, like the Mujahedin with their mountain passes. This still leaves hovering the question of what might have drawn the foxes to the depot in the first place. But maybe Raf will find that out when he gets back inside.

On three sides the depot is surrounded by a high palisade fence topped with barbed wire and security cameras, and on the fourth side is the railway viaduct. Before he left home, he checked Google Maps, so he knows that the next warehouse down makes a right angle with the railway viaduct to the south-west, but the depot doesn't quite line up squarely with either of them, creating the sort of annoying gap you might find in a badly assembled flatpack dresser. No more than a couple of metres wide at the base, it's just a fuzzy tine of brown and grey on the satellite photo, so he can't tell if it will be any use until he sees it for himself.

Standing in the weirdly clean and unsmelly alleyway beside the Serbian café, however, he observes that the depot's fence is contiguous with the north-east wall of the adjacent warehouse, so there's no way to sneak in between them. For a while he wonders if it might have been better to get up on to the railway line somehow, pick his way along the track for a bit, and then climb down, but he decides he certainly would have fucked it up, even if Isaac used to have adventures like that all the time when he was still into tagging. (That hobby came to an abrupt end the night Isaac and his spraycans fell through rotten boards into a kebab-shop septic tank.) Instead, at ground level, Raf will have to loop clockwise all the way round to the other side of the warehouse, hoping there'll be access from that end. Tightening the drawstrings of his hood, he looks up at the silver pill half dissolved on the tongue of the night, and when a slow cloud interposes itself, muffling the moonlight a bit, he takes that as a good omen. Nonetheless, he feels as if a whole nest of maxillary dentures are snapping around in his stomach.

He's almost at the back of the warehouse when he sees exactly what he was hoping to see. A fox is sauntering down this cul-de-sac towards the brick flank of the viaduct. But, like the recollection of a dream, the animal seems to disintegrate the moment it feels the clumsy breath of conscious observation on the back of its neck, and before he even has a chance to quicken his pace, Raf finds himself alone in the shadows again. Still, he has some confidence now that he's going in the right direction. The rusty metal gate on the right leads to a long narrow yard between warehouse and viaduct that he hadn't noticed on the satellite photo. Unlike the depot's fence, the bars of this gate are spaced a few inches apart – convenient for foxes – and it's only a couple of metres high – convenient for Raf. If he climbs over it, that will officially be trespassing, but he thinks this warehouse might be derelict: almost every window is a grid of smashed and blistered panes like the back of a used pack of aspirin, and although there's a sign at the entrance that says PROTECTED BY TEYMUR SECURITY SYSTEMS, the phone number underneath starts with 0171 instead of 020, which means it must be at least ten years old.

The gate is padlocked shut with a burly chain, but the chain has enough slack that it actually helps him: with the gate pushed open as far as it will go, he puts one foot on the chain and boosts himself up as if it were a stirrup. Getting both legs across is a lot harder, and he nearly sodomises himself with one of the spikes at the top, but soon enough he drops panting to the tarmac on the other side. At the opposite end of the yard there's a white van, just like one of Lacebark's, that must have been towed here after an engire fire: speckling the mound of blackened offal beneath the propped-open hood are paler flakes from the grey impasto of the melted paint-work. Above, the clouds have consolidated, and it's starting to rain. Since there's nowhere else to go, Raf climbs up on the creaking roof of the van and takes a look through the chink of space between the terminal wall of the yard and the overhang of the viaduct.

Beyond, there's yet another purposeless, rectal yard, and this one is even less inviting. Slumped against the wall to the right is a beach of junk rising almost to chest height: tyres, cardboard, styrofoam, paint cans, bin bags, telephone directories, computer keyboards, fake flowers, broken wooden pallets, and a surprisingly extensive library of what look like books of carpet samples.

All that, and the Bic flame of a fox's tail, flickering down under the morass as Raf watches.

He hops to the ground and starts pulling stuff aside to make a tunnel, smelling stale rainwater and musty glue and maybe a few dead rats down at the bottom. For a while he can't work out where the fox could possibly have gone, but then, at last, he finds it: a small cavity in the brickwork, with a square collar of missing rivets, that might once have had something to do with ventilation or plumbing. On any other day, if someone bet him he could fit through it, he wouldn't take that bet.

He lies down on the ground, hunches his shoulders, and jams himself into the hole. His head bumps against a barrier on the other side. Here in the dark there's evidently lots of vertical space but not much horizontal space. In other words, he can only get into the hole supine, but he can only get past the hole upright. He feels like Santa trying to climb back up a particularly brutal flue, wishing he had a series of necks and waists all the way down his body.

Inch by awkward inch, Raf snakes inside, until at last he's on his feet again. The cold corridor is too tight to turn around in, so he's stuck facing forward. And because he's still too cautious to switch on the torch he brought, he can't see a thing, and instead gropes along the sides as he crabwalks to the left. He has an odd sense of being trapped backstage in the middle of a play.

Quite soon, on the exterior wall, his fingers find a ladder – but not a real ladder with metal rungs, just a column of wooden slats bolted at regular intervals into the brick. Still, a ladder has to go some-where. So he starts climbing.

By the time he's about twelve feet up, he's relaxed into the rhythm of hand over hand, and he's trying to decide how much farther it would be sensible to climb before giving up and coming back down. Then, as if he weren't distracted enough already, he realises he can hear music from somewhere. So when he reaches for the next slat, and it isn't there, it catches him totally off balance.

He topples backwards. Somehow, the wall behind him yields. And light explodes in his eyes.

Fitch looks down at him. 'Oh, hi,' he says.

Raf is lying in a fridge. Or, in fact, he's lying half in a fridge and half out of it, just like when he was squeezed part of the way through that hole in the wall. From the thighs down he's still dangling on the other side. The fridge, he realises, must be open at the back, operating as a hatch between this kitchen and the space behind the wall. In terms of props and set design, everything else looks just as it did when Belasco gave him the tour of the core scenario installation, although of course he hasn't seen it from this angle before; light streams in through the small window over the sink, toasted to a high-colour temperature to suggest daylight. Only the foxes are new.

There are at least a dozen of them hanging out here, some on the floor and some on the kitchen table and some out in the corridor. When you see so many in one place, that's the first time you can get a real sense of how much they vary. One is stout and fangy, like a crossbreed with Rose or some other bull terrier; another is gymnastic, surgical, almost arachnoid; another has a broad leer of a mouth to match a skull the shape of a flattened diamond. Raf is stricken to his ventricles by their gaze, their scent, their colour. The foxes, on the other hand, don't seem intrigued by him at all.

Slathered from head to toe in damp grit, Raf shunts himself all the way out of the fridge and gets to his feet. 'Am I safe here?' he says.

'For a minute,' says Fitch. 'Probably won't be any more simulations until morning – real world morning.'

Not having paid much attention the last time they met, Raf now looks Fitch up and down with renewed interest. He's only about five feet tall, with darkish skin even for a Burmese guy, and delicate, sombre features that contradict his demeanour. 'I know you're "Fitch" on Lotophage, but what's your name, really?' says Raf.

'Win.'

'Do Lacebark know who you are?'

Win tuts. 'You a retard? Of course not! They don't know I'm a chemist. They think I'm just an actor they hired to play a chemist. Otherwise why they still hunting me all over town?' Interrupting his heavy Burmese accent is the occasional pronunciation that sounds distinctly American, giving his speech a cut-and-paste quality, and he has the syntax of someone who's made a diligent study of English from coke rap and specialist messageboards.

'And the guy in Zaya's flat who answers to your name?'

'Some asshole with nothing better to do.'

Raf began to understand all this the minute he saw that graph. Cherish has a fake chemist in a real kitchen, like a false real morel, while Lacebark – without even realising it – have a real chemist in a fake kitchen, like a real false morel. The guava juice incense burner is here because Win actually made it himself, but the passionfruit juice incense burner was in the kitchen in Camberwell Green because Cherish thought it would make her fake Win look more realistic to Raf. Perhaps it didn't occur to her that by reproducing a minute detail that Lacebark would never have been able to get right on their own, she was bringing the two models so close together that the logic of her story got squeezed to death in between them. (After all, if Cherish had the real chemist and Lacebark had a fake one, then the two kitchens should have looked dissimilar, because Lacebark didn't know Win personally and they were just guessing at his habits. It was only if Cherish herself was the counterfeiter that the two kitchens could have matched so exactly, because she knew Win well enough to build a near-perfect imitation of his workspace.)

'What happens to the foxes when Lacebark are running simulations or showing people around?' Raf says.

'They hear anyone coming, they bail.'

'They didn't this time.'

'They know you not a threat.'

'How would they know that?'

'Maybe they been watching you for a while.'

Raf thinks of the fox on the bus, the fox by the basketball court, the five foxes in the video. 'Are they . . .' He hesitates. 'Are they getting more intelligent?'

'Don't expect them to start talking. But, yeah, they are. The *glo* does that. They get more social. And they spatial memory gets better. I think maybe they start using light the same way they already use smell. They make these three-dimensional maps in they heads.'

'You mean *glo*, the plant?'

'Yeah. They love to eat that shit. And they come here because I feed it to them. You understand how glow made, right? Glow, the drug.'

'No.'

'Foxes metabolise the precursor in they bodies from the alkaloids in the plant. Then I purify it out of they excreta.'

Again Raf thinks of Isaac and his autogenous rocket fuel. 'Wait, so glow comes from fox piss?'

'And fox shit, yeah. Don't look so surprised. How you think those Siberia shamans started getting high on fly agaric? You can't just eat the mushrooms out of the ground – they toxic. So you wait for a reindeer to eat some and then you drink some reindeer piss.' Fitch shoos a feathery-cheeked fox off a chair so that Raf can sit down. 'Look, you obviously totally fucking clueless. Maybe I ought to start from the beginning.'

Glow might never have come to exist, Win explains, if he hadn't wandered into a bar in Gandayaw one muggy, sour night in 2007 to watch a Muay Thai match they were screening. One of the fighters was getting ground up like fish paste by the other, and the picture on the old TV set was flopping and wincing as if the satellite dish on the roof could feel the punches all the way from Bangkok. The only other customers were a handsome white guy in a sweat-soaked shirt and three drunken Burmese boys whom Win had seen around town several times already in the month or so since he came to Gandayaw.

About ten minutes after Win bought a bottle of beer and took a seat in front of the television, he became aware of angry voices behind him. Evidently the three boys were determined to sell the white guy a carton of cigarettes but their English was so bad that the sales pitch involved snarling 'Cig-et! Cig-et!' The white guy thought they were asking him to give them some cigarettes, and he kept pointing at the carton as if they might have forgotten about it. 'But you already have all those,' he was saying. 'There must be ten packs in there.' By now they'd decided he was being deliberately obstructive and one of them had just taken out a flick knife.

Win got up and walked over to the white guy's table. 'They want to sell you box. Give them five dollar and they leave you alone.' His English wasn't quite as good back then.

'Oh,' said the white guy, and laughed. 'Shit. OK.' He found a five-dollar bill – holding his wallet under the table like a poker hand in that tourist way that's supposed to stop anyone from seeing that you have a lot of cash on you but in fact just makes it immediately obvious that you do – and passed it across. The boys sneered at him and walked out.

'Thanks,' said the white guy, looking up at Win. 'Do you want . . . uh . . . do you want some money too? Or a drink?'

They held eye contact for a waxy second before Win called to the barman for a glass of Johnnie Walker Red and Coca-Cola, which was the most expensive thing you could order in this bar. The white guy turned the carton of cigarettes upside down so that all the individual packs fell out on to the table. 'There are only four in here,' he said, and laughed again.

Win knew that if they went back to the white guy's hotel room later, the white guy would probably offer him cash again at some point, and he wasn't sure whether he'd take it. He had never quite decided whether it was more gangster to turn down money for sex, because a gangster couldn't be bought and sold, or more gangster never ever to turn down money for anything, because a gangster was always on his grind. Anyway, tonight it didn't really matter, because he genuinely wanted to fuck this guy. It had been a long while since he'd had sex with anyone but Hseng, and sex with Hseng was like having ten thousand scalding hot pork dumplings shot at you point blank out of a greasy mortar cannon.

'You Lacebark?' Win said.

'Yeah. Just arrived yesterday from Jakarta. But I live in North Carolina.' There was a wasp in the ashtray, almost dead, shivering in small circles like a mobile phone left to vibrate on a table. After a long pause, as if he was so surprised to be having this kind of conversation that he'd lost track of the rules of banality, the white guy said, 'Are you from around here?'

'No. From Mong La.'

'Oh. I haven't heard of it.'

Mong La was a town on the Chinese border where the United Wa State Army made such extraordinary profits from opium that one year they whimsically used some of the surplus to construct a Museum

186

of Drug Eradication. Win's aunt had sent him to work in Hseng's small yaba factory when he was fifteen years old. The pay was low and the hours were long and the fumes gave him headaches, but at least he knew it was gangster to be so close to the drugs and so close to the money. Also, he was captivated by the chemistry: the logical magic and odorous grammar of the catalytic reactions, the precursor's ascension to new forms like a soul moving through the thirty-one planes of existence, the idealistic, asymptotic pursuit of absolute purity. He even loved to watch the last fastidious hesitation of the electronic scales before they settled on a count, the polar shimmer of the crystallised product in the first few seconds after it was sifted out of the evaporator.

His boss, Hseng, was an obese, mottled Chinese guy with a big appetite for boys. Once or twice a week, he would bring Win into the back office, lock the door, and undo his fake designer belt. But Hseng had what Win would later come to identify as a rare disability among males: he couldn't seem to turn himself on by the use of force. He was happy to let Win suck his cock for the price of a bowl of soup, but if Win ever started trying to fight him off, Hseng would immediately forfeit his erection. This left Win with some bargaining power. And quite soon he asked to be allowed to take some lessons from Hseng's chemists and to spend a few hours a week in the internet café on the corner, browsing websites like Lotophage.

Within two years, he was running the factory for Hseng, and its output had never been higher.

For a while, everything was pretty good. Hseng paid Win quadruple his old wage, and even bashfully presented him with a gift: a shoddy Chinese-made portable CD player so he could take his hip hop with him wherever he went. He took to wearing a home-made necklace based on the hexagonal benzene ring common to all amphetamines. Then, late one night towards the end of the rainy season, Hseng came to Win's aunt's house and told her to wake him up because he was needed at the factory. Win blearily followed him outside, and they stood in the wet shadows under a banyan tree while Hseng explained that a colonel in the United Wa State Army was planning to murder him and steal his business.

'We have to leave Mong La. I have a cousin in a town called Gandayaw about a hundred miles west of here. He'll set us up. We'll start a bigger factory. You can oversee everything.'

'Why would I leave?' said Win. 'My aunt is my only family.'

Hseng looked hurt. 'You have to come with me. They'll kill you too. They'll gut you with hooks.'

Later Win would realise that Hseng had been lying about this – if anything, the colonel probably would have given Win a better job. And it was almost certain that Hseng had done something idiotic to provoke the colonel, because his second-rate business alone would scarcely have been worth killing for. But at the time Win wasn't savvy enough to understand any of that, so he packed a bag, said an inadequate goodbye to his aunt, and set off west with Hseng.

When they got to Gandayaw, however, it was obvious at once that although the town had a lot of drug addicts and a lot of drug dealers it had no place for a drug factory. The Tatmadaw and the Lacebark security force had never been on such spiteful terms, so even if one had tolerated it, that would have been reason enough for the other to shut it down. Also, Hseng's legendary cousin turned out to have left for Thailand almost a year earlier. So Hseng decided he was going to start a casino. He used most of the cash he'd brought with him from Mong La to buy an old brothel that had closed after an electrical fire, with the intention of installing baccarat and black-jack tables. (Also he wouldn't shut up about his idea for a fishtank full of turtles whose shells would be encrusted with tiny mirrors, like autonomous disco balls.) But Hseng didn't have any connections here, plus no one trusted the Chinese, so he ended up paying for most of the materials and labour in advance, and in Gandayaw paying for anything in advance was like giving alms to a monastery: you certainly wouldn't expect to see any direct benefit in your current lifetime. After a month, the former brothel looked even more dilapidated than when he'd bought it. One morning he decreed that

Win should start helping out with the refurbishment, but Win deliberately hammered enough holes in the walls that by lunchtime Hseng changed his mind and banned him from the project. Now he just mooched around Gandayaw, pining for his reactor and his drying oven and his rotary tablet press.

The white guy's name turned out to be Craig. He was an 'internal management consultant' at Lacebark, specialising in 'process efficiency optimisation', and he'd been sent to Gandayaw for three months to find out how to boost the productivity of the mine workers in the Concession. Modern efficiency consulting, he told Win, was all about neuroscience: the old, loose terms like 'alertness' and 'initiative' and 'morale' just gestured at specific brain states that could now be described much more precisely in empirical language. When Win started posing questions about dopamine and norepinephrine, Craig asked him how he already knew so much about all that stuff.

'Back in Mong La, I run factory for yaba pills,' Win said.

'What's yaba?'

'Mix of methamphetamine and caffeine.'

'Really?' said Craig. 'You were in the drug trade?' His hair was dark but there was both ginger and grey in his stubble.

Win nodded and clenched a fist over his heart. 'For life.' He rapped a few lines: '"The chemist is brolic, Pyrex scholars, professors at war over raw, killing partners for a million dollars."'

'Did you do much business with sweatshops in Thailand? They go through amphetamine like it's powdered milk. You can't knock it from an efficiency point of view. But we've done a couple of studies and in the long run we think it works best for small, repetitive, seated tasks. Not so much for heavy resource extraction . . . Godammit, sorry, I've got to stop talking about work.'

Three drinks later, they walked back to Craig's room in the Lacebark-owned hotel on the north side of town, where the American turned out to have the biggest penis that Win had ever seen outside porn videos. Afterwards, as he lay dreamy and exhausted, Craig got up and started rummaging through his suitcase. Even though the windows were wide open, the air in the room was still fuggy and ammoniac, as if within the valvular manifold of their connected bodies they had synthesised a molecule so complex it couldn't filter out through the mosquito screens.

Craig held up a bag of coffee beans. 'You ever had this? Civet coffee. I got it in Jakarta. The civet eats the coffee berries, softens them up in its stomach, and craps them out. Then you make coffee with the roasted beans. Tastes amazing – like cherries. The Indonesians came up with it in the eighteenth century because the Dutch wouldn't let them pick coffee berries from the plantations but they couldn't keep them from scooping up the civet crap.' He started fiddling with some sort of expensive-looking black appliance on the desk. 'I got the company to send this here before I arrived. I'm a coffee nerd, obviously, and there was no way I was going to live in a hotel for three months without my own grinder. You know, back in the States, you can't use the coffee pots in hotels, because people like you use them to brew meth. Even in the good hotels, I heard. Do you want a cup?'

'No,' said Win.

Craig pursed his lips apologetically. 'I'd rather come back to bed but it's still the afternoon in North Carolina and I'm going to have a million emails. It's like they've never heard of time zones.'

Later, Win walked home to the brothel. Craig hadn't offered him money and Win was glad that he hadn't. The room at the back with the turquoise walls was dark when he came in but Hseng was still awake. 'Where have you been?' he said.

Win lay down beside Hseng on the psoriatic foam mattress. 'I was at a bar watching videos.'

'You don't smell right.'

Win realised he should have just rinsed his cock and arse before he left the hotel instead of taking a long, soapy shower – this was the cleanest he'd been in weeks, and Hseng could tell. 'I swam in the stream on the way home.' He spat on his hand and reached under the sheet for the chubby radish between Hseng's legs. If he surprised him with a handjob right away, it would both etherise his suspicions and pre-empt any larger demands that Win was still too sore to satisfy.

Win started meeting Craig at the bar about every other evening while Hseng was back at the brothel accomplishing nothing much. Even apart from the diverse pleasures of Craig's company, he found that simply to carry with him a pleasant secret was in itself enjoyable: growing up, you got so used to all your secrets being sad or shameful that you came to assume that secrets, like alkyl halides, were intrinsically neurotoxic, and now he had learned for the first time that they weren't. One night, after they'd gone at each other like Muay Thai fighters for a couple of hours, Craig got up to work on his laptop as usual, but instead of brewing a pot of coffee he took from his holdall a small clear plastic bag full of what looked like white petals.

'What's that?' said Win.

'It's just a flower that grows out in the forest. Most of the Myanmar guys I've interviewed in the Concession say they don't like our polyphasic sleep schedule, but if they eat this, it makes everything a little easier. I tried some yesterday. It works. I mean, it's no Adderall, but it's better than a cup of coffee if you want to get a whole draft report done in one night, and the really special thing is, you can still get to sleep afterwards without any trouble. We might start prescribing it officially, after a few tests.' He tossed the bag on to the bed. 'Want to try some? You just chew and swallow with some water.'

The effect was mild, as Craig had said, but Win was certain that he could perceive something more in this drug, an incandescence blotted out, an urgent thought left unspoken. It was there in the smallest seams of his awareness, in the instants of absent-mindedness or blurred concentration, when he turned his head or licked his lips or scratched his neck in the first sixty minutes after eating the petals. What had set him apart from the older chemists at Hseng's factory wasn't just that he could pick up chemistry so easily, it was also that he seemed to have powers of introspection that they entirely lacked, as if his eyeballs could swivel all the way round to focus on his own frontal lobes. And he'd tried enough different batches of yaba back in Mong La to know when a phenylethylamine's real potential was still unborn.

'I can make this better for you,' he said to Craig.

'What do you mean?'

'I just need some equipment and some lab chemicals and I can make this a better drug for you to give to your workers.'

In fact, what he anticipated from a more potent formulation of *glo* wasn't the boring and reliable concentration and wakefulness that were needed at Lacebark's mines – it was the lawless, luminous core that he'd already sensed. But he couldn't admit that yet.

Craig was bemused. 'How the hell would I get you equipment and lab chemicals?'

'Same way you got your coffee grinder,' said Win.

'Oh. Right.' Craig admitted that it might not be that hard to put in an order with Lacebark's procurement department and make it look as if it was all needed at the mine for some reason. People still joked about the Lacebark executive – no one seemed to agree on who he was or whether he was still at the firm – who'd managed to use corporate money to set up his Burmese mistress and lovechild in a beach house in Los Angeles five or six years earlier.

When the supplies finally arrived, Win installed them in one of the two defunct indoor toilets in the brothel, telling Hseng that he'd scavenged them from a dump out of sheer boredom. Hseng, who by now had been obliged to sell off all his gold jewellery, accepted this explanation with the same sceptical silence as usual. Craig started bringing back several bags of *glo* a week from the Concession for Win to use in his experiments, and at first he tried to get something out of *glo* roughly as you might get morphine out of a poppy or cocaine out of a coca leaf or ephedrine out of a joint fir. But he had no luck with oxidation or fractal distillation or acid-base extraction or any of the other documented methods. There was something evasive, almost coquettish, about the alkaloids in the flower. It was as if the skin of the ripening molecule couldn't be peeled away without pulping the flesh inside.

Then one day he came into his toilet laboratory to find that all his bags of *glo* had been ripped up. He accused Hseng, of course, because he knew that Hseng had some suspicions now, and this was just the sort of pathetic, thuggish way that Hseng might express his jealousy. But Hseng insisted he didn't know anything about it. It happened twice more, and Win was baffled, until at last he happened to catch the perpetrators in the act.

Two foxes stared back at him as he came in, their jaws still working the petals like cud. He'd never seen a live fox before. Unhurriedly, one of them bent its hind legs and shit on the floor, as if that was the only comment it cared to make. Then they darted out past him down the corridor.

There were at least three new smells in the small room: dung, yes, and fox musk, just as he would have expected, but also a third that stood in some cognatic relation to the aftertaste of *glo* petals. Remembering Craig's civet coffee, he pulled on a pair of latex gloves, picked the turd up off the floor, and began another experiment.

A fortnight later he brought an eighth of a gram of white powder with him to Craig's hotel room. 'Do we snort it?' Craig said.

'No, it really stings.'

Win poured two small glasses of Coke and dissolved half the dose into each. After they'd both gulped down their drinks, Craig kissed him and then looked around the room. 'I can't believe how long I've been living here. I never thought I'd miss my ugly condo in Charlotte.'

Win noticed that Craig had written out a few lines in longhand on a piece of notepaper and taped them up on the wall next to his desk. He went over to read them: 'This laugh at once evoked the flesh-pink, fragrant surfaces with which it seemed to have just been in contact and of which it seemed to carry with it, pungent, sensual and revealing as the scent of geraniums, a few almost tangible and secretly provoking particles.' He looked back at Craig. 'Oh, it's just some Proust I like,' Craig said. 'Did I ever tell you I took French Lit. in college?'

On the internet there were PDFs of the laboratory notebooks that the chemist Alexander Shulgin had maintained in the 1960s when, out of gratitude for his invention of a new pesticide called Zectran, his employer Dow Chemical had funded his experiments with drugs like MDMA and mescalin; and during those experiments Shulgin had made continuous painstaking observations on 'visual distortion', 'mental coordination', 'mental attitude', and so on, sometimes interspersed with hand-drawn graphs. (Despite its complexity, the chemistry was often much easier for Win to follow than some of Shulgin's other references: 'This was a miniature high,' he'd written about one compound, 'in the same sense that I would describe a piece by the jazz pianist Bud Powell as miniature.')

Win had planned to imitate Shulgin's methods, even his irritatingly precise time measurements – why should anyone care about the exact minute that something happened? – and he persuaded Craig to take notes too. But when they checked the next morning, Craig had written only a few lines:

12.30 a.m.   Nothing so far.
12.50 a.m.   OK, quite tingly now – reminds me of that one time I took ecstasy in NY.
1.10 a.m.   No, this is much better than ecstasy.

Then:

LIGHTS!!!

And Win had written nothing at all.

'Did I say anything really schmaltzy to you last night?' said Craig. When they hadn't been flipping the fluorescent light above the bathroom mirror on and off or gazing at the red neon across the road, they had mostly been having meandering, slithery sex, any possibility of orgasm suspended several miles out of reach.

'About what?' said Win.

Craig smiled and looked away.

There was nobody at the brothel when Win got home around noon. This was the first time he'd ever stayed out past dawn, and he wondered if Hseng had noticed. Too tired and stiff to work in his laboratory, with raw patches all over his body where he'd rubbed himself against Craig for too long without any feeling of pain to tell him to stop, he lay in bed eating a couple of poppyseed cakes in such tiny rodent mouthfuls that they lasted the whole afternoon. When Hseng still wasn't back by dusk, he began to wonder if something might have happened, and he put his flip-flops on again to go outside. Blue and gold and pink were piled up on the horizon like bolts of silk on a dressmaker's shelf. Outside the bar where he'd first met Craig, he saw the same three boys who'd wanted to sell their carton of cigarettes.

'Are you looking for your fat Chink boyfriend?' said one. Win, who couldn't be bothered to start a fight, just nodded. 'Try the dump.'

For a while after he got there, Win kneeled watching two black cats gnawing at Hseng's fingertips. A small landslide farther up this hillock of rotten cardboard and burned plastic had already covered parts of the corpse, so it looked more like an old buried thing exposed by erosion than a recent delivery from a van or a pick-up truck. In its back were three exit wounds, not too bloody, the bullets perhaps exhausted by the long slog through Hseng's blubber.

Maybe Hseng had tried to default on a loan, or maybe an old enemy of his cousin's had come back to Gandayaw; in either case, it was a reasonably gangster way to die. Those were Win's suppositions until he talked to a bald rag-picker who told him that the shooting had happened that afternoon outside the Lacebark hotel. The sight of Hseng's body had given him only a gentle churn in his bowels, but as soon as he heard that he was really anxious. He ran all the way there, but he couldn't see anything out of the ordinary, so he asked a woman selling biryani from a cart. She'd seen the whole thing, she explained excitedly. An American had been coming out of the hotel when a fat Chinese man had rushed out of an alley and run him through the belly with a samurai sword. Then a Lacebark security guard who was smoking a cigarette nearby had opened fire on the Chinese man with his AK-47. Win asked about the American's body, and she said it had been wrapped up in a plastic sheet and taken back inside the hotel. After she wheeled her cart on down the street, Win just stood there staring up at the hotel, trying to find the window of his lover's room.

DAY 14

4.54 a.m.

By now, most of the foxes have slunk away, as if they don't like to hear the end of that story. 'How long did you stay in Gandayaw?' says Raf.

'I carried on making glow. I had to pay guys from the Concession to start bringing the flower back for me. They told me a lot of stories about the foxes in the jungle acting like people. I guess I was torn up about Craig, but . . . "It feels good to get paid, regardless of how many homeboys get slayed", right?' Raf doesn't find Win's bravado very convincing here. 'Then one night Sam – he's one of Zaya's – he comes to me, he tells me who he is, and he says Lacebark looking for me and I need to get the fuck out of Gandayaw.'

'But how would Lacebark have known who you were?'

'Zaya worked out how it must've gone down.' Lacebark would have seen that handwritten note on Craig's desk about something 'better than ecstasy', Win explains, and if they sent a femoral blood sample back to North Carolina – standard procedure for insurance reasons whenever an American employee died on Lacebark business – they would have detected trace quantities of an unfamiliar amphetamine-class substance. So they would have known right away that Craig was into drugs. But their suspicions wouldn't have stopped there. Craig's killer, after all, was the cousin of a one-eyed Chinese heroin dealer who had been chased out of town by the Tatmadaw a year earlier for late payment of protection money. Also, in his early draft reports Craig had mentioned a rare flower with promising stimulant properties that was picked by mine workers in the Concession, and later on he'd made a procurement order which had attracted no scrutiny at the time but which now looked a lot like supplies for a drug laboratory. Overall, there would have been enough evidence to imply that their internal management consultant – thirty-seven years old, unmarried, owner of a seven-hundred-dollar programmable espresso machine – had made a preposterous and doomed attempt to set himself up in Gandayaw as some sort of small-time trafficker. As the investigation continued, the hotel staff would have reported that a Burmese boy had often visited Craig in his hotel room, and the local security force would have reported that the Burmese boy was known to be a lackey of the Chinese heroin dealer's murderous cousin.

In other words, it's possible that Lacebark started chasing Win for corporate security reasons long before they realised that he was the only person in the world who knew how to synthesise the substance in Craig's blood. And in fact none of this is enough to explain why Lacebark turned their attention to glow with such urgency. Even if a few young executives were open-minded and entrepreneurial enough to contemplate the possibility that an extraordinary new drug might one day be of more value than an underperforming copper and ruby mine, a handwritten note and a toxicological analysis and a few rumours about a flower in the forest would not have been sufficient to explain diversification. All that stuff is just fruit juice. Which is why Zaya is convinced that Craig, like an idiot, must also have been keeping a diary.

'After Gandayaw, Sam took me to this camp in the forest,' Win continues. 'You ever read that Che Guevara *Bolivian Diary*? I thought it would be pretty gangster, but it's the most boring book ever. "Today it rained and we had to move camp." "Today it rained and we had to move camp." That's what it was like. And they made me eat roasted bats! Zaya wanted to get me out of Burma, but Lacebark were watching too close. Then Nargis happened. That was our chance. They smuggled me out of the country with a condom full of *glo* seeds while everything was still fucked up.'

Raf takes a sip of his tea. 'So why London?'

'Foxes,' says Win. 'Foxes everywhere here. Plus people take a lot of pills. We need both of those to operate. That don't leave a lot of cities.'

'Does it really have to be foxes? It can't be another animal?'

'I don't know. I heard Berlin has wild boar right in the middle of the city. And they take a lot of pills there too. So that might have worked. But we didn't want to take the risk.'

'So how did you end up in a Lacebark training facility?' Raf says, suppressing a small yawn, because it's now dandelion on the flower clock, a couple of hours past tonight's bedtime. Darkness has settled on the fictive transect of south London outside the window, the notional sun beginning another three-hour whirl around this classroom globe, even as the weeks skipping past in Win's memoir superimposed yet another chronometry on the short span that's elapsed since Raf came into this kitchen. Isaac once told him about the two competing theories of time: according to the A theory, tenses are real, and the present is a meat-grinder that converts the future irrevocably into the past, but according to the B theory, tenses are a subjective illusion, with all the different instants bound like pages into a book, sequential but static, or maybe not even sequential. Here in the training facility, Lacebark could make the B theory real, swapping one of the three dimensions of space for a dimension of time: a single upright plane would be extended into an infinite smear, like one of those multiple exposures of a golf swing or a tennis serve in a magazine, so that as you walked forward, you'd never travel even an inch farther down the street, but instead you'd slide from dawn to dusk, an army of extras brought in to represent a single individual existing at many different times in the same spot.

'You know why all animals got a blind spot, right?' says Win. 'Because the gap where the optic nerve attaches to the retina is the only place you can't fit photoreceptor cells. That's what this place is. They running surveillance all over London. Except here.'

'But there are cameras all around us.'

'Those cameras on a separate, closed system. The footage don't get processed by they facial-recognition algorithms.'

'So you're just hiding here inside the blind spot?'

'Yeah. Been here since they set this place up. Half the extras, they really working for Zaya. They bring in *glo*. I feed it to the foxes. The foxes shit in my bathtub. I filter out the precursor and do the hard chemistry. What I end up with is, like, one reductive amination away from pure glow. I give that to the extras and they take it back to Zaya. Then his guys finish off the process. If that was happening anywhere but here, Lacebark would've traced the supply line to me months back, but they don't have the imagination to see, right? That the centre of Zaya's network could be . . . fuck, what's the word?' – he snaps his fingers – 'could be homotopic with the centre of they own network. The journeys they extras make between they cribs and the facility, the interactions between the extras while they here together – the hilarious thing, Lacebark take care to cut all that stuff from they ImPressure• mapping, because they don't want any artificial distortions in the data. But we live in those distortions. "The calls are coming from inside the house!" You ever see that movie? Anyway, we couldn't have done it without help. Right now, most of the money we make from slinging glow goes to paying off the guys in the control room above the "pub". They make sure everything tilts our way.'

'Lacebark have completely lost control of their own training facility, and they don't even realise?'

'They starting to. They don't understand what's happening yet, but they starting to realise something fucked up here. Nobody wants to admit it, though. Nobody wants to get fired. That's why they so slow to catch up. You know, they run simulations in here every day? They bust in and put a hood over my head and drag me into a van. They already caught me a hundred times. They just don't know it. Wish I could see Bezant's face when he finds out.'

For Lacebark, Raf thinks, it must feel like a locked room mystery, with south London as the locked room. 'So what are you going to do? You can't leave the blind spot or they'll catch you for real.'

Win smirks. 'Of course I leave. I got to get laid like everybody else.'

'What do you mean?'

'I go see my boy Jesnik at the café. It's easy. I get out like you came in. And I know where the cameras are pointed.' Every time he tunnels through that beach of rubbish in the yard, he admits, it reminds him of Hseng's body on the dump in Gandayaw.

'Does Cherish know?'

'She knows I have a thing going with Jesnik. But she don't know I leave this place to see him. She thinks we just jerk each other off when he comes in to deliver coffee and baklava for Belasco and the others.'

'They let him in here?'

'Yeah. He gets paid to keep his mouth shut same as the rest.'

Raf wonders about the photos on the fridge in the flat in Camberwell. He realises that although they looked like disposable camera pictures, they could just as easily have been webcam pictures printed off some cruising site. 'Why haven't you told Cherish there's a way out of the facility?'

'I have to keep my options open. Here's the thing: Jesnik's uncle's a gangster. Like, a real live one.' And he's famous in the Serbian mafia, Win explains, partly because in the toilets of a puppet theatre he once took down three big men who'd come to kill him using only a broken fluorescent tube lamp. When Win finally leaves the facility for good, the plan is to smuggle him to a farm outside Majdanpek – the countryside there is full of foxes – where they'll start a *glo* plantation and a glow factory big enough to export hundreds of kilograms of the drug a year. Jesnik's uncle was sceptical at first, since he'd never managed to make any real money from ecstasy, but now he's starting to negotiate terms. Of course, he doesn't realise his nephew is gay – as far as he knows, Jesnik is just Win's business partner.

Matryoshka dolls again, Raf thinks, except this time each doll is kept a secret from the one that contains it: the depot is disloyal to the city and the laboratory is disloyal to the depot and the chemist is disloyal to the laboratory, as if inside the Hopi reservation inside the Navajo reservation inside the state of Arizona there was yet another reservation which had a population of only one.

'You're going to betray Cherish and Zaya?' he says.

Win shrugs. 'I don't care about that Shining Path shit. I just want to get rich and live in a big house with Jesnik the rest of my life. "My laboratory story keep me flowing with glory."'

'The rest of your life? Really?'

'Sure.'

'So, I mean, do you love him?' says Raf, feeling like someone's dad.

'You think I could love a bitch who hates rap music?' says Win, but he says it in a way that means 'Yes.'

Raf thinks of those old men playing cards in the café. Win's deluding himself, surely, if he thinks the Serbian mafia, of all people, are going to give him a fair deal. And although there's real tenderness in the chemist's voice when he talks about his boyfriend, Raf is certainly glad that none of his own inevitable break-ups took place when both parties were stranded on a rainy Balkan crime farm.

'Win, you wouldn't be alive right now if it weren't for Zaya,' he says. 'Lacebark would've caught you back in Gandayaw and tortured you until you told them how to make glow. Cherish and Zaya need you so they can keep fighting. And you owe them.' Raf can see from Win's expression that he's not getting anywhere. And ever since he heard Win's story about Gandayaw, there's been a question he's been longing to ask, even though he knows he should save it for another time. 'So if Lacebark were planning to use *glo* to regulate polyphasic sleep schedules in the Concession, that means it must do something to your circadian rhythms, right? Make them easier to change?'

'Yeah, maybe.'

'Does that mean . . . Do you think there could ever be a derivative that . . .' Raf realises he's going to have to explain from the beginning. 'Listen, I have this condition—'

Then he hears footsteps in the corridor behind him. He turns to look.

A Lacebark soldier stands in the doorway.

He's wearing full black ops gear, like a golem built out of the darkness inside a sensory-deprivation hood. There's a pistol in his thigh holster and he looks as if he could pop kneecaps like bubble wrap between finger and thumb. Raf's first instinct is to try to escape through the fridge, but he knows that will expose Win's route out of the freight depot, and they'll probably both end up dead. In any case, a feedback squeal of terror is drowning out any orders Raf could possibly send to his limbs.

The soldier stares at him. 'What the fuck are you doing here?' he says. 'The call sheet just says one ethnic high-value target, as usual. No Caucasians.'

The soldier thinks Raf is just another extra. But Raf has no idea how to reply. His heart is stamping out each beat like a factory die.

The soldier strides forward, picks up Raf's mug of tea, and pours the lukewarm dregs out into his lap. 'Do you speak English? Or are you another of the Polacks? When the simulation starts, you'd better be gone, you mompie cunt, or I promise you Bezant will stick his Taser right down your fucking throat. All right?'

Raf nods, feeling the surrogate piss soak into his underwear. The soldier gives him a final long look. And then he turns and marches back down the corridor.

12.49 a.m.

From the front, there's no evidence that a coup has taken place here. The warehouse looks just as it did when Isaac showed it to him last week. But with Lacebark gone, those two million litres of empty space sing a new anthem. Patting people down for weapons around the back is a squat bouncer with pouches under his eyes that bulge like hospital blood bags, and Raf recognises him from several of Isaac's previous raves, so they have a little chat. The soundproofing, apparently, has been more trouble than Isaac could have anticipated: almost everyone who turns up asks if the rave's been cancelled, because they weren't able to navigate down the street by the bass, and then they're even more restless than usual in the queue, because usually it's the heartbeat of the music inside that keeps you interested while you're waiting. The steel door here reminds Raf of a particular gag in old cartoons: from total silence to loud noise as soon as it's ajar and then back to total silence as soon as it's shut. And when he pays his nine quid and gets inside, tears rush to his eyes just like they did when he was watching the fake rain in the freight depot, except this time there's a grin on his face too.

Isaac's done it. This is a genuine full-scale early nineties illegal warehouse rave of the type Raf thought he might never get a chance to experience, except that the music they're playing is the same music you hear on Myth FM every day. As far as anyone knew, there were almost no gaps left in the surface of London, just an impermeable glossy sheath, but Lacebark bored some holes and now hundreds of people are crawling in after them. The bouncer told him that before long they're probably going to reach 'capacity', which is Isaac's semi-arbitrary estimate for the maximum number of people that can fit in here before it's no fun to dance any more. As he feels the subwoofers licking his ribs with their rough Staffie tongues, Raf knows that after tonight he can never go back to that laundrette. All that's nagging at him is the thought that the last time loud bass tones were played in this room, they were to tenderise someone for interrogation. But he decides this is just the most thorough possible reconsecration of this ground, chasing away the poison from every frequency.

On his way to the trestle-table bar for a beer, he brushes past a sweaty couple holding hands, and he realises delightedly that it's the boy and the girl from the dryer the weekend before last – they're rosy, seraphic, with pupils the size of howitzer barrels, and he wants to tell them that if they feel as if this is the best night of their lives, they might actually be right. Then he feels a touch on his arm. And he knows this. He's been here before.

'This is pretty awesome,' Cherish says into his ear.

He never sees her arrive or leave anywhere, he thinks. She's just there. Like Batman. One day he'd like to watch her untangling her headphones from her scarf from the strap of her bag as she comes into a pub. He kisses her straight away, just as if she was his girl-friend. 'Yeah, it is,' he says. Then he remembers the reason he's not supposed to enjoy himself. 'Hey, I really have to talk to you about Fourpetal.'

She puts a hand on his arm. 'It's fine. We're watching him.'

'You know where he is?'

She nods.

'So he can't do anything stupid and get himself interrogated?'

'Raf, relax. It's fine. I promise.'

There's something a little bit slippery about Cherish's casualness here. Just watching Fourpetal isn't going to be enough, surely. That won't stop Lacebark from getting him. Cherish should have snatched him up herself and locked him in a room somewhere. Coming to a rave with Raf should not be the priority tonight. Unless she already has a reason to be certain that Fourpetal isn't a threat any more.

Is it possible, Raf thinks, that Fourpetal is already dead, and Cherish doesn't want him to know? Zaya is a soldier, after all, and he probably wouldn't think twice about killing someone who was about to wreck the whole operation. Of course, Zaya couldn't have physically accomplished it himself. But Ko could have. Or Cherish. Raf looks at her, wondering if she would have been capable of a pragmatic murder. It doesn't feel plausible. But maybe that's just because she's so pretty and he doesn't have any imagination. After all, she's a soldier too. Raf doesn't know how he'd feel about the right and wrong of it all if he learned that Fourpetal really had been stubbed out. For the hundredth time, he runs through all the people Fourpetal could doom. Cherish and Zaya and Ko and Win and Jesnik and Raf himself.

But Cherish is right. He should relax. Even if Lacebark had conquered the whole of the rest of London and driven every other cuckoo out of every other nest, for the next few hours it wouldn't matter. Tonight this warehouse is a demilitarised zone. 'I need to say hello to Isaac.'

They swim through the crowd towards the low platform where the decks are set up. Isaac is sharing a spliff with the MC. When he sees Raf, he waves and hops down off the platform. 'Mate!' he shouts. 'You made it!'

'Of course I made it.'

Isaac looks at Cherish. 'Is this her?'

'This is her,' says Cherish.

Isaac turns to Raf and makes such a diverse and protracted series of gestures and facial expressions signifying 'Good work!' that even Cherish giggles.

'When's your set?' says Raf.

'At three. Assuming the next DJ turns up. Otherwise it's in twenty minutes.'

'Make sure you play that track with the harp sample.'

'Listen, Barky finally managed to get hold of some real glow,' says Isaac. 'Do you two want any? I know this is sort of the wrong way round, given where it . . . You know.' He looks at Cherish. 'Comes from.'

Raf panics. Isaac might as well be wielding a syringe full of sodium thiopental. If Raf gets high with Cherish, the oxytocin will make him feel like nothing in the world could be more pleasurable than spurting out all his secrets. She doesn't know that he visited the real Win in the training facility, nor does she know about Win and the Serbian mafia. Even if Win is ready to betray Cherish, it doesn't seem to Raf that he has any right to betray Win after Win confided in him like that.

'I don't want to take any tonight,' he says.

'Why not?' says Cherish.

This is especially frustrating because for obvious reasons he is desperate to find out for himself what glow is like. Also, he knows Cherish would look more gorgeous than ever as the drug took its effect on them both – objectively gorgeous because of the bloom of elation it would put in her face and subjectively gorgeous because of the lens of elation it would put in his eyes – the love they'd find in each other until it wore off would be silvery and fathomless like the small universe between two mirrors. A rave like this deserves glow. But he just can't.

Improvising, he says to her so Isaac won't hear, 'When we fuck later, I want to be able to come.'

He's almost sure he can see a flicker of relief behind her smile, and he realises she probably had just the same worry as him. She has plenty of secrets to keep too. That much he knows for sure.

'OK,' she says. 'I guess if you're not taking any, I'm not taking any.'

'So it's "love is the drug" with you two now?' says Isaac. 'All right. More for me.'

'Let's get some shots and then I want to dance,' says Cherish.

Raf gives Isaac a hug. 'See you in a bit.'

DAY 15

5.26 a.m.

Because Raf wasn't paying much attention back in the shop, he's confused to see that all Cherish has brought for the 'picnic' is two cans of Guinness, a bottle of Tabasco, and a bag of lemons. When they emerged from the rave into an exceptionally warm and brilliant dawn she said she didn't want to go back indoors for a while, and as much as he was looking forward to taking her back to his flat and undressing her he couldn't really disagree. The yard at the back of the warehouse was acrid because of all the people who'd got bored with queueing for the Portaloos and gone outside to piss behind the wheelie bins, so it was a relief to get out on to the street. Now they sit cross-legged in the centre of the derelict tennis court, which was only about half an hour's wobbly stroll from the warehouse. At this time of the morning the quills of sunlight flaring through the trees at the side makes it feels less like a gravesite and more like a garden. This would be a good place for Linnaeus's *Horologium Florae*.

Cherish takes from her bag a foil blister pack containing eight mauve lozenges and passes it to Raf. 'Put one of these on your tongue and let it dissolve.'

'I thought we weren't doing any drugs tonight.' The ringing in his ears from the rave is like a thin cloudy liquid trapped in his cochlea.

'Just take one.'

The lozenge tastes fruity. 'What is this? Flavoured temazepam for kids?'

Cherish uses the edge of the bottle opener on her keyring to saw a lemon into quarters. She passes one to Raf. 'OK, bite into this.'

'But it's a lemon.'

'Trust me.'

Raf apprehensively does as he's told. There's an interval of controversy in his mouth, like when you put your finger in a basin of cold water that you were expecting to be hot, and then he realises that the lemon is delicious.

'What did you just give me?' He turns over the blister pack and finds only a quotation printed on the back: '"Again, it is proved that sweetness is not really in the sapid thing, because the thing remaining unaltered the sweetness is changed into bitter, as in case of a fever or otherwise vitiated palate." – George Berkeley.'

'They're made from miracle berries,' says Cherish. The fruit of a West African plant called *Synsepalum dulcificum*, she explains, contains a glycoprotein that distorts the shape of the sweetness receptors on the tongue so that they respond to acids instead of sugars. 'Ko gave me some. I've been wanting to try them for so long.' She opens both the cans of Guinness. 'Now this.'

Raf takes a swig. 'Chocolate milkshake!' And the Tabasco is a piquant syrup. Cherish tries everything after him. Perhaps somewhere in the Concession there's a shrub that can be fermented into eye drops to make everybody look as beautiful as her. She leans forward to give him a long kiss and he puts a hand inside her top. 'You taste as sugary as all the other stuff,' he says afterwards.

'Yeah, but that's because all the other stuff is still coating my tongue. I don't think miracle berries do anything for saliva. Otherwise you'd taste your own mouth. OK, now rinse with Guinness like you were at the dentist.'

'Why?'

'Because I don't want any Tabasco left in your mouth when you go down on me.' She starts to wriggle out of her skirt. Surprised, Raf looks around like a meerkat. 'I come here all the time with the Lacebark guys and I've never seen anybody else come near here,' she reassures him.

Raf wishes she hadn't mentioned Lacebark, because it reminds him that he's still concerned about Fourpetal. He thinks of Win, there in the lion's mouth, so cocky but so defenceless. But then it occurs to him that in fact Win would be safe even if Fourpetal got interrogated, because Fourpetal still knows only about the fake Win. Every Lacebark mercenary in London would swoop down on that flat in Camberwell, but the real glow chemist would still be in Lacebark's blind spot. Which makes Raf think of a question he's been meaning to ask Cherish.

'Why were you outside my flat last week? You were in the van with those Lacebark soldiers. But back then I had nothing to do with any of this. So why were Lacebark already watching me?'

'They put you under surveillance because I told them to.'

'Why would you do that?'

'Because you're so handsome and I wanted some candid shots to take home with me.'

'Really?'

'No.' Part of Cherish's job as a double agent inside Lacebark, she explains, is to distract their attention. She tries to make sure they keep a lot of people under surveillance who have nothing to do with glow. But she can't just pick those people at random: to retain any credibility, she has to find subjects who look as if they plausibly might have some connection to Zaya's network. Raf was basically in the same position as someone who's hired for a police identity parade because he happens to have the right facial hair. When he gave her that fake glow at the rave in the laundrette, he established himself as a candidate. And after Lacebark found out he worked for Myth FM, they didn't need any more encouragement.

'But after they searched your flat, and watched you for another day or so, they gave up and moved on.'

'Did you tell them we had sex?' he says.

There's something especially creepy about the thought of Lacebark mapping sexual commerce in their ImPressure• network like a village gossip. If Fourpetal did tell Lacebark that Jesnik was in a prelingual relationship with Win, they'd note it down eagerly (even if they still had the wrong referent in mind for that name). Maybe the real Win is safe for a while, but Lacebark could still take Jesnik from him. Raf tries to imagine how he'd feel if those mercenaries did something to Cherish. With Jesnik gone, Win would presumably lose interest in defecting to the Serbians. In fact, he might be so furious with Lacebark that he'd pledge allegiance to Zaya and what he called 'that Shining Path shit' for the rest of his life.

'I didn't tell them everything,' says Cherish. 'I just told them I made out with you, so you wouldn't be suspicious.'

He remembers that afternoon, and looks down at the pack of miracle berries. 'Hey, did I say something to make you think I don't like the way you taste? Because—'

'No! I just want to know what this is like. Take off your pants and get on your back.'

She settles herself over him on all fours so that she can suck his cock at the same time as he licks her from underneath. He can feel when his tongue is in the right place because it makes her bobbing mouth falter and purse for a second before it hurries up again. After a while she pauses and says, 'OK, what do I taste like?'

They're both out of breath. 'Pretty good but not as sweet as the lemons.'

She runs a fingernail down the dorsal vein of his penis and he shivers. 'Are you disappointed? Were you expecting, like, cookie-dough ice cream?'

'Kind of, yeah.' He remembers Isaac telling him about a photographer's assistant he went out with for a while whose prescription mood stabilisers not only diminished her secretions but also left them disconcertingly odourless and flavourless. Isaac, who is devoted to cunnilingus, said it was like having sex with a Scandinavian welfare system. To Raf there's something persuasive about the finding that a person's capacity for joy might percolate into their glands and follicles. If you wanted, you could say that the sweetness of Cherish's clitoris on his kinked chemoreceptors is just a sort of oral hallucination. But the taste of her seems more

211

truthful to Raf now than it ever did before. Take these miracle berry tablets often enough and you'd begin to believe that they revealed the real sweetness hidden in external objects in just the same way that MDMA sometimes seems to reveal the real joy, a coy pith of luminance like the alkaloids Win had such trouble refining from *glo* petals. After all, sweetness isn't just a taste, it's also the pleasure stitched inextricably into that taste. And you can't be mistaken about pleasure: like pain, if you think you feel it, then you feel it. Then again, there's not much that's sweeter than antifreeze; he's read that they discourage people from drinking ethylene glycol by accident by mixing it with something called an 'embittering agent', which is presumably distilled from pillowcase tears.

'What do I taste like?' he says.

'I don't know yet,' she says, and puts him back in her mouth. He moves his hands over her body, mapping her vectors of influence. From this angle the sun reflects so brightly off the edge of her hip that it could be a coin or the face of a watch, and when he comes he feels as if he's siphoning the light back into her mouth like a periscope. Afterwards, she spits a couple of times on the ground and then reaches for an open can of Guinness.

'How was it?' he says.

'Worse,' she says hoarsely. 'Way worse than usual.'

'How could it be worse?'

'I don't know but that was a terrible idea. Oh my god.' She starts laughing.

Starlings are hassling one another in the trees. 'I wish Rose were here,' Raf says.

'Because she loves sperm so much?'

'No! Because I haven't been walking her enough recently and she'd like it out here.'

'We could totally go get her from the roof if you want.'

'She's not on the roof. I've been keeping her at home the last few days – I don't give a shit about guarding the transmitter if Lacebark are running Myth now. But, yeah, let's go and get her, that would be nice.' He gets to his feet and starts collecting up the picnic rubbish, still naked from the waist down, the backs of his thighs patterned by the gravel.

'She's in your apartment?' Cherish says. Something behind her expression has reconfigured.

'Yeah. Maybe we could have a nap while we're there. I don't think I could sleep out here with the sun coming up.'

'Let's not go to your apartment.'

'Why not?'

'I told you, I don't want to go back indoors.'

'Well, we don't have to stay for a nap. You can just wait outside while I pick her up.'

'Let's stay here for a while,' she says. 'We can get her later.' She leans her head against his leg in a gesture that feels not quite natural. One of the weird double qualities of bodily intimacy in relationships is that it gives you an excuse for those times when you're so exasperated that in some trivial but not entirely symbolic way you find yourself trying to physically coerce someone, tugging at their wrist or sitting on their lap like a child, and that's what Raf is reminded of here.

'OK,' he says cheerfully, and sits down again, because although he's suspicious now, he wants to give himself time to think.

Does Cherish think Raf might be in danger somehow if he goes back to his flat? In danger from Lacebark? She said earlier that Lacebark quickly dismissed him as a false lead. Yes, they'd turn their attention back to him right away if they found out from Fourpetal how deeply he's involved in all this. But that can't happen if Fourpetal is already dead. And it certainly seems as if Fourpetal is already dead, since that's the only explanation Raf can think of for Cherish's nonchalance about the whole issue.

Unless for some reason Cherish wouldn't care if Fourpetal was captured today. But of course she would care, because then she and Zaya and Ko and Win and Jesnik and Raf himself would all be under threat.

He stops to revise that. Not Cherish or Raf, because they're here at the tennis court. And not Win, because Lacebark don't know about the real Win, only the fake one. And not necessarily Zaya or Ko, because if they really are watching Fourpetal, they'd have plenty of notice if Lacebark snatched him.

In fact, the only people in real jeopardy would be Jesnik, the fake Win, and any other Burmese guys from Zaya's organisation who weren't warned in time. If Fourpetal told Lacebark everything he knew, they wouldn't have to wait for the first of June to start trampling. They'd launch immediate raids all over London, expecting to declare victory by morning. But they wouldn't catch anyone very important. They'd just waste a day in a pointless convulsion. Which makes Raf recall what Cherish told him about her plan to get Win out of the city: 'It's too dangerous to move him at the moment. Lacebark have too many eyes. Until we can find some way of making them blink . . .'

Just like when he adjusted that line graph and realised the truth about Win, the understanding surges through him all at once as if administered intravenously, except this time there's a colloid of venom suspended in the mixture.

Zaya wants Lacebark to catch Fourpetal. Zaya wants the raids to happen.

By the end of today, Lacebark will have only Jesnik, the fake Win, and a handful of other expendable Burmese guys. And Zaya will have all he really needs, which is a heartbroken, angry, loyal chemist, ready to leave London.

The reason this can work is that Fourpetal will give Lacebark a lot of false information. But he'll believe it's all true, because he learned it from Raf. And back then Raf believed it was true, too, because Cherish made sure that he did when he went to the flat in Camberwell. When she took him to the kitchen, it wasn't an accident that he saw those pictures of Jesnik up on the fridge. Raf was meant to find out Jesnik was in a relationship with Win. And when she took him to the bathroom, it wasn't an accident that the bin bag had fallen away from the window, or that they fucked in just the right place for Raf to see it. Raf was meant to think the location of the flat was a big secret so that he'd present it as such when he next talked to Fourpetal. He couldn't have been more gullible.

This has got to be Zaya's scheme, Raf decides, not Cherish's. He can see how she might do nothing to prevent Lacebark from capturing Fourpetal. Maybe that has a sort of moral logic. And maybe that's why she didn't want to take glow with Raf last night. But there is just no way that she would be willing to see Jesnik go to his death in order to manipulate Win when as far as she knows the boy has nothing to do with any of this. Cherish must be following Zaya's orders without understanding the whole picture. That's the only explanation that makes sense.

Raf is trying to make up his mind whether to tell her all this when she says, 'Are you zoning out already?'

'Yeah, a bit.'

'What time is it for you now?'

'Only about midnight.'

'I have to pee.'

She gets up, pulls on her high tops without bothering to lace them, and walks off towards the trees. Her phone is lying there on the ground. Raf picks it up, wondering if he'll be able to find any clues in her text messages or her call log, but it turns out Cherish has a PIN lock on it.

There is one other thing he can do. But he has to decide right away, too fast to think about it, and there won't really be any going back afterwards.

Raf slides the back of the case off the phone, takes out the SIM card, and bends it hard enough that it cracks down the middle without actually breaking in half. Then he replaces it exactly as it was, and puts the brain-dead phone back down. By the time Cherish comes back, he's pulling on his trousers.

'Are you going somewhere?' There's no concern in her voice. She's a much better liar than Belasco, he thinks.

'I just want to go back to the shop to pick up some water or some juice or something. We should've got some before.'

'I'll come with you.'

'No, don't bother, I'll only be a minute.'

He thought maybe he could get away with this. But he can see it straight away: she's guessed that he's guessed.

The truth has been dragged out of the undergrowth and dumped there on the ground between them, flayed and steaming and membranous: the moment he leaves, Raf is going to do whatever he can to stop Zaya's plan from going ahead, and Cherish is going to do whatever she can to stop him from stopping it. Each of them is going to fuck over the other, and it's going to be irreparable, and each of them knows it, and neither of them wants to acknowledge it out loud. Since there's no chance they're going to change their minds, there's nothing to be lost by talking about it. But he won't until she does. And she won't until he does. They're locked together in an ouroboros of silence the same shape as the sex they just had, playing these underwritten roles like the extras in Lacebark's training facility, and when he looks into her eyes it's so frustrating he thinks his heart is going to pop like a light bulb in a microwave.

'OK,' Cherish says. He can tell that she's trying not to cry now, which is contagious like a yawn. He takes a step forward to kiss her, and at first they're both stiff with the awareness that if this kiss is any more passionate than the usual dutiful parting kiss you might give someone preparatory to a minor errand, it will spoil this pointless game they're determined to play; but then it seems to occur to both of them at the same moment that if you've recently been entwined it's customary to make your next kiss a small aftershock of what you just did to each other. By the time they reluctantly pull apart, they're both too tearful to hide it any longer.

'Do you ever feel like there's . . . you know . . . a hole in things?' Raf says softly.

'No,' Cherish says, shaking her head as if this is quite important. 'No, Raf. There's no hole in things. There's just a hole in people.'

Raf steps back and gives her a small chest-level wave. Maybe every break-up is basically the same, he thinks, no matter how strange the circumstances. All that oxytocin is wonderful until you try to escape with it and somehow it's transmuted into embittering agent, the same way that when you rob a bank the cashier hides a dye pack in your bag of money that will explode ten seconds after you pass the radio transmitter in the door frame. 'See you in a bit,' he says. Cherish looks at the ground. VOID VOID VOID VOID.

10.06 a.m.

When Isaac arrives at the playground opposite the Myth studio, his pupils are different sizes, but otherwise he seems lucid, which is a relief because Raf was worried that by now he'd be too far gone to be any help. Since the last time Raf was here someone has dumped one of those old-fashioned gumball machines in the bushes, its empty glass dome reflecting the sky like an astronaut's helmet. 'When did the rave finish?' he says.

'It hasn't. You made me leave my own fucking party. What's going on?'

Raf tells Isaac what he now knows.

'And you worked all this out because Cherish seemed a bit shifty just now?' Isaac says afterwards.

'Seriously, Isaac, I'm sure of it. We have to warn everyone so they can go into hiding before the raids start.' But it's hopeless to carry the warning door to door like evangelists, Raf explains, even if they knew where to find Ko and the rest. There's no way to be sure whom Zaya will decide to protect – maybe just himself and Win and Cherish, on the basis that the more bountiful the raids look to Lacebark, the longer it will take them to realise that the whole fox hunt has been deliberately allowed to happen. And even if Raf and Isaac could get to a few people in time, it wouldn't be enough. When the captives from the first wave of raids begin to powderise under interrogation, they'll implicate their contacts, and the danger will multiply out through all the dendrites of Lacebark's ImPressure• network. Raf still doesn't know how many Burmese immigrants Zaya has spread across London in honeycomb cells, but it might be dozens, and the second and third wave of raids might snare nearly all of them.

'So what are we going to do?'

What Raf really wants to do is organise an assault of about a hundred foxes on Lacebark's training facility. But even if Win could arrange that, Raf can't. Instead, he gestures at the council block opposite. 'Get on the radio.'

'During the Burmese show?'

'We can't wait for that. But a lot of the people who listen to the Burmese show listen to Myth the rest of the day as well. If we can warn some of them, they'll spread the news to the others.' His plan is to get inside the studio and either trick the DJ into handing over the microphone or just overpower him with Isaac's help.

'What are we going to say?'

They won't have much time before they're thrown out of the studio by Dickson or whomever else is managing the station this morning. '"If you have anything to do with Burmese anti-Lacebark activity or the production and distribution of glow, go somewhere no one is going to be able to find you, and stay there. Otherwise Lacebark may capture and kill you."' If they can accomplish that much, then maybe the last two weeks won't have been a total failure.

'We'll also mention that my rave is now down to six quid on the door.'

As they cross the road, Raf catches sight of the old gasometer in the distance, the sunset-coloured cylinder today pushed most of the way up inside its steel foreskin. At the council block, they get into the lift with Raf's keys and go up to the fifth floor. Raf dials the mobile phone number that's supposed to get him inside, but there's no response. Even before Theo disappeared, this sometimes used to happen in the evenings when Dickson was so stoned he couldn't be bothered to come to the door, and Raf wonders if discipline here has relaxed even further now. He tries the number a second time and then a third.

'We should find a radio and check they're at least on air,' says Isaac.

But at that moment they hear bolts sliding back. As the door opens Raf is planning to whine about how long this took so he can avoid explaining why he's turned up here without Rose on a Saturday morning.

The seven-foot Lacebark soldier in the doorway looks back at the two of them and frowns. At some point his big nose has been broken and reset so awkwardly that he now resembles a cartoon character trying to smell his own ear.

Raf, who isn't quite as scared as he was last time, is hoping to stay calm and try to bluff their way out of this. But then Isaac bolts. And if one of them bolts then both of them have to.

The soldier was slow to react but by the time they get back around the corner and into the lift he's not far behind. Raf punches the ground-floor button and then, frantically, again and again, the door-close button, trying to remember whether it's a myth that those buttons do anything or whether it's a myth that they don't. Either way, as the doors begin to thrum shut, the soldier lunges forward with an outstretched hand. But instead of the safety sensor activating, the doors just keep closing, and as the soldier whips his hand back Raf gives thanks for poorly maintained social housing infrastructure.

'Jesus!' says Isaac as they begin to descend. 'That was one of them? That's what they look like?'

'Yeah.'

'What the fuck was he doing there?' says Isaac.

'Lacebark must be locking everything down.'

The soldier's probably taking the stairs, so when the doors open on the ground floor they start running again. They get to the bus

219

stop outside the carwash in time to follow three teenage girls in hijabs on to a westbound bus, and when they look back from the rear window of the top deck they can't see anyone following.

'You still have the keys to the roof, right?' says Isaac.

'Yeah.'

'We should go up there, cut the infra-red link and plug a mic right into the transmitter. We can work out how. I spent yesterday setting up the world's dodgiest PA system.'

'No, Theo put glue in all the ports on the transmitter that he wasn't planning to use. The wily cunt.' They both smile sadly. 'Anyway, if Lacebark are guarding the studio now they're probably guarding the transmitter too. We should give it to the Serbians.'

'What do you mean?'

'The transmitter and the aerial together have got to be worth, what, at least ten grand? We go to Jesnik, give him the keys to the roof, and tell him his uncle can have all the gear for free. If he wants he can start a station playing Serbian wedding music.' The Mexican drug cartels, Theo once told him, have built their own military-grade radio networks in parts of the desert where mobile phone coverage is unreliable or insecure, but perhaps that wouldn't be so much use in south London.

'What would the point be?'

'To steal Myth back from Lacebark before they find any more uses for it. We've got to start thinking like Cherish. Anything that distracts their attention is a good thing.'

The other option is to tip off Ofcom, who until all this started were the only bastards driving around London in unmarked surveillance vehicles that Raf ever had to worry about, but the thought of helping them out is just too sickening.

'Don't you remember when Barky got mixed up with the Serbians?' says Isaac. 'Maybe Jesnik's OK but some of them are really fucking scary guys. If we're going to give away the transmitter, we should at least give it to someone like Jonk. He's been wanting to start his own station since we were kids.'

'He won't be able to get past Lacebark if they're on the roof. But the Serbians must have guns.' The sweaty bald guy in the seat in front of them has been in the process of mixing a milkshake in a Thermos flask with a bag of strawberry-flavoured protein powder and a carton of semi-skimmed, hugging all three receptacles to himself every time the bus brakes.

'If we give up on the radio broadcast, how are we going to warn everyone about the raids?'

'We can't. So we have to make sure they don't happen.'

'But the only way to do that is to make sure Lacebark don't catch Fourpetal today.'

The bald guy downs the milkshake and burps.

'Yeah,' says Raf.

'And we have absolutely no clue where he might be. Absolutely no clue.' Isaac looks at Raf. 'Right?'

12.13 p.m.

By the time he gets near the climbing gym Rose is straining anxiously at her leash as if she can already guess that something important is about to happen. The noon sky's such a steely blue that every dull mass in the foreground seems to spark at the edges like the flint in a lighter as your retina struggles to arbitrate the contrast. If Raf is right, Fourpetal will be watching the entrance of the warehouse, but he has to make sure that he sees Fourpetal before Fourpetal sees him, so he does a bit of rough mental trigonometry with the sightlines to decide on his route. After that, he pendulums back and forth from point to point, moving a bit closer each time, feeling like an authentic vengeful ghost now. The place he saves for last, even though he thinks it's the likeliest, is the yard of the builders' merchant, which he enters hoping he looks as if he might be on his way inside to buy some joist hangers. And maybe it's because he deserves some good luck today but that's where he finds Fourpetal, crouched behind one of those pallets of breeze-blocks, eating from a bag of prawn crackers.

'Hey,' he says. Fourpetal looks round. Raf knows that Fourpetal is going to run, because Fourpetal always runs, so he's not obliged to await that formality before he lets Rose at him. Just as he does so, Fourpetal hurls *Lacunosities* like a brick, but the book misses by several inches and the dog has her jaws around Fourpetal's left calf before the handle of her nylon leash has even slapped the tarmac. Fourpetal starts howling, and Raf calls Rose back. He's always liked to imagine that she knows a total prick when she sees one, although in this case the enmity might simply be class-based.

'I should let her really fuck you up but I'm not going to,' he says. Fourpetal is now holding on to his leg with both hands and rocking back and forth but Raf can see that Rose didn't even break the fabric of his trousers.

'You followed me?' Fourpetal says.

'No. I just worked out what you'd probably try next. You thought taking one of Nollic's kids hostage would be easier than getting Nollic himself.'

'Yes.'

'What were you going to do when they came out? Punch the nanny and then run off with one of the kids?'

'I was going to find some way of distracting the nanny. Only if that didn't work was I going to punch her. The trouble is, they haven't arrived yet, and I don't even know if this is the gym they go to. I think there's one in London Bridge. Still, I wonder if Martin only started coming here as a way of sucking up to Nollic.'

Raf looks around. 'Get up. We've got to go.'

'Are you taking me back to your girlfriend for some sort of para-military tribunal?'

Raf wishes she was still, or was ever, his girlfriend. 'No.'

'Where, then?'

'I'm not telling you where we're going.'

'Well, thank you very much for the invitation, but in this case I'll have to send my regrets.'

'The alternative is either Lacebark kills you or Zaya does.' Raf looks down. 'Or Rose, who would really like to.' Then he sees Fourpetal raise his eyebrows in surprise, and he turns.

Ko is standing there with one hand in the kangaroo pocket of his sweatshirt, and from his posture Raf can guess he must be holding a weapon there, although there's no way to know what it is. Raf's hope had been that it wouldn't matter if one of Zaya's men was watching Fourpetal, because he would have been ordered not to intervene under any circumstances, both to make sure Fourpetal didn't know he was there and to avoid getting captured himself when Lacebark arrived to abduct him.

'Hi, Ko,' Raf says. 'Cherish sent me here to pick him up.'

Ko shakes his head. 'No.' Maybe he's already spoken to her.

'All right – next ploy?' says Fourpetal behind him.

Raf takes a deep breath. 'Ko, you know I'm not on this cunt's side. You saw me set the dog on him just now. And you know I'm not on Lacebark's side. They killed my friend. But I need to take him away.'

'Can't let you,' says Ko.

'Zaya is going to let Lacebark take him. And he'll tell them everything. And all the people he tells them about will die unless Zaya decides to save them. That can't be right.' This has a much better chance of working if Ko hasn't already been taken into Zaya's confidence, but right now Raf can't tell much from Ko's face. 'Listen, I know Fourpetal deserves to have something fucking awful happen to him. But it should be one of us who handles that. Not Lacebark. And I know you're loyal to Zaya and Cherish. But all you have to do is tell them you couldn't stop us from getting away. Ko, please. You told me the reason you got involved in all this was that you didn't want to see anyone else get killed. That's how I feel too. Come on. Just let us go.'

Ko is still impossible to read, and Raf reluctantly finds himself running the odds on a physical fight. If Ko only has a blade, not a gun, then Rose might be fast enough to get him on the ground before he even has a chance to use it on her. On the other hand, she might not. And he doesn't know whether he's willing to make her take that risk.

But then Ko spits something in Burmese that sounds like a curse, takes his hand out of his pocket, and stands aside.

6.31 p.m.

Raf has been up now for about thirty hours. He'd always hoped that his syndrome might turn out to be not only a bug in his programming but also, in some contexts, a superpower. But if that was ever going to happen, it would have happened since Theo disappeared, and it hasn't. Yes, there are sometimes hours of the night when he's more alert than the average person. But that's nothing a few hundred milligrams of caffeine can't replicate. There's no secret time of day to which only Jack-go-to-bed-at-noon has entry, no 3.67 or 25.04 accessible through the back of a prop fridge. All he's got is his deviant wavelength. If Lacebark's conspiracy had been operating on a twenty-five-hour schedule, perhaps he would have noticed it before anyone else in London, and that would finally have vindicated his suprachiasmatic nucleus. But Lacebark keep their deviant schedules for their mines and their training facilities. He's like Monet, who apparently gained the ability to see ultraviolet light after he had cataract surgery, if Monet had lived in a world with no known sources of ultraviolet light. That's not much of a superpower. So right now all he can say is that he's not quite as exhausted as he would be if he'd got up at nine in the morning on Friday instead of two in the afternoon.

The handover probably isn't that different from Martin's in Pakistan, except that instead of driving outside the city they've just assembled in the car park of a discount carpet shop. There are still a few rolls of carpet pressed yearningly against the plate glass at the front, but otherwise it looks derelict, and someone has pasted up a few of those garish purple circus posters that are so common on shopfronts around here (despite Raf never in his life having heard of anyone actually going to the circus in south London, not even when he was a kid, which makes him wonder if they could be a species of ivy that has evolved a shrewd but dated mimetic camouflage). Raf has brought Fourpetal and Rose, and two Serbian hulks in embroidered bomber jackets have come in a van.

'This is him?' says one of the hulks. The helix of his left ear is bandaged and Raf can't work out how you'd get injured there until with a wince he thinks of an earring being ripped out in a scuffle. 'Deal is, we take him all the way to farm with others?'

'Yeah. And keep him there. In exchange for the radio station.' Isaac negotiated this deal on Raf's instructions, and he wanted to be here to see it happen, but Raf told him it would be an unnecessary risk. Earlier, Raf wondered whether the Serbians were going to take any precautions before rescuing Win. Unlike Zaya, they knew that Lacebark didn't really need to be made to 'blink' for Win to leave the training facility, and it seemed probable that they had a better infrastructure for smuggling people in and out of London than the Burmese did, but that didn't mean it wasn't going to be tricky. Raf got his answer a couple of hours ago when he was sitting in Happy Fried Chicken with Fourpetal, trying to pass the time until this meeting. A twenty-four-hour news channel was playing on TV and during the traffic alerts there was helicopter footage of a warehouse fire near Elephant and Castle that was causing mild traffic congestion on the Old Kent Road. He already knew from Google Maps what the freight depot looked like from the air.

'So he stay on farm?'

'Yeah, you don't let him go,' says Raf. 'If you want you can put him to work for his bed and board.'

'Board?'

'Food and stuff.'

The hulk nods. His cologne smells like an alcopop. 'OK.'

'What the hell is "farm"?' says Fourpetal. 'Which farm?'

Raf hands him *Lacunosities*. 'When you're not scraping up frozen fox shit you can pass the time with that.'

The other hulk slides open the back door of the van, which looks just like one of Lacebark's, and Raf catches a glimpse of Win and Jesnik sitting on the floor kissing. They pull apart hurriedly and either the hulk didn't notice or he pretends he didn't. In the last few hours all the battery acid seems to have drained out of Fourpetal, and he meekly climbs inside. Raf realises this is his last chance to talk to Win in person. He has to finish the conversation that was interrupted in the training facility. 'Win.'

'Yo.'

'You know we were talking about how *glo* can alter your circadian rhythms? I have this sleep disorder called non-24-hour sleep/wake syndrome—'

'Oh – you want to know if *glo* could do something for you?'

'Yeah.'

'I don't know, man. Talk to Pfizer.'

One of the hulks slides the door of the van shut. Then both get back in the front and drive away.

Raf decides to look for a pub. As he walks, he thinks about Fourpetal and Win and Jesnik all leaving London for good, and for the first time in what feels like centuries he remembers that he promised himself he'd do the same.

But he doesn't want to.

It's not just that he'd rather live in south London than in a mudhole in the Serbian countryside. He'd rather live in south London than anywhere else in the world. All he needs to do is tape up some honeycomb over his door. Nothing is so bad that it can leave an indelible stain on this place, not break-ups, not Lacebark, not Theo's death, not anything: however frightening the last couple of weeks may have been, they should have reminded him of that. Cherish was right. There is no hole in things. Right now, if he saw a fox sidling out from under a parked car, that would feel so appropriate, so fated, so perfect, that he almost can't believe it won't happen, and

226

he's looking around optimistically when his phone vibrates in his pocket. He sees an unfamiliar number on the screen and guesses straight away who it's going to be. 'Hi.'

'Do you have any fucking idea what you've done?' Cherish says. 'Win's gone. We think the Serbians have him. But maybe you know better than I do.'

'He didn't want to work for you any more.'

'This wasn't about what he wanted. This wasn't about you or me or Win or Zaya. This wasn't even about Lacebark. This was about revolution. We were going to take over northern Burma and turn it into a narco-state. Like Bolivia. Like Guinea-Bissau. The world's first and only benign narco-state. We would've laundered our money through the same banks Lacebark use. Al Qaeda's annual budget is twenty million dollars. Even Hezbollah's is only four hundred million dollars. Do you know what we could have done with ten billion dollars a year from a monopoly on glow? Every man, woman, and child on this earth working as a slave to some corporation, we would have gone out and given them their freedom. First at the Concession, then everywhere else. Can you even begin to imagine the good we would've done? The lives we would've saved? And you stopped us, because now the Serbians have glow. You just made sure your friend Theo died for absolutely nothing.'

'But you were going to let all those other people die too. They were on your side and you were going to give them up.'

'Letting people die is something you have to do sometimes when you want to do good. Killing people is something you have to do sometimes when you want to do good. Do you really think whacking a snake against a tree was the worst initiation Zaya put me through when I went to visit him in Burma?'

Raf doesn't even want to think about what she's implying. He remembers Zaya's pious claim about how he didn't want any of the Burmese extras in the training facility to get into trouble as collateral damage. 'You have to stop listening to Zaya. I don't know how he convinced you to do this but—'

'Convinced me? You're just going to assume that it would have taken a man to come up with that stuff? Do you know how fucking condescending that is? Raf, it was my plan. Passing Fourpetal to Lacebark was my plan. Not Zaya's.'

'And feeding me all that false information about Win was your plan too.'

'Yeah.'

'So when we had sex in the bathroom, you weren't even turned on, it was just business.'

'I guess it would never occur to you that maybe the reason I was so turned on was exactly because it was meant to be just business.'

Graupels of crushed styrofoam packaging skitter across the pavement as the breeze picks up. Rose walks off to piss against a lamppost. Raf felt pathetic asking that last question but somehow it seemed important. And maybe also it was a way of working up to the question he really wants to ask, which is whether it means anything that she tried to protect him. This morning, she must have thought that if he went back to his flat to fetch Rose without knowing what was about to happen, there was a chance he'd be there when Lacebark launched their raids. So she tried to make sure he didn't go home. But he knows there are any number of reasons why she might have made that choice. 'Cherish, you knew I was going to do this, right?' he asks instead. 'At the tennis court, I could tell that you knew. But you didn't try to stop me.'

After a pause, Cherish says, 'I didn't know you were going to sabotage my fucking cellphone.'

But that isn't really the point, Raf thinks. He wishes that somehow they could be face to face again for this. 'Am I ever going to see you again?'

'Seriously? You are seriously asking me that question? No, of course you are never going to see me again. And you're never going to see London again, either. I hope you know that.'

'What do you mean?'

'Lacebark are going to come looking for you soon.'

'Are you going to give me up to them?'

'No, Raf. I could, and maybe Zaya would say that I should, but I won't. But when Lacebark realise Win's not in London any more, they'll start to wonder how things went so wrong here. And I know for sure that when they take another look at their ImPressure• metadata, it'll tell them to take you in. You have to go somewhere they won't think to look for you.'

'But I want to stay in London. I've only just decided I want to stay. Summer's starting.'

'No. Leave. And stay the fuck out of Burma, too.' She hangs up.

Raf puts the phone back in his pocket and looks around. He doesn't see a fox.

ÞJÓÐVEGUR 1,
ICELAND,
DECEMBER 2010

AFTERNOON, SUPPOSEDLY

Isaac has been following the white van for nearly five hours. Because he already knows the route the van is taking – þjóðvegur 1 loops around Iceland like a giant M25 and there's no other sensible route from Reykjavik to Dalvík – he hasn't needed to stay within sight of it all the time, so it's possible that the other driver won't even have noticed him. While he's been driving, the sun has hauled itself up to the parapet of the horizon, hung on there panting for a while, and then fallen away with a bronzy moan of resignation, leaving no trace but the last drag of its fingernails in the clouds to the south. Now it's night again. During that long fermata of dusk, when the motorway was snaking alongside what he is reasonably confident in identifying as a fjord, he saw four ponies grazing on the hillside opposite, bear-like in their winter duffles, not far from a gingerbread farmhouse with a red roof; some of the time this place could pass for a kind of steroidal, mythic Yorkshire. In his wallet he has the phone number of a tall blonde he met at the airport whose genotype must be perfect in the same way that the circles and squares described in mathematical proofs are perfect. She told him four or five times how to pronounce þjóðvegur but he couldn't even get the first syllable right.

Somehow even in the darkness you get a sense of the huge cliffs rising over Dalvík across the bay. On the approach to the harbour Isaac pulls closer to the white van, because for the first time he doesn't know exactly where it's going and he doesn't want to lose it among the warehouses and containers and derelict fishmeal plants. This must be one of those Icelandic towns that over the course of the previous decade started to feel a bit embarrassed that it was good for nothing but fishing and now is learning to feel proud of that again. The van carries on all the way to the second-farthest jetty, where a boat is already waiting for its exceptionally precious cargo. Isaac parks not far away. For a little while he's worried that there'll be no one here to meet him but then there's a knock on the window. He gets out of the car. When Raf gives him a hug they're like sumo wrestlers in their jumpers and parkas. Out here it's several degrees below zero and a razor-edged wind is blowing in off the water.

'Jesus, I can't believe this is really where you live now,' says Isaac.

'I live down the road.'

Isaac saw a sign for Akureyri just before he turned off the motorway. 'Yeah, but I mean, Iceland. The sixtieth parallel. This time of year it must be like living in one of those West African cities where they get only about ten minutes of electricity a day. Except instead of electricity it's daylight.'

'You should have been here in June.'

If he ever had to acclimatise himself to a new latitude, Isaac thinks he would do better than Linnaeus's tea but not nearly so well as Win's *glo*. Shivering, he looks over at the van. 'Ready for this, then?'

By now the bearded driver has opened the back and a second man has come down the gangway of the ship to help him unload. From inside the van comes a mess of noises. As Isaac and Raf come near, the other two men turn to see what they want. '*Já?*' says the driver.

Isaac watches Raf take a moment to decide how to put this. The harbour lights cast long shadows. 'I've come to say hello to my dog.'

'Sorry?'

'I just want to say hello to her on the way from the van to the boat.'

The driver shakes his head. 'The animals have to be taken directly to quarantine on the island.'

Driving here, it occurred to Isaac that if he were the government of Iceland he would quietly ensure that Hrísey were set up to receive people, too. Coronavirus was coming eventually and you couldn't be too careful.

'I don't need to take her out of the transport kennel or anything,' says Raf.

'They're not allowed any human contact. That's the whole point. I hope you didn't come all the way from Reykjavik for this?'

'I did,' Isaac says. 'Listen, he hasn't seen his dog in more than six months. He's not going to see her again for another month after this. The dog doesn't know where in fuck's name she's been taken and she also doesn't know if she's ever going to see this guy again in her life. Just let them say hello to each other through the little grille.'

This was the best plan that Raf and Isaac could come up with. If they understood more about how the Burmese got Win to London, or how the Serbians later got him to Majdanpek, then maybe they would have known how to smuggle Rose to Akureyri, perhaps using some sort of intermediate safehouse on the Faroe Islands. But they didn't. For an animal to enter Iceland legally, it needs to obtain a sheaf of certificates and a microchip in its ear, and there wasn't time for any of that before Raf fled London at the start of the summer. To be safe, Isaac couldn't follow too soon, because they didn't know who might still be watching. So he waited six months and then organised Rose's emigration. When she passed all the blood tests, Isaac assumed it could only have been because veterinary science did not yet have the means to detect or even really conceptualise the pandemonium of spores and endoparasites surely languishing in her tissues after a lifetime on the streets of south London.

Then Raf could have gone down to Reykjavik this morning, but because of security there would have been no way for him to get into the section of the airport where the pet chaperones wait to get their certificates checked before their pets are taken into thirty-day quarantine. And they had discovered that, of the two competing accredited quarantine stations in Iceland, the cheaper one happened to be on an island less than thirty miles from the town where Raf was living. So it made sense, relatively speaking, for Raf to meet Isaac here at the harbour.

'Please,' Isaac says. He tried to get the blonde at the airport to teach him how to say 'We would be eternally grateful' but, again, it was too hard.

The driver looks at the other man and then back at Isaac and Raf. 'If you are here when we take the dog out of the van . . .' He shrugs his shoulders. 'Well, then you are here.'

When the Icelanders start loading the transport kennels on to the boat, they work much faster than Isaac was expecting, and he can't ask them to slow down in case they change their minds. So for a while he's worried that Rose might slip past them like a drum of sassafras oil past a customs check. But in fact when the seventh kennel comes out of the van, it starts shaking and barking as if it's warming up for a thermonuclear fusion reaction. Rose has caught Raf's scent. So the Icelanders lower the kennel to the ground and Raf gets down on his hands and knees for the prison visit. This reunion can't be that satisfying for either of them, but at least it might give Rose a bit of hope for the future while she's serving out her sentence so far from her friends.

Isaac's going to miss Rose too, of course. He's already thinking about getting a pet to replace her. For a while he wondered about a star-nosed mole, and did some research into moles in general, but he's now more interested in naked mole-rats, which aren't actually related to moles but are singular in various ways. First of all, a naked mole-rat looks like a wrinkly cock with fangs, and mole-rats are the only mammals that have queens and workers the same way bees and termites do, so a photo of a naked mole-rat nest reminds him of a nineteenth-century Toyokuni woodblock print that Hiromi once showed him, depicting the 'penis god' and his offspring. Second, naked mole-rats never get cancer, which is pretty weird. Third, the skins of naked mole-rats don't have a neurotransmitter called substance P that administers pain in other animals. Because the lack of ventilation in their nests fugs the air down there with carbon dioxide, a lot of acid builds up in their tissues, and if they had substance P then they would be in constant discomfort.

To Isaac this is an example of evolution's brusque mercy.

Evolution hasn't bothered to prevent human childbirth from being agonisingly painful, because the pain of childbirth doesn't make a woman any less likely to reproduce. But it has gone to some lengths to soothe the pain of these mole-rats, like a boss who grudgingly lets you have a nap every three and a quarter hours because it might make you more productive. The more Isaac reads about the question of consciousness, the more persuaded he is that the shortest route to the answer will come from understanding the relationship between the functional roles of pain and pleasure and their phenomenology – between what purpose they serve in the brain and what they actually feel like. The subjective experiences of colour and pitch and temperature don't seem to have any intrinsic meaning, any intrinsic push. But the subjective experiences of pleasure and pain have 'Yes!' and 'No!' built into them. How can that be? How can banal matter achieve that?

After a while Raf reluctantly gets back to his feet and waves goodbye to the kennel as it's taken off down the gangway. The Icelanders seem to relax a bit now they've seen that Raf was sincere, and when they've finished with the kennels, the driver says, 'Where are you two from?'

'London,' says Isaac.

'But I live in Akureyri now,' says Raf.

'Oh, I went to London once! Great for clubs.'

'Yeah, I put on some nights myself,' says Isaac.

'Have you been out in Reykjavik yet?'

'We're going to drive down there tomorrow night.'

'Do you want to buy some glow?'

Isaac exchanges a bemused look with Raf. 'There's glow in Dalvík?'

'A friend of mine has a lab nearby.'

'How much?' he says.

'Fifteen thousand kronur for a gram.'

'That's a lot.'

The driver smiles. 'This is Iceland.'

237

'Yeah, but it's not like your friend is paying VAT and import duty,' Raf says. 'Ten thousand.'

In the end, Isaac and Raf hand over twelve thousand kronur, partly just for the sheer novelty of buying phenylethylamines in Dalvík harbour. They say goodbye to the Icelanders – although the man from the boat still hasn't spoken a word – and then get back into the hire car to warm up while they watch the ark set sail for Hrísey.

'Six months ago no one outside London had heard of glow,' Isaac says. 'And now it's here?'

'The Serbians were never going to be able to keep it themselves. We knew that.'

'MDMA took seventy years to get popular. And do they even have foxes around here?'

'Arctic foxes are the only mammals that got to Iceland before people did. I've seen them a few times but it's not as cool as seeing a fox in London. Do you still want to go and watch the northern lights tonight?'

'Of course I fucking do. I brought a VLF receiver. We should take some glow, too.'

'But glow only works with artificial light,' says Raf. 'That's what everyone says.'

'First of all, I never really believed that anyway, because how would that work, scientifically? Second, the aurora borealis is nitrogen and oxygen atoms giving off photons as they return from an excited state to a ground state. That's just like fluorescent tubes, LEDs, cathode rays. The northern lights are a lot more similar to artificial light than they are to sunlight.'

'OK, well, we can give it a go.'

They decide to drive back to Akureyri to have dinner first.

'So what's it actually like to live here?' says Isaac on the way. He's realised that the black ice on these roads is mostly harmless until it smells fear.

'Nice. Boring. Cheaper than Reykjavik, which is useful – I'm doing more rendering work than I used to but the money's still crap. And some English teaching.'

'Are you going out with anyone?'

'I was for a bit. But she broke up with me a couple of weeks ago.'

'Shit, really? Do you avoid her?' Isaac knows what Raf is like.

'Are you joking? Akureyri is tiny. There are only four bars. And only one of them's open after three in the morning. I see her all the time. It's OK, though.'

'And how's your menstrual cycle?'

'I don't notice it so much,' Raf says.

'Like you were hoping?'

'Yeah. In the middle of summer and the middle of winter everyone's rhythms are erratic here. You get up. You go to sleep. It's day. It's night. The clock isn't so important.'

'Did you know that all moles – except Japanese and American shrew-moles – are equally active day and night? They just come out whenever they feel like it. You could find acceptance among the moles. You, the moles, the Martians, and the northern Icelanders.'

'Thanks, mate. That means a lot.'

They eat bad hamburgers in Akureyri, fill up the car at a petrol station, and drive halfway back to Dalvík to get some distance from the town's gentle light pollution before they pull off to the side of the road. Isaac reluctantly takes off his woollen gloves so he can make the two quarter-gram tortellini of glow that they'll wash down with local beer.

'I can't believe after all this time I'm finally going to find out what this stuff is like,' Raf says.

'These are for Theo,' Isaac says, clicking his beer can against Raf's.

'These, and all the rest.'

While they wait to come up, Isaac puts the batteries into his VLF receiver, which he ordered from one of the same websites from which Myth FM sometimes used to buy its spare parts. With the right equipment, the aurora borealis is not only visible but audible, a celestial radio station transmitting on the same marathon wave-lengths that government time signals use to keep radio clocks synchronised with atomic clocks. And indeed before they see the lights they hear them, like dead leaves crunching under someone's boots as birds whistle and peep in the background. Only much later does the sky begin its dim emerald churn.

They get out of the car for a clearer view, and while it's probably not the most spectacular display in the history of the auroral zone, it's still enough to make Isaac wish he could see it every night for the rest of his life. He thinks of the afternoon nine or ten years ago that he bunked off school with Raf to go to Nunhead Reservoir. They climbed in through a gap in the fence and sat down together on one of the graffiti-covered concrete hatches at the top of the mound, not so much to watch the sun go down as to watch the city light up afterwards. The two of them had only just started to become friends and when you're a teenage boy it doesn't feel quite right to admit that you've gone to a lot of trouble just for a nice view. But that afternoon it was fine. He's missed Raf these last few months and he's glad to be here with him now as the magneto-sphere smoulders far above.

The 'glow', on the other hand, has done absolutely nothing. 'Those guys ripped us off,' he says, lurching from foot to foot to keep warm.

'I don't really care,' says Raf.

'No, me neither. They let you see Rose.'

'Yeah. By the way, how are the Japanese girls?'

'I'm sorry to say this but they've really let themselves go in the last few months.'

'Seriously?'

'No,' says Isaac. 'As always, they are magnificent.'

The signal on the VLF receiver is getting even stronger. Isaac imagines the neurons in his visual cortex sparking in patterns that mirror the ionisation in the sky, just smaller and with a bit of a lag, like a little girl dancing in front of a pop video on TV. 'You know he said the lab was "nearby"? I bet it's on that island somewhere. Can you think of a better place for it?'

So far tonight they've hardly spoken about what happened in May. Talking about the past with Raf isn't always easy. He can be surprisingly bitter for someone so young. Nostalgia's like an ImPressure• network: most of the database is harmless but there are connections you don't expect and you're never more than a couple of clicks away from the high-value targets, the redacted entries. Isaac decides not to put it off any longer. 'You know Lacebark are getting taken over byXujiabang Copper and Gold?'

'Fuck, I didn't know that.'

'Announced this morning.' But nothing has ever come out in the press about Lacebark's activities in the Concession or in London. Isaac knows Raf sent anonymous tip-offs to a lot of journalists and bloggers. But it was hard to be sure how much to explain to them. If you tried to dump the whole story at once, there wasn't much chance they'd believe it. And there was no real evidence to attach as ballast. The video with the foxes has disappeared from YouTube and Raf never had a copy of the original Pankhead email that got Fourpetal involved.

'Do you know what's going on at the farm now?' Isaac says.

'About a month ago I got a private message on Lotophage from Win. He said he's still out there with Jesnik making glow. He sounded cheerful. But apparently Fourpetal's gone. One night he stole the keys to one of the four-wheel drives. They have no idea where he went.'

'Have you heard from anyone else?'

'No.'

'What about Cherish?'

Isaac feels as if it's all right to ask the question because Raf seemed so equable about his ex in Akureyri. But his friend doesn't answer and Isaac doesn't want to press him on it. So for a time the silence between them is broken only by the chirruping of the lights in the sky.

SIMANDOU, GUINEA,
AUGUST 2011

6.03 a.m.

The problem started when rumours reached the camp of what had happened in Mauritania. Three weeks ago, after the collapse of their financing, a Chinese oil syndicate had abruptly pulled out of the country, leaving behind nearly a hundred low-grade private military contractors who had already been hired as security for the project. The rations began to run out, and the men soon realised that they were not going to be paid the wages they were owed, nor were they even going to be flown home. They'd been abandoned like a litter of kittens. So they spent a few days half-heartedly pillaging the countryside before they were dispersed by a series of confrontations with the army, and by now most of those who hadn't already been killed or jailed had reportedly found their way to the streets of Nouakchott, where they were eking out the money for plane tickets by any means they could. There is no such thing as a consulate for mercenaries.

When Bezant's boys found out about this, they started to worry that the same thing might happen to them. That was nothing new. Mercenaries on deployment are always needy and neurotic. In other circumstances, instead of indulging them, Bezant would simply have reminded his boys that Xujiabang Copper and Gold was not some tinpot oil syndicate, that its annual turnover exceeded Guinea's entire GDP, that the cash registers in its staff canteens were more solvent than most of the banks in their home countries. In other words, they should shut up about Mauritania because they were certainly going to get paid. But then Angus Yu announced that to 'restore confidence' they were all to receive an immediate advance on their wages. He hadn't consulted Bezant and it made the entire command structure look feeble.

What arrived on the courier plane last night was not even a steel briefcase, just a white cardboard mailing box, as if someone had ordered a pair of high heels off the internet, and inside that a mylar bag, and inside that a few dozen vacuum-sealed stacks of hundred-dollar bills. Because the box was too big to fit in any of the camp's safes, three men were posted outside the door of the metallography shed, which nobody ever uses, to guard the box until the money could be disbursed. Bezant did not mention to those men that he was going to spend the night dozing on a camping mat in the nook beside the eyewash station. So when Angus Yu comes into the windowless shed just after six o'clock in the morning, he must be expecting to have the place to himself. Bezant waits until Yu shuts the door and flips on the lights before he gets up from the mat with a pantomime of yawning and stretching.

'G'day, Angus,' he says. 'Have you brought me breakfast?'

To watch Yu flail is going to be a real pleasure. Since his arrival he has been so prissy and condescending and autocratic that Bezant sometimes lulls himself to sleep with fantasies of feeding the boy limb by limb into the impact crusher. He can't do anything of the sort, though, because Yu is the son of one of the vice-presidents of Xujiabang Copper and Gold. For this princeling who spent four and a half semesters at Harvard to have been sent to manage a mine in Guinea, he must have done something exceptionally naughty. Someone must have died, maybe on American soil, maybe in baroque circumstances. Yu knows nothing whatsoever about mining, and although he once announced that he was 'too busy' to appraise himself of the difference between Guinea, Guinea-Bissau, Equatorial Guinea, and Papua New Guinea, he spends most of his time here watching sitcoms and video chatting over the satellite broadband.

Admittedly, Bezant doesn't have much to do here either. It's quiet out on these scrubby hills. There have been a few silly rumours about the Gandayaw Liberation Organisation operating in West

Africa, but he knows for certain that the cunt who called himself Zaya has been dead of unknown causes since at least the start of the year, so Bezant isn't exactly gnawing his phalanges off with apprehension. And the workers here are docile. The turquoise pills that arrive on the courier plane every week make sure that they don't sleep and they don't make mistakes and they don't complain. They might look like voodoo dolls of themselves by the time their contracts finish, but Yu claims the pills are chemically analogous to the nootropics some of his friends used to take when they were studying for exams at Harvard, so they can't be so bad for you.

Still, Xujiabang are keeping those prescriptions a secret. They're even more obsessed than Lacebark were with 'process efficiency optimisation', but they also don't want the reputation for human rights abuses that was just beginning to break out like herpes sores on Lacebark's face before the takeover. Last year they announced with plenty of fanfare that they would welcome inspections by human rights charities and television crews even at short notice. Apparently the first of these inspections took place at a mine back in Shaanxi. Because Xujiabang had access to the NGO's email servers, they knew about the visit several weeks in advance. So they simply built a second mine, a temporary fake, a few miles away from the real one. The inspectors never knew the difference. Bezant has heard that a lot of the people who used to work on MOUT training facilities for Lacebark are now doing set design and special effects for these Potemkin mines, including one English guy whom everyone calls either the Invisible Man or the Gimp because on sunny days he walks around in one of those latex masks that Chinese women wear at the beach to avoid getting a tan. The investment's worthwhile because they won't have to play the trick many times. When there's too much good news people lose interest.

'Who opened this package?' Yu says, pointing at the box that sits on the steel table in the middle of the room. Predictably, he's going to try to bluster his way out of this, but when he's nervous he keeps shooting the cuffs of the shirt he wears under his ridiculous designer blazer.

'I did,' says Bezant.

'You aren't authorised to open it.'

'Yes, I am.'

'I should have been present.'

'I counted. There's three hundred and fifty grand in there. That's five thousand each for seventy men.'

'So?' Young Angus is now alternating between his cuffs with such force that he looks like a skydiver trying to deploy a faulty parachute.

'As you know, there are only forty-eight grunts on site at the moment. So we only needed two hundred and forty grand. That's a difference of a hundred and ten. You must've thought no one would check the paperwork. Like one of those Chinese restaurants where they don't bother to itemise the bill so you never know if you're getting ripped off. Is that where you learned how to do it? The old moo shu switcheroo, eh?'

'That is racist language,' said Yu.

'So you're desperate. You owe someone a bundle. Fair enough. What I don't understand is, how can it be so urgent? Whoever it is, they're not coming to collect. We're in fucking Simandou.'

'You should leave right now.'

'Listen, Angus, we both know what you were going to do and we also both know I can't prove anything. But if you think you're keeping any of this, you've got tailings for brains. And you'll show a little bit more respect from now on, eh?'

Since the takeover Bezant has been trying to learn Mandarin from a language tape but it doesn't cover any of the words Yu is muttering as he leaves the shed. For an instant before he slams the door a rectangle of dawn nudges limply at the fluorescence within. After making sure the latch is closed, Bezant retrieves his rucksack from the nook beside the eyewash station and goes back to the box on the table. He's in the process of counting out the twenty-two stacks of bills he's going to take back to his quarters when he feels something hard against the back of his neck.

'That doesn't feel like a firearm,' he says evenly.

'It's not,' says the person behind him. 'It's a cordless rivet gun. It won't make much noise. Put your hands behind your head.'

She has an American accent. He doesn't recognise her voice.

ACKNOWLEDGEMENTS

I lived in at least ten different flats and houses (depending on how you count it) during the two years it took me to write and edit this book, so I'd like to express special gratitude to all my hosts, land-lords and flatmates, including the Akademie der Künste in Berlin and the Omi International Arts Center in upstate New York, plus the British Council for all the travel. I'd also like to thank Professor David Sulzer and Dr. Carl Hart for talking to me about the chemis-try of pleasure, although I must emphasise that I never offered them the opportunity to check the manuscript and so they cannot be held responsible for the outrages against serious neuroscience committed within. Finally, for all their help, I'd like to thank Jane Finigan and everyone at Lutyens & Rubinstein; Drummond Moir and everyone at Sceptre; David Forrer and everyone at Inkwell; and Gary Fisketjon and everyone at Knopf.